Guardians of Zion: The Paladin of Panama
Copyright © 2017 by Michael Chrobak

This is a work of fiction. Names, characters, places, and incidents either are the product of the author's imagination or are used fictitiously. Any resemblance to actual persons, living or dead, events, or locales is entirely coincidental.

Seneschal Publishing; Oakley, California
www.seneschalpublishing.com
Twitter: @SeneschalBooks

Book Cover Artist:
Kristyn / Drop Dead Designs
http://www.dropdeaddesigns.com

ISBN paperback: 978-0-9981350-4-5
ISBN eBook: 978-0-9981350-5-2

First Paperback Edition
Printed in the United States of America

Also by Michael Chrobak

Brother Thomas and the Guardians of Zion Series
Book One: Foundations of Faith

Other Books:

Where Angels Dwell

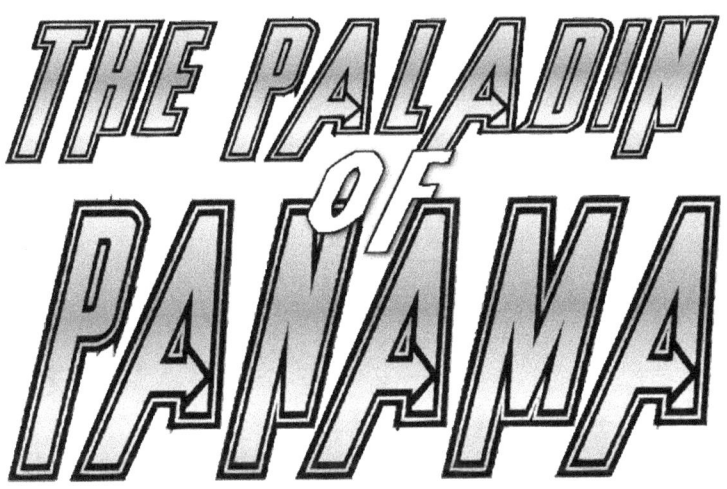

THE PALADIN OF PANAMA

A NOVEL
by
MICHAEL CHROBAK

To all the young people
who have touched my heart.

INTRO

Welcome to Book Two of the *Guardians of Zion* series. This series began in Book One, *Foundations of Faith,* with the story of Thomas at fifteen years of age. Like most teens, Thomas has serious doubts about his faith—until he attends a high school church retreat. As he begins to understand the depth of the faith he does have, his life starts to fall apart. Through these challenges he recognizes that even though he may still have doubts, he knows now what his faith really means.

Faith is one of the twelve fruits of the Holy Spirit, and, in my opinion, the most important of the twelve. The rest of the fruits are: *charity, joy, peace, patience, kindness, goodness, gentleness, generosity, modesty, self-control,* and *chastity*. Each book in this series will explore one of the fruits through the lens of fantasy. The primary characters, otherwise known as the Guardians of Zion, will each have superpowers based on these fruits.

As the title suggests, the first book was about the fruit of *faith*. The superpower that manifested within Thomas was the ability to see the feelings and emotions of others —their true feelings and emotions. He sees them as symbols that float above their heads. As his power grows, he finds that he is able to interpret the emotional state of the individual by the shape, color, and scent that the symbols give off. Darker colors, irregular shapes, and unpleasant smells indicate negative or harmful emotions, whereas bright colors, smooth shapes and pleasant smells represents healthy emotions.

Thomas also has the ability to extend himself beyond normal limits of strength or speed. Though these superpowers are based on fantasy, a strong faith in the real world does give us the ability to stretch our limits. When we lack faith, we approach life with fear, doubt, worry or concern, causing us to remain timid. This keeps us from taking risks and limits the trust we have in our own abilities. In a sense, a weak _faith_ life leads to a weak _real_ life. Whereas a strong faith life, one in which we suspend our judgments and accept that everything has a purpose—including us—leads to a life of confidence and grace. When we believe that our lives have meaning, we believe that our actions are not wasted. We become altruistic, virtuous champions who are willing to stand for those who cannot stand for themselves. We forgo our own needs for the greater needs of the world.

This is why I started the series with the fruit of _faith_. In my opinion, the life of a superhero is deeply rooted in faith. Their choices are based on an altruistic understanding. They know that their lives have meaning and purpose and that their actions really do matter. They also believe that those of lesser power can be raised up through their example. They don't fight evil and tyranny because it's fun—they fight because they want others to see that it is possible to take a stand.

This is where _The Paladin of Panama_ comes in. The character who becomes _The Paladin_ chooses a superhero life for one reason: they want to help. They want to help others heal the wounds of their past, find purpose in their challenges, and discover strength within themselves. Their power comes from denying their own wants and desires and putting others needs first. This superpower manifests from the fruit of _chastity_.

I believe this fruit is the most misunderstood of the twelve. *Chastity* goes far beyond choosing whether to engage or refrain from sexual relationships. Instead, it delves into our understanding of purity and discipline. It is not just our actions that we need to monitor but our thoughts as well. When we do, our faith has a greater opportunity to develop and grow. Think of it this way: when the seeds of our faith are planted in fertile soil, they have the best chance to grow. But, as any home gardener will tell you, the better the soil, the better the chance that weeds will grow as well. Following a chaste life is like being a careful gardener. We must understand that these weeds must be pulled as early as possible to avoid damaging the health of the plants. In the same way, impure thoughts must be set aside in order to prevent damage to our faith.

Chastity is not a decision we make once but one we are faced with over and over again. It is a conscious desire to return to the purity we had at birth, to remember who we were before impure thoughts or desires began to establish themselves within our hearts and minds. It recognizes that these impure thoughts do not come from what is good and true. Instead, they are there to lead us away from what is good. They break and damage our relationships; with ourselves, with others, and with God. But remaining chaste repairs that damage. This is the power of *The Paladin*—to heal the damage, returning things to how they were before they were broken.

Now, once again, it is time to prepare for an adventure! Suspend your doubts, your judgments and your disbelief and follow me as we journey into the land of *The Paladin of Panama*!

PART ONE

The nation doesn't simply need what we have
It needs what we are

— *St. Edith Stein*

CHAPTER ONE
JUST VISITING

"Hi, honey! I'm home!" Thomas sarcastically called out as he opened his apartment door.

"Welcome back," Terence responded casually from his reclined position on their living room couch. "How was the trip?"

Grunting softly, Thomas dropped his bags with a 'thump' and then lumbered over to the only other piece of furniture the two roommates shared: a navy blue clamshell chair with a bamboo frame, most likely left over from the 70s. Taking a position in front of the chair, Thomas didn't sit down but instead simply gave up standing. His body landed squarely, though a bit more aggressively than he had planned, causing the chair to tip backward before settling back in place.

"Exhausting…" Thomas sighed. "Remind me never to fly that far for a weekend. Ever again."

His roommate chuckled lightly, giving Thomas a quick glance, and then turning his attention back to the television.

Terence was an athletic young man with thick, sinewy arms, and legs the size of trees. He had bushy, blonde hair that fell loosely over his shoulders, sky blue eyes, and a perfect tan. He reminded Thomas of the surfers he used to watch on the beaches back home. The young man was dressed in black cargo shorts, a t-shirt, and a gray hoodie sweatshirt. A pair of Birkenstock sandals were close by—the only shoes Terence wore.

Along with having natural good looks, Thomas found his roommate to be a fairly outgoing guy. The kind who easily made friends wherever he went. He was opposite to Thomas in just about every way, though, in truth, the pair were perfectly matched for each other. Terence had a way of drawing Thomas out of his introverted, studious, socially awkward world of books and contemplation, while Thomas helped dampen some of Terence's free-spirit, life-of-the-party, openly flirtatious behaviors. Though, Thomas knew, his roommates' public persona was just for show. Inside the boisterous, playful, energetic young man was a gentle, kind, and giving spirit that only those who got to know him would ever see.

"I told you you'd regret it," Terence laughed.

Thomas wanted to nod in agreement, but couldn't find the strength.

"Yeah, you did," he admitted. "Next time you have permission to break my ankles, or tie me up with duct tape. Something I can't just shrug off."

Terence laughed more robustly as he moved from reclining to lying flat. Thomas knew that laugh. It was the one Terence used to, as he put it, 'close the deal' when he was trying to get one of the female student's phone numbers. Even though he couldn't see his roommate's face, he knew that if he could he would see a wide, toothy grin, decorated on each side by a deep pair of dimples.

"Oh, well. Did you at least meet any cute girls?" Terence inquired.

Thomas shook his head, a move that made him feel more than a bit dizzy.

"First of all," he responded, "it was a high school retreat. Second, it was a church retreat, and I was there as spiritual counsel. And third…"

"Yeah, I know, I know," Terence interrupted. "Your 'personal vow of celibacy'. I don't know why you did that, though. You're not going to be a priest for at least, what, four or five more years? Seems like you're wasting some precious freedom to me."

"Why? What purpose would it have? The only reason to get into a relationship is to find out if you like the other person enough to move all the way to marriage. Relationships aren't meant to just fool around and have fun like most of the world might believe."

"Well, I don't know how you do it, Thomas. There's no way I could cut out dating. But, if it works for you, that's great."

Though his roommate wasn't the type to ever take advantage of his 'golden boy' good looks, he was still a consummate flirt, never missing an opportunity to flash his perfect smile and twinkling eyes. As Thomas considered what to say in reply, a deep and powerful yawn came over him. He could feel his mind drifting towards sleep, and wondered if he had the strength to extricate himself from the chair. Curled like a kitten enjoying a bit of sunlight, he knew he could just as easily sleep right where he was. Just in case, he pulled out his phone and set an alarm for the morning.

"Anyway," Terence said, causing Thomas' eyes to flicker back open, "tell me about it. Did you meet anyone at all? Was your friend Lily there?"

Lily. Why did Terence have to bring up that name? Other than a conversation a few months ago when Thomas had shown his roommate a few photos of Lily, her name never came up. Now that it had, he began to recall how she would sneak into his room late at night so they could talk. That was back when he lived at the

Thompson's house, back when his mom was in her coma and his father was in jail. Thomas suddenly wished Lily was with him now. How he missed their late night conversations.

His thoughts drifted to the people who *had* been on the retreat. People like Stephen, the music minister, who had such a wonderful talent getting teens to sing. As he pictured the musician's face, Thomas thought he heard music playing. Next, he thought of Beth, the young adult volunteer with the wonderful, caring and compassionate spirit. Beth brought to mind the sound of laughter, along with the faintest scent of strawberries. The room around him began to grow fuzzy, and his eyelids grew heavy.

His next memory was of Theresa, the young woman who called herself The Endlessly Dying Girl and claimed to have the power of invisibility. He wondered if it was true or just a teenage girl's fantasy. Superheroes were myths, weren't they? As her the features of her face became focused, the room around him began to fade. Suddenly, Thomas felt a sensation of movement, as if the chair he was in was tipping over. Instinctively, he flinched, grasping wildly for the arms of the chair as his eyes opened wide. The first thing he realized was that Terence was gone. As was the couch, the TV, and the clamshell chair he had been curled up in. In fact, the entire room was no longer there.

Feeling both stunned and a bit frightened, Thomas' eyes leaped around his new surroundings, trying to make sense of where he was. The first thing he noticed was a small, twin-size bed with a puffy, pink bedspread and far too many pillows. On the left side of the bed he saw a small desk filled with art supplies and partially completed sketches. Above the desk, a pair of bookshelves hung on the wall, filled to capacity with books of every size. Mixed in with the books were several candles in glass jars, their wicks glowing brightly, filling the air with the scent of cinnamon and vanilla.

An old-fashioned rocking chair was on the other side of the bed. The array of clothes draped over it told Thomas the chair was no longer being used, (at least not for its intended purpose). Next to the rocking chair was a nightstand, with another small shelf on the wall above it. This one held several porcelain and crystal figures and a few more candles, also lit. Random items lay on the floor: a pair of denim shorts, several shoes, a backpack, a sweatshirt, and a girl.

Thomas froze when he saw her. She was lying on her stomach on the floor beside the bed, facing away from him, absentmindedly drawing on one page of a large sketchpad. She wore a faded gray Metallica t-shirt, a pair of denim cut-offs, and a navy baseball cap worn backward. Her hair was twisted into a ponytail to keep it from falling over her shoulders as she drew. Her feet, crossed at the ankles, were raised above her waist, twitching just slightly to the rhythm of the song playing from the cell phone nearby. Next to the phone was a large box of pencils in every color. The girl held a bright red pencil in her right hand, and a cluster of half a dozen others in her left. The only illumination in the room came from the small pockets of light from the candles, leaving most of the room in dim shadow.

Thomas took a slow, quiet breath. A musty, stale smell tickled his senses, barely perceptible under the mixed odors of the candles. He knew he had smelled that scent before. He had also seen the same fluid, blue-gray shape his power was now showing him above the young woman's head. Putting the two together, Thomas realized where it was that he had appeared. This was not just any girl's bedroom, but the bedroom of Theresa, The Endlessly Dying Girl.

Unaware if he was dreaming, seeing things, or simply losing his mind, Thomas stood as still as he could, watching her draw. From where he was standing, he could see only see the edges of her drawing, as her head and shoulders blocked the rest. On the right side of the page, he saw a dark, foreboding forest, with fearsome eyes shining out from the shadows. On the left stood a brilliant, luminous, crystal cathedral, with several angels floating above. A dust-gray road led from each side, winding through a verdant, green valley. Thomas guessed that the road most likely connected in the middle.

On the forest side of the page, standing just on the edge of the road, Theresa had drawn a demon, complete with fire-red skin, a pitchfork, and a long, barbed tail. On the cathedral side, she was adding the final touches to the figure of a man dressed like a monk. The monk was holding a cross in one hand. In the other was a bundle of short, red lines that reminded Thomas of tiny ropes. He knew immediately what they were.

Red vines.

"Oh my God," Thomas gasped, "that's me!"

At the sound of his voice, Theresa yelped, leaping to her feet. Her hand struck the tray of pencils sending a rainbow of colors into the air.

"What the hell?" she said in a frightened voice.

"You can see me?" Thomas gasped.

Theresa, her face frozen in shock and her eyes locked on Thomas, nodded her head slightly. Suddenly Theresa's room, her candles, and the music faded away, leaving Thomas wondering where he would wind up next. When nothing but inky black shadows appeared, Thomas closed his eyes. When he opened them again, he found himself once more in his apartment at school.

"What just happened?" he said quietly.

"What's that? Did you say something?" Terence replied from the couch.

"Um, no…sorry. Forget it. I was just talking to myself," Thomas mumbled.

"Okay, if you say so," Terence responded.

"I must have fallen asleep," Thomas considered silently, thinking that was the most plausible explanation.

How else could he clarify what he had just seen, other than that it hadn't been real? Otherwise, wouldn't Terence have noticed that Thomas had suddenly disappeared? Before anything else truly strange happened, he pushed himself out of the clamshell chair.

"I think…" Thomas began as he shifted his weight, once more feeling more than a bit dizzy. "I think I'm going to bed. I'm exhausted."

"Yeah, I'll bet. You look like hell, Tommy. Like you just saw a ghost or something."

Thomas didn't like when Terence called him 'Tommy', but he had never asked him to stop. Having gone for so many months without saying something, he knew it would seem weird to mention it now. Rather than make this moment more awkward than it already was, he simply 'huffed' once and then headed to his room.

On the way down the hall, he thought about what had just happened. A myriad of questions flooded his muddled, exhausted mind. What if he really had somehow transported to another location? What if, like the strange colors and shapes he was seeing more and more often, some new phenomenon was beginning to develop? If he had actually shown up in Theresa's room, how would he be able to explain it to her? Was this somehow linked to the quest he had been given by Saint Thérèse? With far more questions than he felt he would ever find answers to, Thomas checked once more that he had set an alarm, closed his eyes, and drifted off to sleep.

※

Theresa finally pulled her eyes from the corner of the room where she could swear she had just seen Brother Thomas standing. Blinking several times to wet her now very dry eyes, which had been held open for quite some time, she slowly stood up. Her senses on full alert, she moved cautiously towards the wall. Something *had* been there, she knew it had. She could feel a warmth in the air where his image had been, as well as a slight scent that immediately brought to mind how he had smelled when she had hugged him Saturday night. If he had, in fact, been here, then the next question she would need to answer, was why?

After the two had talked, Theresa had gone to reconciliation with Father Jorge, as Thomas had suggested. Though she would never have chosen to do so on her own, she had been very glad she went. Afterward, she had found Beth waiting for her, and the two had gone back to the large meeting room. They had found a quiet corner where they could talk, and, for the third time that night, Theresa had retold her story.

Of the three who had heard her tale, Beth had been the one who showed the most compassion, giving Theresa the feeling that Beth more than understood what she had been through. The two had exchanged phone numbers, with Theresa promising to reach out for support if she ever needed, though inside she had known she never would. Trusting someone else meant becoming vulnerable, leaving her open to being hurt again, and that was something Theresa had had more than enough of.

Still, somehow that night Theresa had felt something more than a friendship had developed with both Beth and Brother Thomas. Though she couldn't put her finger on it, she also hadn't been able to rid herself of the feeling that her future depended on them, and, in turn, theirs would depend on her.

Still unsure if what she had just witnessed in her room had been real or not, Theresa returned to her drawing, gathering up the colored pencils from where they were strewn scattered across the floor. She put the final touches on the image of Brother Thomas near the crystal cathedral, her interpretation of what heaven might be like. Satisfied, she sat back and examined her work.

※

When the alarm sounded the next morning, Thomas didn't dare shut it off. He knew if he did, he could easily fall back asleep. And if that happened, as exhausted as he was, he might not wake again for days. Though he didn't have a class scheduled until later in the afternoon, he did have an early morning assignment. It was his turn to assist during morning liturgy. Rolling over, he dragged his legs unwillingly out of bed, and then sat there for a moment, slumped like an abandoned marionette. Though he attempted to stand, his muscles refused to respond. All he could coax out was a deep, whimpering groan.

Thomas tried clearing his throat, finding it dry and scratchy. He hoped he wasn't coming down with a cold. He placed the back of his hand against his forehead. He did feel a little warm, but not hot. Satisfied that he wasn't sick, he pushed himself up from the bed. Then, plodding one foot after the next, Thomas lumbered into the bathroom. The face that greeted him in the mirror wasn't recognizable at first. His eyes were puffy and red, and his whole face drooped as if his cheeks were sliding off.

Thomas leaned over the sink, splashing a good amount of cold water on his face. The chill helped revive him slightly. A cold shower would do the rest. Somewhat more awake (and by far the cleanest he had been since Thursday night) Thomas put on a pair of black denim pants, a white t-shirt, a long-sleeve navy blue thermal shirt, and an unbuttoned red flannel 'lumberjack' shirt over that. He stuffed a black hoodie in his backpack, just in case it was colder than it looked, and headed outside.

The cold, late winter air made him shiver, but he decided to keep his hoodie tucked away as he knew the chill would help wake him up. So would caffeine, which he suddenly craved more than anything. On his way to the chapel, he stopped in a small coffeehouse near his apartment and ordered two cups. He asked for one to be served extra-hot, and the other, slightly chilled. The young woman behind the counter smiled as she rang him up, then turned to fill his cups. As he watched her work, Thomas was drawn to the colorful shape she unknow-ingly displayed above her head. He hadn't seen this combination before.

The shape was wound together tightly, as if there was something the young woman was trying to hide. It was mostly light pink, with some white highlights and deeper red undertones. Thomas couldn't be sure, because of the strong smell of coffee in the café, but he thought he could detect a slight scent of flowers. Though perhaps that was just her perfume or shampoo. He was about to ignore it when something captured his attention back.

As she was in the process of adding frozen coffee crystals to the slightly-chilled cup, she turned her head just slightly, looking at him from the corner of her eye. As he gave her a warm smile, his left eye twitched, causing it to wink. Her cheeks flushed as the tightly wound shape burst open, becoming what looked like a crimson rose. She gave him a shy, embarrassed grin, and then quickly turned back to her work.

As she secured the lids on the coffee cups, the blossom petals folded back, once more forming the tightly wound shape he had seen before. However, this time the crimson color remained. She handed the cups to Thomas, flashing the same shy grin once more, and then quickly turned her head, blushing deeply. Thomas caught sight of her nametag as she did.

"Thank you, Gemma, These should wake me up," he said, not sure what else to say.

"Well, if not," Gemma replied, her face still turned away, "you know where to find me."

As she said these words, her cheeks blushed even more, and the petals of her emotional rose opened ever so slightly. Brutally aware that Gemma had misread the wink he had unintentionally given her, Thomas struggled to find the right words to say. He didn't want to leave her with the wrong impression, but he couldn't get his brain to work. Unsure of what to do, he simply nodded his head, turned around, and walked out the door. A part of him wanted to look back, just to see if she was still looking. Even if she was, what could he do? Hard as it was, he had made a promise when he pledged to follow the path he was on. A promise he had no intention of breaking. Still, he had to know.

Raising one of the cups to his mouth, he turned around, walking backward now. Gemma was still looking. As soon as their eyes met, she blushed once more, turning her head and wiping the top of the counter, pretending as if she hadn't been looking his way. Still, Thomas could tell she kept one eye on him. He smiled, tilting the cup back as he did, and then turned and continued on his way. The cool coffee washed easily down his throat, giving him hope that the dark liquid would work its magic quickly, helping to clear the remaining cobwebs away. With four more mighty swallows, Thomas finished off the chilled coffee, tossing the cup in a trash can along the way. With one hand now free, he fished in his pocket for his cell phone to check the time. He would have to hurry.

Rushing across the campus, he reached the chapel a few minutes later and slipped in through the unlocked rear door. He made his way to the sacristy, tossing his backpack on a chair in the corner. Taking a small sip from the remaining cup, he looked around the room, spotting Father Lawrence in the process of cleaning vestments.

"Running late, are we, Brother Thomas?" Father Lawrence said, passing a lint roller over a chasuble.

Father Lawrence was a small, frail, older man with bony hands that were bent and twisted from arthritis. His face was deeply furrowed from far too many years worrying about things outside of his control. This gave him the appearance of being permanently upset, though Thomas knew that was far from the truth.

"I apologize, Father," Thomas said, meekly. "It was a very long weekend."

"Ah? Was it now? And by your bedraggled appearance, a particularly festive one at that. Too many beers and too little sleep, I'm guessing."

"Actually, Father, this was the week I flew home to work the confirmation retreat for my old parish."

Father Lawrence's hands stopped mid-motion, his eyes looking at Thomas over the top of his glasses, which were riding half-way down his nose.

"Really? And what, pray tell, were your responsibilities on this retreat?"

"Spiritual counsel," Thomas replied proudly.

"You? A second-year Initiate? You haven't even taken the Permanent Commitment yet, have you?" the priest huffed in reply.

Thomas bowed his head, not looking Father Lawrence in the eye.

"No sir, Father Lawrence, sir," he whispered.

"Well, then," came the haughty reply, "they must have been fairly desperate, I would imagine."

"Oh, undoubtedly, Father" Thomas said, trying not to laugh.

"Next time you plan on being late for Mass, you should do us both a favor," Father Lawrence instructed.

"What might that be?" Thomas asked, unable to keep from smiling.

"You should at least bring enough coffee to share," Father Lawrence said, turning towards Thomas with a grin.

The two stood for a moment in silence, then both men burst out laughing. Father Lawrence dropped the lint roller on the counter, stretching his arms out wide.

"Come and give an old man a hug!" Father Lawrence said through the laughter.

Thomas walked over and wrapped his arms around the priest, squeezing tightly and lifting him slightly off the ground.

"Woah, woah, easy now. I am old, remember!"

"Hey, you're the one who said 'fairly desperate', old man," Thomas joked.

"Come, come. You can tell me all about it after Mass this morning. Unless you have class right away?"

"Not until after lunch, actually."

"Well, then, hop to it lad! Go, get thee to your duties! And not a single water spot on my chalice, or I'll have you saying rosaries until you graduate!"

Thomas shook his head, sighing deeply. Then, turning to retrieve the items Father Lawrence would need during Communion, he paused just a moment, pointing at the chasuble the priest was once more cleaning.

"You missed a spot," he said with a grin.

"Where? I don't see anything," Father Lawrence replied, pushing his glasses back up the bridge of his nose and squinting slightly.

"Yeah…I guess you were right," Thomas said as he disappeared around the corner, "you are old."

"Still young enough to kick your skinny backside if I wanted!" Father Lawrence said. "Don't forget, I've been at this much longer than you. God owes me a favor or two. Don't make me ask Him to punish you!"

"Yes, sir, Father Lawrence, sir!" Thomas joked.

"What was that? I'm not sure I heard you correctly," the priest retorted.

"Yes, sir, your holiness!"

"That's better, my boy. That's better."

CHAPTER TWO
THE ROAD

A cool breeze brushed across Thomas' face, causing him to stir. His eyes opened slowly, as if coming out of a deep sleep. The brightness of the day startled him, and his eyes blinked several times. As his eyes adjusted to the glare, he stifled a yawn and then took an idle, relaxed look around. He found himself in the shade of a large tree. The tree sat in a small depression, surrounded by grassy hills on all sides. Though the bark was rough and the ground was nowhere near as comfortable as his bed, he had slept on worse. Hardwood floors, the back of his parent's station wagon, and once on nothing but rock.

Considering the position his body was in, which was more reclining than lying flat, he found it highly unlikely that he had come to the base of this tree with sleep in mind. Instead, he had most likely been drawn here as means of escaping the heat of the day. After which he had spent some time lazily watching the afternoon pass. Eventually, sleep must have found him, and not the other way around.

That, he considered, may as well be what had happened, since, for the life of him, Thomas couldn't remember anything else. Not why he was where he was, or where he had come from, or what he might have been doing when the thought of resting in the shade of this tree had first crossed his mind. Try as he might, he couldn't find even the scrap of a clue. Waking under this tree was just one more item in a growing list of strange events.

This realization should have filled him with certain familiar emotions. Fear, being one. Anxiety, another. Or trepidation, in the least. But he had no fear, no worry, no concern. Nor did he sense happiness, joy, or sadness. His heart seemed as devoid of feeling as his mind was of memory. It was as if, rather than waking in this place as he had assumed, he had instead simply arrived. And without two of his most valued possessions, those being his heart, and his brain.

There was only one way to test this theory. Thomas pinched himself. Hard. The sensation of his fingers powerfully clamping the skin of his forearm registered immediately. As did the pain that followed just nanoseconds behind.

"I must have my brain, then," he thought, *"or I wouldn't have felt that."*

As for his heart, well, the rhythmic pulsing in the swollen and quickly-bruising circle that the pinch had left behind was evidence that he must have his heart as well. Perhaps, he considered, rather than forgetting to pack them, he had simply forgotten what it felt like to feel. This made more sense, since his memories of everything else were vacant, too.

Well, not everything else. He still had distant memories from days of his youth. And he had some more recent ones as well, such as the day he had met Father Dominic. He could also recall the events that had taken place after that meeting, too. Right up until…

That was the problem. Until when? When was it that his last memory had been recorded, cataloged, and stored away for future use? Try as he might, he couldn't recall. Rolling first to his side and then to his knees, Thomas got up. Yawning fully this time, he stretched his arms as high as he could, glancing up at the branches above. The limbs were so tightly intertwined, there wasn't even a glimpse of the sky.

With his brief fitness routine complete, Thomas took one last look around, then walked the dozen or so steps that brought him out from under the tree and into the sunlight beyond. At first, all he could see was grass. Long, green grass. Broad blades standing at attention, refusing to bow or sway in the breeze. Thomas found this curious. Grass always swayed in the breeze, didn't it? Now that he thought about it, don't trees sway as well?

Climbing to the top of the rise just behind the tree, he glanced back down. Though the tree grew far taller than the low rising hill he stood on, it didn't move. Not even one leaf. Even more curious now, Thomas looked at the landscape around him. Nothing seemed to move. Not the grass, clouds, or even the pockets of flowers that dotted the gently rolling terrain. What's more, there was no sound. Though Thomas felt the breeze, it passed over him noiselessly. Silence. No birds, no animals. Nothing.

Feeling perplexed, Thomas began descending the hill, and then scrambled up the next. This one was slightly higher than the last, and provided a much better view. As he crested the peak, he saw the valley open up before him and, at the base of the hill he now stood upon, a dust-gray road traveling in both directions. A narrow, barely visible path broke off from the road, winding between the knolls, leading to where he now stood. At the place where the path splintered off, a wooden signpost was planted firmly in the ground.

"That's as good a place to start as any," Thomas said as he made his way to the path below, watching as the blades of grass continued their stoic stance.

Arriving at the signpost, he saw it had two words written in large, black letters. Below each word, a white arrow pointed. One to the left, and the other to the right. The arrow pointing to the right had the word "Hell" written above it, and the arrow pointing left was below the word "Heaven".

"I think that's a pretty easy choice!" Thomas announced, as if the signpost cared what he thought.

Pivoting his feet, he pointed his body to the left, and started walking. As he walked, he wondered about what he would find when he reached his destination. He also wondered how many people, if any, had ever chosen to walk the other way, if even just for curiosities sake. Finally, he pondered how long the walk would take, and how he would know that he had reached the end.

The day was warm, but the ever-silent breeze kept him from getting too warm. Though he could see that the terrain around him undulated, he still couldn't get rid of the feeling that what he was looking at was flat, almost two-dimensional. Still, he continued on, hoping he would find the answer to the questions colliding in his mind.

Thomas walked for what felt like an hour, but it could have just as easily been half that time. With nothing to reference, it was hard to tell. All he had was the moderately similar hills on each side of the road, and the inaudible steps his feet made upon it. In the distance, it appeared as if the sky was growing brighter, with silver-white streaks highlighting the blue.

"Ten more hills," Thomas huffed as he trundled on. "Ten more hills and then I'm going to rest."

Luckily, he only had to pass eight more before he spotted something up ahead. It looked like a building of some sort, or at least the top section of one, made out of mirrors or glass. The light bouncing off of the reflective surface was what had created the streaks of silver-white light he had seen. The building looked like a palace, or a temple, or…

Thomas froze.

"A cathedral!" he shouted, not believing the words, even though they were his own. "But it can't be."

Thomas glanced at the landscape around him. If his suspicions were right, then it would explain why everything appeared to be flat, why was there no movement or sound, why he had no memory of how he got here, and why he seemed unable to feel emotions. Taking a few tentative steps forward, Thomas began moving towards the cathedral again. Steps became a fast walk, and then a jog. Eventually, he was sprinting. Faster and faster Thomas ran, his feet flying beneath him until he could no longer tell the left foot from the right.

In mere minutes he reached the church and paused about fifty feet away as he took in the magnificent sight. Every inch of the building was made from the same translucent, crystalline material. Walls, door handles, hinges, window frames, everything. Looking through the transparent doors, he saw that the same held true for the interior as well. He had never seen anything like it. Though, like the landscape he had just traversed, the crystal cathedral still had a two-dimensional feel. Still a bit befuddled, Thomas shrugged his shoulders, walked the rest of the way to the massive front doors, opened them, and then went inside.

"I'm in her picture," he said, laughing uncomfortably, the sound echoing around the cavernous chamber. "I'm literally inside Theresa's drawing. But, how did I get here?"

"I can answer that if you'd like," an unfamiliar voice called out.

Thomas turned in surprise, finding a man standing on the dais near the altar. He had a friendly face, a round, balding head, and a long beard stretching down to his chest. He wore circular glasses that rested halfway down his nose, and the chocolate brown robes of a Conventual Franciscan Friar. Thomas recognized the man immediately, being that he was currently studying the history of Catholicism in the Far East.

"Saint Maximillian Kolbe?" Thomas whispered, only half-surprised at this turn of events. "I'm dreaming again, aren't I?"

Saint Maximillian flashed a half-smile as he nodded his head.

"In a way, Thomas, yes," he said with a heavy accent. "The power you have been granted is one based on faith, by far the most powerful of all the Fruits of the Holy Spirit. Scriptures tell us that faith is 'being sure of what we hope for and certain of what we do not see.' This gives you the ability to create what you believe."

"So, this is real? This cathedral, and the land that I walked through to get here…it's all real?"

"As real as you believe it is. Now, don't get me wrong, you will not be able to find this place on earth. It doesn't exist in the physical realm. Here, we are in the spiritual realm," Saint Maximillian explained.

"The spiritual realm? What's the difference?"

"Think of it this way. When you eat a meal, the physical food you take in breaks down and becomes chemical compounds. Protein, carbohydrates, or fat. Your body then uses those chemicals as energy to maintain your health. When you eat healthily, your body is healthy.

But if you eat too much sugar, or foods with too much fat or salt, you create an environment where it is harder to maintain health.

"It's the same with the spiritual realm and the physical realm. The actions of the physical world, the 'food', if you will, breaks down into positively charged and negatively charged energy. For example, let's say you decide to help someone in need, which you would probably consider to be a positive action, which it is. But, just like the food in the physical world, not everything that appears healthy really is."

"So, how does that compare to helping someone in need?" Thomas inquired, a bit puzzled.

"What if the person who decided to help only did so because they knew others were watching? What if they had no true concern for the person they were helping at all? What if they did it to boost their own stature?"

"Oh, I see," Thomas said quietly as he contemplated the implications of these words. "So, what you're saying then, is that intention is far more important than action, is that right?"

Saint Maximillian smiled.

"Exactly, Thomas. When the action is broken down as it comes into the spiritual realm, the true intentions are revealed. Those that promote a healthy spirituality move the balance between good and evil in the direction of good. But those underlying, unhealthy motives, even if they are invisible in the physical world, become like poison here in the spiritual world. They move the balance in the direction of that which is evil. And the more evil there is in the spiritual realm…"

"…the more evil gets created in the physical one," Thomas finished.

"Now you understand. The true battle for good and evil never happens in the physical world. It happens here, in the spiritual world. However, the spiritual world is completely dependent on the physical world for the energy it needs to survive. Just like the health of the human body does not depend on what happens on the outside, but what happens within."

Thomas turned his eyes away for a moment, his mind racing as he thought about what he had just learned. The way Saint Maximillian explained it made sense, he just still didn't understand how he moved between.

"How can I travel between the two?" he asked.

"Because of your faith. Those shapes you see above the heads of people you know, and the smells too, come from your ability to be confident in what you do not see. It allows you to see what is real, what is true. It helps you discern between an individual's actions and their true intentions. This creates a bridge between the spiritual and the physical worlds, providing you with the power to directly affect the spiritual realm. But, to do so, you must first travel here."

"I think I understand," Thomas said. "But I'm still not sure what all I'm able to do while I'm here."

"First of all, the way you perceive the spiritual realm is up to you. You have the ability to see what you believe it to be. This time, your perception created the environment based on an image that resonated deeply within your mind.

"It was the Holy Spirit that led you to Theresa's room. You needed to see the image she was drawing so that our meeting here today would be possible. You see, you are here for a purpose. I have a gift for you, Thomas."

"A gift?" Thomas asked. "What sort of gift?"

"One that the Devil has tried for many years to acquire, or, at least, to destroy," Saint Maximillian said earnestly, holding Thomas' eyes with his own.

"But, this gift is not for you. Though it will help you in your quest, it is meant for another, one who will be a Guardian of Zion, like yourself and Theresa. They will be the one to use this gift. Through its use you will also find benefit, though you must not use it yourself."

Thomas knew by the look in Saint Maximillian's eyes that there was a seriousness in what he said. He wasn't just asking Thomas not to use the gift himself, he was warning him against it.

Nodding, Thomas replied, "You have my word."

The serious look in Saint Maximillian's eyes faded, returning the orbs to a gentle, comforting look. He gave Thomas a relaxed, friendly smile.

"Then, come. Follow me," the saint said as he stepped down from the dais, turned his back to Thomas, and began walking away.

Thomas followed close behind. As they made their way to the far side of the church, he took the opportunity to look around even more.

"So, why are we inside Theresa's drawing? Why couldn't we just meet in my dreams, like I did with Saint Thérèse?" he asked tentatively.

"We needed a safe place, somewhere the Devil couldn't follow you, where I could give the gift to you without his knowledge."

"What is it, this gift you have for me? And who am I supposed to give it to?"

"What it is, you are about to discover. But who it is for, you cannot know. If you knew before the time was right, there is a chance the Devil would find out. All it would take would be for you to treat the person differently than normal, trying to protect them. That could lead the Evil One to find out before they are ready."

"Ready? Ready for what?"

Saint Maximillian paused, reaching into his cloak and drawing forth a large, crystal key. He inserted the key into a lock. As it turned, Thomas could see the transparent tumblers falling into place. Before the door was open, Thomas already knew what they would find.

"Thomas, please trust me in this. You are being granted as much information as we can provide. Everything we tell you, the Evil One will discover one way or another. The less you know, the better it will be for all involved. He almost got to you before we did four years ago. If it hadn't been for the way you suddenly called upon God's help as you ran past that chapel, we might have lost you. Forever."

Saint Maximillian turned and walked through the now open door, beginning to climb a crystal stairway that wound up the inside of one of the cathedral's towers.

"What do you mean, lost forever? And why is this place safer than any other?"

"We are safe here because of the way Theresa drew this land. You couldn't see the center of it from your perspective. All you saw were the two sides. Do you recall what her drawing showed?"

"Yeah, one side had a cathedral, which I assume is where we are now, and the other had a dark forest, with a demon standing nearby. But, are you saying I actually traveled to where she was? That it wasn't just a dream?"

"Let me answer your questions in order. First, let's talk about Theresa. As you learned in your dream with Saint Thérèse, this young woman is special. She is one of the Guardians of Zion. We could tell you who she is because she is protected. First, through the way she perceives the world. And, second, because she has someone watching over her. Someone who will also be a Guardian of Zion, though we cannot say just who that person is yet, as their powers have not yet come.

"As you learned from Saint Thérèse, these powers that Theresa and the others have all come from the Fruits of the Holy Spirit. Theresa's power comes from charity. Though she feels it as a desire to be unseen, that is just an aftereffect of the Fruit she carries. It is what allows her to turn invisible."

"I'm sorry to interrupt, Saint Maximillian, but I'm not sure I see the correlation here. Don't most people want others to see their charitable acts? I mean, they post about it all the time on Facebook or Twitter. How does that make them invisible?"

"That is a good question. You see, whenever someone gives to another with the purpose of getting something in return, then it is not charity. Call it a transaction or an exchange if you want. But it is not charity. Not true charity, anyway. Though they are doing good works, they do them because of what they gain from them. Perhaps it makes them feel better about themselves. Like the rich people Jesus spoke of who gave only from their abundance. This is like the fruit we spoke of earlier that appears healthy on the outside, but bears within it pesticides and poisons that are unseen.

"True charity, or untainted fruit, is like the scripture of the poor widow who gave two small coins. She gave all she had, simply because she knew there were others who had less. She didn't make a show of it. She did it quietly, expecting nothing in return. That is an example of great faith, Thomas. She gave simply because she had something to give, knowing that God would provide for her even more. This is true charity, and this is the Fruit that Theresa has. It enables her to become invisible. She has no need of anyone knowing what it is that she does or to see how she sacrifices herself for others."

"Oh, I see now," Thomas interrupted again. "Charity is selfless acts of love, not public displays for attention or personal gain."

"Exactly. But, that is not the only power Theresa has. As I said before, she has a unique way of viewing the world, brought about by her call to charity. This view of the world, which she interprets as endlessly dying, has a dual nature to it."

"I'm not sure I understand," Thomas said as he glanced out at the landscape below, wondering how high they had climbed.

"Consider this. If she is endlessly dying, but yet never dies, then isn't she also endlessly living?" Saint Maximillian questioned.

"I hadn't thought about it like that, but yeah, I guess she is," Thomas replied.

"This is what gives her the power to create and exist within dualities. Where these dualities exist, nothing can cross between. This is what Theresa formed when she drew that picture. Heaven on one side, and hell on the other. She created a version of reality where the Devil could not cross over. If he had followed you to this reality, or sent any of his demons here, they would be stuck on the side with the dark forest, helpless to cross the divide."

"Why doesn't God just create the world like that? So Satan can't do harm?" Thomas asked, a bit puzzled still with the way these dualities work.

"Ah. So many before you have asked that question. And the answer is simple. Because that would deny the right to free will. God doesn't want robots. He wants people to seek Him of their own choice. But that is a discussion for another time. I believe we have arrived."

Thomas was so engrossed in the conversation that he hadn't realized they had reached a landing. Before them stood an archway, decorated with crystal images of cherubs, flowers, and rosaries. Beyond the archway was a large room furnished like a small museum. There were items stored in transparent display cases and others hanging in crystal frames on the walls. In one display Thomas saw a leather slingshot. Three small stones lay next to it. Another display held several wooden staffs.

"What is all of this stuff?" Thomas asked.

"Relics, mostly from Old Testament times. The staff Moses used to part the Red Sea, Aaron's rod, David's slingshot, the ram's horn trumpet from the Battle of Jericho. Come, over here is the item we came to collect."

Thomas followed Saint Maximillian to a large display in the center of the room where a full suit of armor hung on a crystal rack.

"What is this?" he asked, reaching out to touch the armor on display.

"That," Saint Maximillian stated proudly, "is the Armor of God."

Saint Maximillian brought forth another key, this one made of gold, and unlocked the chain that secured the armor to the stand.

"Finally, be strong in the Lord and in the strength of his power. Put on the whole armor of God, so that you may be able to stand against the wiles of the Devil." Saint Maximillian quoted as he removed the chain.

"Ephesians, chapter six, verses ten and eleven," Thomas responded, a bit in awe.

"Well, now," Saint Maximillian said, pausing his work to give Thomas an approving glance, "I see you know your scripture."

"Yes, although never in my wildest dreams did I imagine the armor was real!"

Saint Maximillian placed his hand on the crystal and gold armor and said softly, "For man this is impossible, but with God all things are possible." He then turned to face Thomas more fully as he explained, "You seemed very aware of who I am when you first came into the cathedral. Now tell me what you know."

"I know you were a Conventual Franciscan, and that you were martyred at Auschwitz. Before that, you were nicknamed the Apostle of Consecration to Mary for your devotion to Our Lady, and that you started two organizations. The first was named Militia Immaculata, or 'Army of the Immaculate One'. The other was a monthly periodical you published, though I cannot pronounce the name in your language. In English it translates to Knight of the Immaculate. This earned you the nickname Knight of the Rosary."

Saint Maximillian smiled. It was a broad, wide smile that exposed most of his teeth, which were normally hidden behind the full beard.

"Very good. Here is what you don't know. I started those organizations not simply because of my devotion to Mary but because I was once asked to wear this armor myself."

The corners of Thomas' mouth dropped slightly as he nodded his head in understanding. "Hmm..." he said. "That I didn't know."

"Few are called to wear it and, of those called, even fewer accept. It comes with great responsibility and even greater sacrifice. When one puts it on, they become a Knight of the Immaculate, a Holy Paladin. They must give up the ways of the world, forgo any temptation, and give total control of their life to God's plan."

"And the one I am supposed to give this to, they will be willing to do that?"

Saint Maximillian shrugged, frowning slightly as he did, saying, "That is in God's plan. But, as we already discussed, God cannot force anyone to do what they do not want. The choice must come from their own free will. They must willingly accept the responsibility and sacrifice this knighthood brings."

Saint Maximillian paused a moment, as if collecting his thoughts or trying to decide if he should, or could, say anything more. Then he simply returned to his work, pulling the chain that held the armor in place as he quietly continued to quote from scripture.

"For our struggle is not against enemies of blood and flesh, but against the rulers, against the authorities, against the cosmic powers of this present darkness, against the spiritual forces of evil in the heavenly places."

He bundled up the chain, laying it on the floor at the foot of the armor stand and then began to unfasten a thick, golden belt from around the armor's waist.

"Therefore, take up the whole armor of God, so that you may be able to withstand on that evil day, and having done everything, to stand firm. Stand, therefore, and fasten the belt of truth around your waist…"

He handed the belt to Thomas who accepted it with reverence and awe.

"…and put on the breastplate of righteousness."

Thomas accepted the main piece of the armor, a crystal breastplate that shone with a thousand rainbows.

"As shoes for your feet, put on whatever will make you ready to proclaim the gospel of peace," Saint Maximillian continued.

Thomas accepted a pair of well worn, leather sandals with long straps that would wrap several times around the lower leg before securing near the knee.

"With all of these, take the shield of faith, with which you will be able to quench all the flaming arrows of the evil one."

The shield that Saint Maximillian held out was made from the purest white gold. On the front were several symbols: a cross, a shepherd's crook, unrolled parchment, and a dove carrying olive branches. Thomas juggled all of the items he was now carrying as best he could. How he would get them all the way back to the tree where he had entered this reality, he had no idea. Saint Maximillian stood holding the final two items, waiting for Thomas to finish juggling the pieces already in his hands.

"Take the helmet of salvation," Saint Maximillian quoted, putting the helmet on Thomas' head, giving him one less thing to hold in his hands, "and the sword of the Spirit, which is the word of God."

"Um...I don't have a free hand," Thomas apologized as he tried once more to shift all the pieces to free a hand so he could hold the sword.

"Why don't you try carrying them where they are meant to be carried, Thomas," Saint Maximillian said, placing his hand on Thomas' chest. "In your heart."

Thomas gave him a curious, sideways glance, garnering a shaking of the head and a deep sigh from Saint Maximillian.

"Thérèse was right about you. Very little imagination," he said, closing his eyes and placing his free hand on the side of Thomas' chest, just over his heart.

Saint Maximillian whispered a few words in a language Thomas was unable to understand, though he could feel their power. He closed his eyes, focusing on the flow of energy he felt coming from Saint Maximillian's hand. A comforting warmth surrounded him, flowing from his hands, up his arms, and into his chest. When the saint finished speaking, Thomas opened his eyes to find he was no longer holding the armor. The sword Saint Maximillian had been holding was also gone.

"Where are they?" Thomas asked.

"In your heart, where they belong. And where they will stay until you realize the time has come for them to be used, which…"

"I know, I know," Thomas interrupted. "You can't tell me, because then the Devil will know God's plan and try to use it against us. Can I at least ask what the words were you were saying when you had your hand on my chest just now?"

"That? Oh, I was simply repeating the beatitudes," Saint Maximillian told him.

"Will I need to repeat them to get the armor back out when the time comes?"

"You can if you want to. It isn't a requirement, or some sort of spell. I say them simply to help focus my thoughts, and to remind me of one of the cornerstones of our faith," Saint Maximillian said, pointing towards the archway where they had entered. "It's time for you to head back. There are only a few days remaining until the moon is full. Use them wisely, Thomas. Prepare yourself, prepare your heart. Trust your faith.

"When you have found the one who this gift is for, return to the spiritual realm. Because the armor exists only in the world of the spiritual, it is here that you will have to pass it along. Do not try to pass it on in the physical world. The Devil will sense it, and will be able to steal it away. It cannot get into his hands, Thomas."

Saint Maximillian stared at him for a long, long moment, ensuring that he understood what he just heard. Finally, Thomas nodded his head.

"I understand," he said confidently.

"There is one last thing I must tell you," Saint Maximillian began. "When you are ready to pass it over, the only way to enter the spiritual realm is through their heart. They must open their heart to you, trusting you fully and completely. Do you understand?"

"I think so. How do I make that happen, though?"

"There is only one way, Thomas. You must connect through love. Pure, honest, holy love. Not physical attraction, or wanton desire, but love like Jesus taught us to have. When they trust that you will never hurt them, that you will always protect them, then, and only then, will their heart be open to you. When that happens, they will enter the spiritual world with you.

"The Devil will most likely follow you, or send one of his demons, so be prepared at all times. Remember, you have power within this realm. However you believe it to be, it will be. Your intuition will help, as will the Holy Spirit. Your faith will support you. Trust in it always."

With that, Saint Maximillian was gone. Thomas took one more look around and then walked back through the archway and prepared to climb back down the long, winding stairs. Yet, as he placed his foot on the first step, his vision blurred and the crystal cathedral began to disappear. As the world around him faded, Thomas felt disoriented and dizzy. He stumbled forward, his arms reaching out instinctively for anything to prevent his fall. As his body began to tumble towards the ground, he heard the voice of Saint Maximillian once more.

"Remember, Thomas, the Devil doesn't need your cooperation. Only your complacency. Never stop believing in the power you have!"

"Wait!" Thomas shouted, realizing there were still a dozen questions colliding in his mind. "You promised to answer my questions!"

But it was too late. The cathedral, Saint Maximillian, and the strange duality of Theresa's drawing were all gone. All that remained was a brilliant, white light that filled the entire sky. Slowly, the light coalesced, becoming dim at the edges until it was no more than a single point. That point, Thomas realized, was the flame of a candle, and the candle, he knew, was the Paschal candle, the one that stood on the dais of the chapel at school. He had returned.

CHAPTER THREE
THE DEVIL'S CURSE

Thomas looked around, noticing that Mass had just ended. Around him students and faculty were filing out, heading to their classrooms or lecture halls. No one paid him more than casual attention as he returned to the sacristy to complete his duties for the morning. Father Lawrence, a smile emblazoned on his face, joined him a few moments later.

"No, no, Thomas. Just leave all that. I can take care of it. You need to rest," the priest admonished as he began returning his vestments to the closet.

"Are you sure, Father?" Thomas inquired, hoping the priest would say that he was.

"Yes, yes, I'm sure. I've done this hundreds of times on my own. I'm sure I can manage once more."

"Honestly, thank you, Father. I really am having trouble even just standing up. Maybe I'm coming down with a cold or something. I just don't feel right."

Father Lawrence finished placing the chasuble on the rack and then came to where Thomas was standing.

"You do look a bit pale. Come here, let me see what I can do to help."

Father Lawrence granted Thomas an Anointing of the Sick. Thomas thanked him for his concern.

"Now, off to bed for you, young man!" Father Lawrence commanded.

"Yes, Father, and thank you again. I'll call you later so we can figure out a time to meet."

"Yes, yes! That's fine. Now go! And no stopping to flirt with anyone along the way!"

Thomas gave Father Lawrence a shocked look.

"Father!" he exclaimed, shaking his head as he held the rear door to the sacristy open, about to step outside. "You are too much."

Father Lawrence laughed heartily as he shooed Thomas away with a wave of his hand.

Thomas had walked barely ten feet from the chapel, the door closing behind him with a soft click, when the world around him began to spin.

"Ugh! What is it now?" he complained, a little louder than he had planned, drawing a few curious looks and more than a few snickering grins.

A sudden bout of nausea hit him, freezing him in place. His vision continued to blur, and his heart began to pound loud and fast. Glancing ahead, Thomas saw an empty bench. Willing his feet to move, he inched his way forward. Every step felt like walking on a ship caught in a storm. And then, he smelled it. The familiar scent of fireworks and hot steel. The aroma bit the back of his throat, causing him to cough. He tasted bile and blood.

Reaching the bench, Thomas sat down, his fingers gripping the edges tightly as he tried to steady the world. He wasn't sure if Satan's power had increased, or if he was simply in a weakened condition, having gone the past four days with barely any sleep. Whatever it was, this attack was far worse than any he had felt before.

"I can make it all go away, Thomas," an evil, chilling voice raked through his mind. *"Just give me what you hold in your heart."*

"So," Thomas thought, *"the Devil knows I have something. I wonder if he knows what it is as well."*

"Yes, I know what it is you have, Thomas, just not how you came to acquire it. It will be mine, one way or another. You will hand it over to me."

"So, you're violating my mind now, and reading my thoughts?" Thomas growled in silence, hearing a maniacal, sinister laughter as the Devil's reply.

"Knowing what is in the mind of man is simple," the Devil's voice echoed in the depths of his thoughts. "Predictable, even. But, I'm not here to answer your foolish questions. I want what you have, Thomas. Now."

"As long as I have breath with which to pray," Thomas challenged back, "I will not surrender to you. Not my mind, not my body, and never my heart."

"Then, you will suffer. The power you have been given, the one that lets you see what others feel, can be used for evil as well as good. I know when you had your first visions, you thought you were losing your mind. You have one last chance, Thomas. Give me what I desire or you will know what it feels like to lose your mind."

"Never," Thomas replied in silence.

Inside his mind, Thomas felt a thunderous crash. The ground around him seemed to shake, though no one near seemed affected. A moment later came the screams, millions of voices crying in pain. Thomas didn't just hear their agony, he felt it. His body lurched to one side as he doubled over in pain. Twisting and writhing, Thomas was bent to the point of breaking. Every bone felt ready to snap. The weight of so many terrified souls crushed down on him, making it impossible to breathe.

Then, just as he felt as if he had breathed his final breath, the pressure released, and the screams were gone. Next came a terrible sensation of heat, as if his body was on fire. Slowly, Thomas opened his eyes, expecting to find that he had been cast into the fires of Hell. Yet, instead, he found himself still on the bench, his hands placed gently on his lap. Thomas heard the sinister laughter once more.

"Soon, you will beg me to take what's in your heart, Thomas. Though you think you can resist, one day, you will come to me. One day, you will surrender."

With that, the darkness was gone. Thomas sighed deeply, believing he had somehow just endured the worst that the Devil could dish out. Yet, as his vision cleared, and the world around him came back into view, he realized how arrogant that thought had been.

The activity on campus was steadily increasing as more and more students and faculty began their day, but that wasn't what Thomas noticed. What he saw instead was a phantasmagoria of images. Directly above the head of every person he saw, and everywhere he looked, Thomas saw ghostly images in every shape and color. Where lone individuals walked, the images were discernable. But when they clustered in groups the shapes would blend and mix as if all those in the group were sharing the same emotions. He could see the shapes even when the person they were attached to wasn't visible. He saw them behind walls, inside cars, in the lecture halls and dining rooms. At times the groups were so large, he couldn't make out where one ended and another began.

And as if seeing them wasn't enough, Thomas could feel them as well. Anxiety, despair, joy, passion, anger, hope. Every sensation imaginable mixed and conjoined in an emotional stew. Had they appeared in small groups, they would have been far easier to digest. But they didn't. They assailed his senses as one, like an emotional tsunami, crashing over him with a powerful, destructive force.

Finally, there was the smell. Every scent imaginable bombarded him, making his stomach turn. Thomas gasped, his eyes growing wide. With the onslaught of feelings, he had no way of knowing which emotions belonged to him. He had never felt this many signatures at once. It was far more than he could withstand. He had to get away. He had to find somewhere where the onslaught couldn't reach. Or at least somewhere with a lot fewer people. Where that might be, he hadn't a clue.

The only positive part of the situation was that since he could see every place where people were he could also see places where they weren't. As long as he moved in the direction where the symbols were less dense, he might find a way out. Taking a deep breath to steady himself, Thomas stood. Spinning in a slow, tentative circle, he searched for the best place to start his retreat.

The main campus, where the classrooms, labs and lecture halls were, was straight ahead. Though that part of the campus was just beginning to come alive, a rapidly increasing flow of colorful shapes was heading that way. Just to the right of the main campus was where he would find the sports fields. This area was less populated, but the strong sense of competitive egos that awaited him there was grossly unattractive. Directly to his rear Thomas knew he would find the residence halls. That part of the school grounds was currently the most populated, with thousands of emotional signatures grouped tightly together. But, to his left, there were few signatures visible, and far greater spacing between.

Thomas started off, headed in the direction that would wind past Christ the King Chapel. Beyond that, the sidewalk split. One path heading towards the parking lot and the other path dipping into a wooded area. He knew that within these trees he would find several of the spiritual landmarks of the campus, including the Tomb of the Unborn Child, the Marian Grotto, Stations of the Cross, and the Portiuncula Chapel. Only a few signatures were present within and around these sites. Plus, the emotional flavor emanating from within these trees had a more relaxed, palatable feel.

The first structure Thomas came to was the Portiuncula Chapel, commonly known as The Port. The small stone building with the large wooden doors beckoned him. Within these walls Thomas knew he would find the Blessed Sacrament exposed for adoration. There also seemed to be no emotional displays present within, giving him hope that he would find the building empty. Yet as he quietly pulled the door open and stepped inside, he realized that was not the case. On one side of the small chapel, a group of three female students huddled in a tight group. Two of them were standing behind the third, their hands resting on their friend's head and shoulders as they whispered quiet prayers for their friend. On the other side of the room Thomas saw two other students, one male and the other female. These two were separated by a large enough space that Thomas could tell they were not together. They were both kneeling before the Sacrament, heads bent forward, hands clasped in front.

The door closed behind him, shutting off the tumult of emotions he had endured, leaving Thomas with a profound sense of peace. He sighed heavily, a little louder than he had intended, causing two of the people in the room to glance his way. Nodding an apology, Thomas took a seat in the least occupied corner of the room. His hand dipped into his pocket, drawing out the sandalwood beads of his rosary. Taking another half-dozen deep breaths, this time releasing each one slowly and quietly, he began to slow his pulse and quiet his mind.

The prayers came easily, having said them hundreds of times before. This allowed Thomas to let his mind float peacefully, his thoughts simply drifting away. He didn't need to tell his hands what to do; his fingers knew the way. Two hours later, having completed all four mysteries, Thomas felt far more relaxed and in control. He wondered if he would find the emotional chaos waiting for him outside. Since he couldn't live the rest of his life inside The Port, he would have to find out sooner or later.

Opening his eyes, Thomas noticed that the five people who had been in the chapel when he had entered had been replaced by new faces. Now, however, rather than five others in the chapel with him, there were eleven. Thomas had to carefully scoot past two of them as he made his way to the door. Steadying himself for what he might find, and knowing that he could always return to the sanctuary of this chapel should the Devil's curse prove too much for him again, he gently opened the door.

As his feet crossed the threshold, the onslaught did return, though not as severe or as damaging to his mental state as it had been before. He knew he would have to talk to someone about what was going on. He had held this secret for far too long. For now, he needed to find something to distract him from the kaleidoscope of visions, the rollercoaster of emotions, and the pungent odors that had become a permanent part of his world.

Following the same pattern as he had two hours before, Thomas looked for the places where the signatures were less condensed, or at least felt quieter and more relaxed. This time, the second floor of the Saint Pope John Paul II library turned out to be the perfect place. With semester exams about a month away, he could use the time to study. Realizing he hadn't eaten yet this morning, Thomas made a quick detour to the same café he had purchased his coffee a few hours before. It was still early enough for breakfast, but he didn't want to waste time in the café with so many people coming and going. Instead, he picked up a pre-made turkey and avocado sandwich on multigrain bread, an apple, two bottles of water, and two of the largest lattes they had.

He asked the clerk who made his lattes if Gemma was still working, and was informed that she had already ended her shift for the day. Inquiring if he could leave her a note, the clerk handed him a small pad of paper and a pen. Why he felt like contacting Gemma, he wasn't currently aware. He simply had an inexplicable urge to speak with her. He went through five slips of paper trying to get the wording correct, and then simply gave up and wrote, 'Please call me. It's urgent we speak.' He added his phone number below, and then signed his name, making sure to include his title, as he hoped that would give Gemma more reason to call. The clerk handed him his receipt and he handed her the note, watching as she took it with her into the back room. Satisfied his note would be delivered, Thomas headed out the front door.

CHAPTER FOUR
PROPOSITIONS

When Thomas arrived in the library, he found the least occupied area happened to be near the section on Quantum Mechanics. Appropriating a small reading nook where he could be alone, he grabbed a book at random, only glancing briefly at the cover. He had a genuine interest in subjects that dealt with the intersection of science and spirituality and this book looked like it fit. The cover said it was about distance healing, medical intuition, bilocation, and prayer, all within the confines of a quantum world, of course.

Settling into the almost comfortable cushion of the bench seat, Thomas began to let his mind absorb the words, temporarily distracting himself from the chaos of emotions surrounding him. As he scanned through the book, one section immediately jumped out. It read:

"You will also learn the deeper awareness of true spontaneous bilocation, where a person may physically manifest in more than one place at one time."

Thomas jumped from his seat shouting, "Oh my God! That's what I did!"

Suddenly far more interested in his random book selection, he began to pour himself into the pages, letting the words wash over him as he jumped from chapter to chapter, learning all he could about bilocation. Between what he read in the book and what he learned from several Internet searches, Thomas discovered that bilocation was not only a scientifically accepted phenomenon, but a spiritually endorsed one as well. Within the history of his church, Thomas learned that several of the more popular saints had had episodes similar to the ones he had recently experienced. Saint Paul of the Cross, Saint Padre Pio, and Saint Joseph of Cupertino were just a few who had displayed this ability.

If he had in fact experienced a bilocation, it would explain why Terence hadn't noticed anything when he had suddenly transported to Theresa's room the other night. Thomas had never left his apartment, but had instead been in two places at the same time! Though this information answered some of his questions, it also raised a few more. For one, from what he read, it appeared that the individuals who had experienced bilocation in the past had been both aware of and active in both locations at the same time. Conversely, Thomas had only been aware of one. Perhaps, like his ability to read emotions, this new ability would also take time to fully develop. He also wondered about any practical uses that bilocation might provide him in the future.

As his thoughts drifted deeper and deeper into these questions, his phone buzzed. Picking up the device, he read a text message from Terence.

Where are you? I have a proposition for you.

Knowing Terence would bombard his phone with urgency until he replied back, and so he quickly typed:

Library Studying What's up?

The reply came seconds later.

Stay there - OMW

Thomas relaxed a bit. Whatever it was that Terence needed to discuss, it was something that could be talked about in public. Setting aside his explorations into and questions about bilocation, he placed the book back on the shelf and then dug through his backpack for his red Nalgene water bottle. As he waited for Terence to arrive, his mind beginning to drift, thinking about the strange, supernatural experiences he had had over the past few days, starting with the way the sky had seemed to open up to him on Saturday night during the retreat, just two days ago. Then there was the dream he had with Saint Thérèse, which he now understood hadn't been a dream at all, but a visit into the spiritual realm. Next was the experience last night where he had appeared in Theresa's bedroom. Finally, the events today. The dream vision with Saint Maximillian, the confrontation with Satan, and the emotional assault he was now experiencing. It all fit together, he just couldn't figure out how.

Deep in thought, Thomas didn't hear Terence approach, nor did he hear Terence call his name. He didn't even flinch when his roommate removed his backpack and dropped it on the floor. But when Terence dropped a heavy book right in front of him, Thomas leaped in surprise. As he did, his right foot caught the Terence's backpack, sending him sprawling to the floor.

"What the heck did you do that for?" Thomas said in a harsh, loud whisper.

"Dude, I called your name five times at least! What were you doing? Sleeping with your eyes open?"

"No!" Thomas sneered. "I was just thinking. Sorry if I'm a little focused right now."

"BroTom, you've been more than focused lately. You've been in absentia," Terence said, tapping Thomas on the forehead.

Thomas didn't like the nickname 'BroTom'. He liked it even less than 'Tommy'. Though 'Tommy' hadn't found roots within their circle of friends, 'BroTom' had.

"Well, now that you've found me, what was it you needed to ask?" Thomas replied, swatting his friend's hand away from his face.

"Like I said, I have a proposition for you," Terence grinned slyly.

That grin. Oh, how Thomas hated that grin. Mostly because he knew that Terence actually practiced making it. He had caught him practicing in the mirror one morning when Terence wasn't aware. He also knew that grin was responsible for his roommate getting out of trouble more often than not. Which was another thing Thomas had witnessed (more times than he could recall). For someone he had met less than a year ago, he and Terence had a long list of near-disasters that his charming, Adonis-like roommate had talked their way out of.

Thomas shook his head, mumbling under his breath, "Unbelievable…"

Terence's grin disappeared, his mouth dropping into a sorrowful frown.

"What did I do?" he pleaded with mock grief that was almost believable if not for the bright, playful twinkle in his eyes.

"You really should go into acting, Terry. You'd be a natural. Seriously," Thomas said, shaking his head and picking up the water bottle he had dropped. He then began pulling notebooks out of his backpack. "Can I go back to studying now? I actually have to try and remember stuff for my exams."

"Yeah, yeah. In a sec. First, the proposition..."

Thomas turned his head to his friend with an exasperated look, letting his head sag down until his chin rested on his chest, his eyebrows raised.

"What?" Thomas huffed.

"You're going home for summer, right?" Terence asked, the familiar grin creeping back to its rightful place.

"Yeah...why?" Thomas asked hesitantly, almost afraid to hear the response. Although Terence didn't know it, Thomas could see the evidence that his roommate was scheming. Above him a silver cloud was in constant motion, never holding one shape for more than a second or so. A metallic scent floated in the air, making Thomas' tongue twinge like when he had licked a nine-volt battery on a dare in first grade.

"Well, a friend of mine needs a ride," Terence stated, and then, seeing the look on Thomas' face, he quickly raised his arms, shaking his hands aggressively back and forth. His eyebrows raised high as he leaned back slightly, saying, "Now, wait, before you say no."

Thomas turned his head away as far as he could without breaking eye contact. His hesitant look told the story for him without the need for words; he didn't trust what Terence was about to say, and Terence knew it. "BroTom! Come on! Have I ever steered you wrong?"

Thomas snorted, a loud "Ha!" escaping his lips. Around him, several students turned at the interruption. Frustrated faces and angry eyes shared their displeasure at having their studies interrupted. Thomas grimaced as he waved a weak apology.

"Seriously? I don't think I can even count that high. Shall I refresh your memory on some of your greatest hits?" Thomas extended his hand as he raised a finger. "One: almost getting charged with breaking and entering at the country club."

Thomas raised a second finger.

"Two: the prank you pulled last fall that somehow I got blamed for."

A third finger shot up. Terence responded by widening his grin.

"Three…" Thomas began.

"Okay, okay. Enough. I surrender!" Terence said, his hands held high above his head, his face stretched tight as his grin reached maximum capacity. "But this time, I promise, no joking around."

Thomas folded his arms across his chest as he glared suspiciously at his roommate.

"Truce?" Terence asked tentatively.

Thomas took a deep breath, letting it slide out as he reluctantly surrendered.

"Okay, I'm listening. I'm not saying yes or no yet though," Thomas said sternly, preparing himself for what he could tell was coming next.

"Cool," Terence said, lowering his arms (and his grin). "So, like I said. I got this friend who needs a ride home. Not all the way to California, though. And they're willing to pay."

"And just how far am I going to have to take this friend of yours?"

"They live a couple hours from here. And it's totally on your way home." Terence replied.

Thomas squinted, his lips pursed tightly. He could tell Terence wasn't sharing the whole truth.

"How many hours?" he asked slowly, his voice low and deep.

"Just a couple. I swear," Terence said, raising his right arm high once more.

"How many?" Thomas asked, deliberately pausing between each word.

"Honestly, I really don't know. But it can't be too far. And, like I said, it's on your way."

"Okay," Thomas began, obviously not trusting the answers Terence was providing, "let me make this easy for you. Within which of the forty-eight contiguous states does your friend need to be dropped off? I have a feeling it's not exactly on my way."

Terence put his arm back down, his wickedly graceful grin appeared once more.

"Darn it, he's good," Thomas thought, watching the wheels of deception spin inside his friend's mind.

"Uh…Texas?" Terence said, his grin expanding.

Thomas' jaw dropped. "Texas? Have you even looked at a map of the United States? How is that on the way from Ohio to California?"

"Oh, come on, Thomas. Take the scenic road for once in your life. I'll bet you've never even been to Texas. Do you really want to go through life knowing you had this opportunity and let it pass?"

"Somehow I think you'd say the same thing about getting thrown in a Russian prison."

"Look, just do me and my friend a huge favor and drop them off, okay? Like I said, they're willing to pay you for the ride. They can even take care of a hotel if you don't want to do the whole trip at once."

Thomas sighed.

"How about I think about it, okay?"

"What? Come on, please say yes. Please?" Terence said, a little louder than he should have, drawing another round of aggravated looks from those studying nearby. Someone made a loud *shhh* sound.

Terence glanced over clearly with the intention of telling whoever it was that had just shushed him to go pound salt. But when he saw the individual was a fairly attractive female student, he instead gave her a look of pure innocence as he pointed the index fingers of both hands at Thomas. The young woman's face changed from a look of aggravation to a playful, flirtatious look, revealing an endearing, shy smile. A warm glow highlighted her bright eyes. Terence returned her smile with his signature grin and a casual wink. She quickly looked away, her face flush, only to turn back a moment later, playfully winking back.

Thomas groaned.

"Casanova, party of one, your table is ready," Thomas said, shaking his head.

"I can't help it. She's cute!" Terence replied, turning his attention back to his friend.

Thomas sighed deeply.

"Okay, okay. Let's say I give your friend a ride…" Thomas began.

"Perfect!" Terence interrupted before Thomas could finish. "I'll go let them know."

With that, Terence grabbed his backpack and spun away, leaving Thomas sitting there with his mouth hanging open. By the time he realized what had just happened, Terence had already walked away. Thomas watched as his roommate walked directly to the table where the co-ed he had flirted with was sitting. Terence stopped long enough to write something on the young woman's palm, then stepped away. He flashed his perfect grin, silently mouthing the words 'call me'. She blushed again, nodding gently as her promise that she would. And then, he was gone.

Thomas looked around the library, shaking his head. Somehow he had just volunteered…no, wait…he had just *been* volunteered for something that he would not have otherwise said yes to on his own. But, as his mentor Father Dominic was always telling him, "Everything happens for a reason."

"I can't wait to find out what the reason is for this," Thomas whispered.

CHAPTER FIVE
FULL MOON

Three rather long weeks had passed since the Devil had placed the curse on Thomas. He was enduring, though barely. He was days behind in sleep, finding it impossible to even close his eyes, as that was when he felt the onslaught the worst. With nothing to distract his visual senses when his eyes were closed, all he saw were the emotional indicators of every human presence nearby. The evening hours seemed to be the worst, too. Perhaps people were just more hopeful in the mornings, as they began their days looking forward to the wonderful adventures that lay ahead.

Thomas could understand. He had been there a thousand times himself. Plans to accomplish brave and wonderful goals always seemed so much simpler and attainable in the morning, especially after his daily allotment of caffeine. Lying in bed at night was the worst as he would suddenly remember the list of items that never got started.

Feeling this way about his own hopes and dreams was one thing. When he added in similar emotions from hundreds of young adults living on and near campus, it became a whole new experience. Lately, he found himself staying up far later than normal, trying to distract his mind with endless hours of late night TV. Eventually, his exhausted brain would simply give up and he would fall asleep. Which on most nights meant somewhere between three to four hours at best.

There had been some solace. Which was why, even with the lack of sleep, he would still rise as early as he could and rush to the chapel for adoration. He would stay there until the start of Mass, and then rush back to The Port until the start of his first class. Throughout the day, Thomas would return as often as possible, finding that even just a ten-minute visit provided respite from the constant buzzing energy.

Today had been the worst. It was Reading Day. Classrooms, labs, and lecture halls were shut down to give students one last chance to study before exams. Finals would begin tomorrow. With no one in class, every library, study room, resource center, and common area was packed. Students stretched out on couches or slouched in chairs. They sat on tile floors, carpeted hallways, or on blankets outdoors on the lawns. Everywhere Thomas looked, he saw them. The combined anxiety from so many students worrying about their grades was more than annoying. Colorful shapes swirled in mixtures of green, gray, and brown. The worst part? The smell. It reminded him of pickle juice. The whole campus reeked.

On top of that, for the past few days his roommate had been distant, aloof. Thomas knew something was wrong, but Terence wouldn't tell him what. He could hear Terence in his room, blasting death metal music a little too loudly. He thought about knocking on Terence's door, trying once more to get him to talk, but he was barely holding things together for himself. Thomas knew there was a good chance that instead of helping he would wind up dragging them both closer to the abyss.

His attention drifted back to the TV as his thumb rapidly pressed the remote. He made one more lap around the channels as he tried to find anything that would take his mind off his troubles. Unfortunately, he came up empty. Frustrated, Thomas shut the TV off, tossed the remote onto the cushion of the clamshell chair, and headed for his room. He didn't intend to stay long, though. He quickly donned a long-sleeve thermal shirt, dark gray hoodie, and a black beanie. Pulling the beanie down low on his scalp, he then headed for the front door. Thomas stopped there just long enough to decide between running shoes or hiking boots. Picking the latter, he slid his feet in effortlessly and laced the boots up tight. Just as he was about to step across the threshold, he stopped and scribbled two words on a whiteboard hanging on the wall.

Needed Air

With his note for Terence posted, he left the apartment and headed outside. It was just after ten o'clock and the campus was mostly empty. The residence halls, which were all around him now, held the main clusters of emotional debris, the very things he sought to escape. Thomas looked for places where the shapes were less dense, knowing there would be fewer people to avoid. Tonight that meant heading towards the northwest corner of campus, far from the constant noise that had lately been his personal hell.

Rounding the residence hall on the northeast corner, he hugged the wide band of trees that lined the border between the campus and the highway. Staying near the shadows, Thomas continued moving north and west until he came to the sand volleyball courts that were just outside Saint Thomas More Hall, one of the larger residence buildings. The emotional kaleidoscope here was thick and heavy, with a wide range of smells that blended into an unpalatable odor. Thomas paused for a moment as he cleared the back of his throat, spitting vile tasting mucous at the grass.

As he stood there, his ears picked up the sounds of the late night traffic as it sped across the bridge where Highway 22 crossed the Ohio River into West Virginia. The sounds provided a slight distraction, like ocean waves gently rolling ashore. It had been months since Thomas had sat by the shore of a large body of water, deep in contemplation on the mysteries of life. The rhythmic surge he was hearing now gave him an idea.

Back on the move, Thomas hurried as he passed two more residence halls. Just ahead of him on the edge of the trees was a large, brightly illuminated parking lot. On the far side of the lot stood the Steel Cross. Thomas slipped deeper into the woods. The shadowy sentinels swallowed him in, respecting his desire for silence. Although he had barely penetrated the woods, the world around him grew abruptly still. Even the wind moving through the upper branches of the trees made no sound. The world of nature understood (far better than any human ever could) the solace and peace Thomas sought. It welcomed him with a knowing embrace.

Picking his way carefully through the darkness, Thomas ran his hand along the bark of each tree he passed and offered a silent prayer of thanksgiving for the comfort they gave. Within the span of a few dozen heartbeats he had cut through the narrow forest and reached the tall security fence that was waiting on the other side. Somewhere along the length of cyclone, he knew he would find a section that had been cut. As he walked along the barrier he was occasionally showered by yellow or blue-white headlights from vehicles speeding past on the highway. Though he doubted anyone would stop if they spotted him, he kept well within the safety of the trees. Finally, he came across the opening. Timing his exit would be crucial. He was concerned both for his safety, and for those driving the road.

Thomas waited several minutes to watch the speed and frequency of oncoming cars. Eventually he saw a large enough gap that would give him the time he needed to cross. Moving quickly, he dashed from the safety of the trees to the small break in the fence, pushing his way through the metal boundary. One of the jagged pieces of metal dragged along his skin, leaving a long, shallow scrape across his left arm. Not stopping to inspect the damage, he barreled his way across the highway, stopping only after he reached the fence on the far side. This one proved a far less imposing barrier and Thomas quickly scrambled over the top.

From there, less than fifty yards separated him from the bank of the Ohio River. Thomas bent low, stepping slow and careful towards the river. A fallen log created a perfect backrest and so he sat down, resting his back against the log with his feet stretched downhill towards the river. The ground was cold and slightly damp, but he could ignore that. At least he was far enough away from the crowds of the campus to finally relax.

Crossing his legs, he rested his hands comfortably in his lap and then did his best to slow his breathing. He could feel his pulse still pounding from the dangerous dash across the highway. As his racing heart slowed, he took a deep breath and held it as long as he could. As he did, he mentally reached out to every part of his body, seeking areas of tension. As he breathed out, he released the tension, repeating the process three more times.

Closing his eyes, he attached his thoughts to the gentle, steady flow of water below him. As each new thought came, it appeared as a leaf riding the current, drifting slowly away downstream. Thomas breathed in deeply again, counted to four, and then quietly sighed. Letting go of the last remnants of stress his mind had fought valiantly to hoard, Thomas was finally ready.

At that moment, his cell phone buzzed. Thomas groaned. This wasn't the first time he had forgotten to turn off the device prior to entering meditation. He knew the single, short buzz the phone had made meant that it was a text, hopefully one that he could ignore until a more suitable time. Thomas reached to retrieve the device, intent on turning it off. As he fumbled for the power button the screen flashed once more, allowing Thomas to see who the text was from. Father Dominic. Although it was nearing ten o'clock for Thomas, Father Dominic was in the Pacific Time Zone, a full three hours behind. Thomas wrestled with ignoring the text until after his meditations were complete or reading it now. It wasn't often that Father Dominic reached out, especially late at night. Sighing deeply, Thomas tapped the screen.

You awake? Got a quick question. Nothing urgent.

Once more Thomas debated his options. He could pretend he hadn't seen the text and wait until the morning to respond. After all, whatever it was, Father Dominic had said it wasn't urgent. Curiosity finally won the mental contest, and Thomas replied:

Yeah…I'm up. Watching TV. What's up?

Lying was unfortunately just easier than explaining that he was trespassing on the bank of the Ohio River after having made a mad (and probably illegal) dash across the highway in the middle of the night. A few seconds later, his phone buzzed again.

Good. I'll call you.

The noise from that text was followed by an even more urgent buzzing as the phone call came through.

"Hello, Father. How have you been?" Thomas said as he answered the call.

"Good, good. Everything here is good. And with you?" Father Dominic replied.

What could Thomas say? That everything was just perfect? Well, except for the bilocation, traveling to alternate realms, the visitation with St. Maximillian, holding the Armor of God in his heart, being cursed by the Devil, and now being forced to see the emotional state of every living person within a mile or so around. But who doesn't love a little bizarre in their lives? Yeah, that would go over real well. Still, he had to say something.

"Well, finals are coming, as you probably know. I should be studying, but I just can't seem to focus."

Not really a lie, but not the whole truth either. He really should tell Father Dominic more. At least about the visions, if nothing else.

"I can understand that. Finals can be tough."

"I'm managing," Thomas said, thinking that 'barely managing' would have been more accurate.

"Well, that's part of the reason I'm calling. No, no, nothing is wrong here. I checked in on your mom and your sister earlier today. They are both doing well, all things considered. Lily and I are having lunch tomorrow, so I can fill you in on her after that. Oh, and the Thompson's wanted to make sure I said 'hello'."

Thomas knew that 'all things considered' was a reference to his sister, Julianna, who had been the victim of cyber bullies at school. Thomas had talked to her about it a few times, reminding her that the opinions and actions of others weren't really something she should try to change. Yet, he knew it was going to be tougher on his younger sibling than it would have been on him. Julianna was far more sensitive, and much more of a social butterfly than Thomas.

Thomas' mom hadn't been much help, unfortunately, as she was dealing with problems of her own. She had never held a full-time job during the years she had been married to his father, which meant she lacked both the skills and the experience to obtain most well-paying jobs. Since Thomas had moved to Ohio, she hadn't been able to keep ahead of the bills. He knew there were nights when his mom and sister had gone to bed without a decent meal, and sometimes no meal at all.

The thought of his mom having to balance between Julianna's demands for the latest fashions or paying their rent and utility bills made Thomas' head spin. He never did claim to understand girls that well, especially teenage ones. He knew Julianna didn't need expensive clothes, but not having them gave her bullies even more to harass her about.

Lily had stepped in, offering to take Julianna shopping, but that just made things worse. The arguments grew so heated that his mom forbid Julianna to speak to Lily. These were the things that made Thomas wish he was home. And yet, at the same time, glad he wasn't.

"What's going on?" Thomas asked, returning his thoughts to the conversation.

"Well, you know the annual summer mission trip I take to Panama?" Father Dominic asked.

"Yeah. That's coming up soon, right?"

"Another few weeks or so, right around the time you start summer break in fact. Which got me thinking…"

Father Dominic paused just long enough for Thomas to sense what was coming next.

"I would like for you to join me this year. Actually, I need you to. There's something that I think we should discuss, and what better time than a few weeks in the jungle! Besides, I think it would be good for you…for both of us, actually."

Thomas paused to think. He really could use an escape. Especially if he hadn't found a way to get rid of the constant emotional overload by then. A trip that would take him to a remote jungle location where there would be far fewer people was just the thing he needed.

"In fact," Father Dominic continued before Thomas could respond, "if you have any friends that might be interested in coming along, I could use a few others as well. I just need people who aren't afraid of getting their hands a little dirty."

"Yeah. That sounds like fun! And I think I might have someone to join us. Two, actually, now that I think of it. Maybe a few others. How many can you take?"

"That's fantastic news, Thomas! We can accommodate at least ten, perhaps a few more. I'll email you a list of everything you'll need to pack, along with the forms that will need to be filled out. You don't happen to have a passport, do you?"

"Never needed one before, sorry."

"Well, then, that's first on the list. As soon as you can. There's usually a lengthy processing time involved."

"Okay. I'll find someplace around campus where I can get it done this week."

"You have made me one very happy friar, my son. Thank you. And please let me know if your friend says they can come. I'll need their contact information and such right away."

"Sure thing, Father. I'll call right now."

"Oh, I almost forgot. I've already booked my flight. I'll be catching a connecting flight in Houston. Perhaps you could find a flight that connects through there as well. I'll send you my travel information."

"Did he just say Houston?" Thomas wondered silently, thinking of the promise he had been roped into to drive one of Terence's friends to Texas at the start of break. There's no way that was just a coincidence.

"Uh, yeah, sure. I'll check it out," Thomas said, his tongue stumbling over the words.

The two said their goodbyes and ended the call. Thomas stretched his legs out in front of him, leaning further back against the log. He glanced down at the slowly moving waters for a moment and then began to scroll through the contacts on his phone. He took a quick glance at the clock. It was just after seven where he would be calling. Late enough for Beth to be home from work but not so late he would be waking her. Tapping on the screen, he started the call and then stood up and walked back towards the highway. His meditations would have to wait. After three rings, a soft voice greeted him.

"Hello?"

"Hey, Beth. It's Brother Thomas! You remember, from the retreat?"

"Brother Thomas! How are you? Are you back from school already?"

"Not quite yet. Still a couple weeks left. Finals are coming up soon, though. How have you been?"

"Busy. Like, super busy. I took on a new role at Project Rachel. I guess that was two weeks ago now? Anyway, lots of new things to learn."

"Oh, then this might not be the best time for this call, I guess," he said.

"Why? What's up?" she replied.

"Oh, nothing, really. It's just, well, I was invited to go on a mission trip to Panama this summer. And, well, I was wondering if you might want to come along," Thomas said, wincing as he waited for her response. When no response came right away, he continued, feeling a bit embarrassed, and more than a little awkward. "The priest who organizes it, Father Dominic, I've known him for a few years now, he's a great guy—anyway, he said he could use a few more adults, people who are good with teens. And, well, you were the first one that came to mind, since I know you work with teens and all."

Again, there was a slight pause. Thomas winced once more. He knew he had just rattled that last part off with the speed of an over-caffeinated rabbit. Speaking to women was never his favorite activity. His social awkwardness always came into full bloom whenever he did. Lily had been the only girl he had ever felt comfortable talking to.

Lily. He missed her so much.

"Well, now," Beth said, obviously taken back by his invite, "That was quite the mouthful! You know, I wasn't aware I had made such an impression! Brother Thomas, I'm flattered!"

Thomas wasn't sure what to say next. "Uh, you're welcome," he said slowly, inflecting the word 'welcome' as if he had asked a question. "But, if you're totally busy at work and all, I can call someone else."

He winced again. Once more, he had spoken without thinking, and with far too much speed.

"Now, you wait just a moment," Beth interrupted. "Let me check my schedule."

Thomas heard papers being shuffled.

"You said a month from now?" Beth asked.

"Yeah. Not sure the exact dates, but that's what Father Dominic said," Thomas replied, this time much slower than before.

"I think I can make that happen. I'm due for some vacation time anyway."

"That's great! Can I have my friend call you?"

"Sure. By the way, does he need anyone else?"

"He might. Why? Who do you know?"

"Someone you already know. You remember Theresa, from the retreat?"

"Theresa?" Thomas exclaimed nervously, his mind flashing back to the night he appeared in her room. "Uh, yeah, of course I do. You guys still keep in touch?"

"Oh my God, we're like besties now! We do everything together!" Beth shared, excitedly. "And I'm going to be her confirmation sponsor too! I can't wait!"

"You think her mom will let her come? She's what, a sophomore, I think, so that should make her fifteen?"

"Yeah, I think so. Anyway, she needs to complete a service project for confirmation. I was going to set up something simple here, but I think this would be far more exciting...and educational, too. I'll talk to her mom. She pretty much loves me, so I don't think it will be an issue."

"Beth, you remember when I told you I thought you were pretty awesome?"

"Yeah?"

"Well, I was wrong."

"Huh?"

"You're absolutely awesome. Let me check with Father Dominic to make sure there's not an age restriction or something. I'll have him call you with all the details tomorrow. This is going to be a blast!"

"I can't wait! I'm literally dancing with excitement right now!"

"Oh, you have to send me a video of that!"

"No way! I do not dance pretty."

"Ha ha! I'll bet you're lying."

"I guess you'll never know. Anyway, I gotta run. Still at the office getting ready for a major presentation we have next week. Can we talk later?"

"Of course! I'll try to give you a call this weekend. My last final is on Friday morning, so I should be back to reality by then. Don't work too hard!"

"Yes sir, Brother Thomas!"

Thomas tapped the button to end the call, then locked the screen and put the phone back in his pocket. He stood looking out over the Ohio River for another minute. The stress he had been carrying the past few weeks was gone. In its place was a sensation of excitement and anticipation that tickled him warmly as he thought about the trip. Turning towards home, he climbed the small embankment, reaching the first of the two fences he would have to cross once more. He looked back for a final glance at the river below. A bright circle flickered and danced as it played across the mirror-like surface of the slowly moving river.

The memory of his dream a few weeks ago sounded deep inside his mind as St. Thérèse spoke to him once more.

"Your quest will begin soon. In fact, in some ways, you are already on it. But it begins in earnest before the full moon rises once more."

In the struggles and challenges of his life, he had all but forgotten the quest she had foretold. Thomas looked up from the flickering reflection on the water to where a break in the clouds exposed a giant orb hanging brightly in the sky. There was no doubt about it. Tomorrow, the moon would be full.

CHAPTER SIX
BETH!

Theresa dropped the phone on her bed.

"What the heck just happened?" she asked the emptiness of her room.

Five minutes ago she had been involved in one of her favorite activities: skulking the popular kids from school. Her social media profile was anonymous. She had established it under a fictitious name. There was no way anyone would link to her. As preferred, she was invisible.

She never posted any comments or engaged in any way. She just enjoyed laughing to herself over the absurdities of life. People who posted pictures of their dinner or poems about how much they loved their cat. As if anyone really cared. She didn't. That was for sure.

Tonight had been a pretty good night, too. The amount of fodder for her snarky humor was more than that of a typical night. A box of tissues was next to her on the bed, evidence of her wet-eyed joy. But that all ended when she answered the call from Beth. Her new friend, Beth. Bestie Beth! Wonderful, intrusive, way-too-positive, Beth. Some days it made Theresa literally want to scream. Although she had to admit that, deep down, she really did like Beth. Most of the time she envied her, wishing she had even half of the energy and excitement for life that Beth did. Plus, Beth had been there for her on the retreat. She had listened without judgment, which made Theresa feel normal for a change. Yeah, Beth was a good person. She was glad that they were friends.

Theresa knew her retreat experience had changed her in more than a few ways. It had helped her realize that although she had always felt that she didn't care about anyone, the truth was that she didn't want them to care about her. That's why she tried to disappear. If they did care, then she might open up, become vulnerable. That was something she couldn't risk. So far, all of the people who were supposed to have cared for her had done nothing but break her heart. She was tired of holding the pieces together.

Becoming The Endlessly Dying Girl wasn't just about learning to disappear. It had become her way of staying safe in a world where emotional pain was far too easy to stumble into. Girls weren't supposed to cry themselves to sleep. Not as often as she did, anyway. Life was supposed to be simple, easy. It was supposed to be filled with cute boys who wink at you and pass notes in class. Parents who love unconditionally and never yell or fight. Friends who never take you for granted. Ever.

Theresa believed that life should be filled with great adventures. And cake. Lots of cake. But, that wasn't the life she had been given. Not even close. And so, Theresa learned to survive. The more she disappeared, the less people paid attention to her, which meant fewer people that could care. And the fewer people who cared meant fewer chances that her heart would get broken again. That was why she had become The Endlessly Dying Girl. She didn't want to be a superhero. She didn't want to fight crime, or do whatever else superheroes did. She had learned to become invisible simply to avoid pain.

She was good at it, too—the endlessly dying part, that is. She had learned that all she had to do was to give a small part of herself away or let someone else get the attention she desperately craved. As long as she sacrificed a part of what she longed for, she could remain invisible. It was all working out just fine. At least, until that retreat.

She first noticed the change a couple days after. She had been skulking Amanda's account on Facebook and had come across a folder filled with pictures from the weekend. One of the young adult volunteers had been there just to take photos. Lots and lots of photos. Plus, Amanda had also created a link so that the teens who had attended could upload their own photos as well. There were hundreds upon hundreds of photos for her to scroll through.

Theresa had looked at every single one. She studied them. She looked beyond who the photo was centered on and focused on the details in the background. She looked at every partial hand, foot, or half of a face. She studied each piece of clothing that lingered at the edge of the shot. She had peered and squinted and wrinkled her face a thousand different times, but hadn't found one image of her. Friday night, all day Saturday, the bus rides, the meals, group shots, panoramic shots, shots during free time and breaks. Not one photo of Theresa.

That is, not until she opened a sub-folder labeled 'Adoration'. And there she was.

The photo hadn't captured just a part of her, either. It wasn't just one hand or only part of her left leg. It was her. Entirely her. There she was, bundled up in a blanket, her head resting in Beth's lap. It was the moment she had tried so desperately to avoid: finding someone who cared. She could tell that Beth cared about her by the look on Beth's face. She had that distant look in her eyes, that somewhat sad appearance that said she was worried. Worried about the girl who was fast asleep in her lap. If only she hadn't gone to speak to Brother Thomas that night. But she had. And now she was paying the price. From that moment on, Beth was now a part of her life.

The first week of their new friendship, Beth had sent Theresa four texts. The first one had come that Sunday night after they got back from the retreat, just before that image of Brother Thomas had appeared.

Just checking in on you. Everything okay?

Theresa had replied:

Yep. All good. Thanks.

She had hoped that would be it. Perhaps Beth was just being nice. She hoped Beth would forget about her, but she wasn't that lucky. The next text arrived the following afternoon.

Thinking about everything we talked about Saturday. Let me know if you need to talk more.

Again, Theresa's reply had been brief. And, again, she hoped that would be it and that Beth would move on. Two days later, she got another text.

Are you going to be at Youth Group this week? I might come help out. It would be good to see you again!

Theresa had replied with one word.

Sure

Theresa understood Beth's concern. After all, she had told Beth the same story about her past that she had told Brother Thomas. Although why she had told him, she still didn't have a clue. After she had told it once, it had been even easier to tell it again. When she thought about it, even as the words had been coming out of her mouth she had still felt like it was a bad idea. And yet, it had felt as if she had to do it; as if something inside her was pushing her to speak and she was just along for the ride.

And now, she was on Beth's radar. Probably on Brother Thomas' as well. Maybe even Amanda's. She could understand why Beth felt the need to check in on her. There were times when even Theresa was scared by her own Endlessly Dying story. She could only imagine how worried they all were. She decided the best thing to do was to let them have their concerns. She would simply try to be as invisible as she could. One day they would no longer notice her. And then, they would simply stop caring. Why not? Everyone else in her life had stopped.

But once more a few days later, Beth reached out.

Make sure you're at Youth Group. And ask your mom if it's okay for me to bring you home. We're going out for ice cream after!

Theresa hadn't known how to say no to that. The last thing she wanted was to tell Beth that she didn't want to go. If she did, Beth would have even more reason to worry. When people worried more, they paid attention more. And when people paid attention, she couldn't disappear. She had responded by saying she would check with her mom, hoping the answer would be no. It was a school night, after all. But mom didn't do the 'mom' thing.

She didn't say no. Instead, she had told Theresa that she thought it was a great idea for her to spend time with people from church. Mom didn't care what Theresa really wanted. Otherwise, she would have asked her if she wanted to go or not. Now she was stuck. Maybe if she pretended to be normal for a bit, their worries would stop. Maybe, if she had ice cream and participated in the conversations, as if she was any other normal teenage girl, that would end their concern.

Funny thing, though, on the way home that night she had realized that she had actually enjoyed herself. It was a small group, which may have helped some. In addition to Beth and Amanda, Stephen and his wife, Jennifer, were there, along with a half dozen teens. It had been the first night Theresa had spent having fun with people her age in a long, long time. She had even been brave enough to make a joke during the conversation. It was everything she imagined normal people might do.

When Amanda had them play a small group sharing game, Theresa had answered honestly. Rather than say what she thought she was supposed to say (like she did every other night at Youth Group) she thought about her answers first. The questions hadn't been of a personal nature. Just weird, off the wall stuff, like; *Would you rather be married to someone who can't speak or someone who can't see?* Theresa didn't remember her responses, except for one. That answer was still haunting her today.

Amanda had somehow brought the conversation to the selection of confirmation sponsors, asking each of the teens in turn who they had picked. The other kids said they had picked an aunt, uncle, or cousin. Theresa had always thought she would pick her mom. That seemed the easiest choice. But after she learned that parents weren't allowed to be sponsors, she hadn't known who she could choose. When it came time for her turn to respond to Amanda's question, she had panicked and said something she now wished she hadn't.

"I was thinking…maybe Beth?"

She regretted it immediately, but it was too late. The words were out there now. Five innocent words when taken each on their own. But when strung together in that specific order they had set in motion a series of events that she had no idea how to control. Almost instantly Beth had said yes, and was 'super excited' she had been asked and would love to do it, as long as Theresa's mom approved. Once more Theresa had counted on her mom to do what her mom did best. Which was to try and protect her little girl. Her mom didn't know Beth. She barely knew Amanda for that matter. There was no way her mom would let Theresa choose someone she hadn't even met yet. Her mom would most likely have someone in mind from one of her small prayer groups, or her Bible study group. Someone her mom could trust.

When Beth had dropped Theresa off at home that night, she had stayed to talk with her mom. The two had talked for over an hour. Theresa waited in her room with the door open, trying desperately to hear what was being said. Eventually, her mom had agreed. She had even hugged Beth, too! Like they had known each other for years! Theresa considered that maybe her mom had been drinking. She definitely hadn't responded like the predictable mom that Theresa had come to know.

Now, there was nothing Theresa could do but accept that she was attached to Beth for the remainder of the year. Beth wanted to do everything together. They had spent an entire afternoon researching saints so that

Theresa could choose her saint name. They had worked together on her essay project, writing and re-writing a four-page paper on why Theresa wanted to be confirmed (even though she really didn't). Theresa's mom had even invited Beth to their house for dinner! Twice!

There was simply no getting rid of Beth now.

During those first few weeks, whenever she fell back to her old ways and tried to disappear, Beth had always found a way of drawing her out again. Last week, when Theresa was in a particularly sour mood (wanting nothing to do with anyone) Beth had brought her to her work. Theresa had never heard of Project Rachel. But after learning about the work they did, she had felt something she had never felt before. She wanted to help!

Prior to that day, Theresa had always thought that girls who got pregnant before being married were stupid. She couldn't understand why someone would wreck their life like that. But the more she heard the stories of some of the teens Beth had worked with, the more she realized that these girls were a lot like she was. They weren't stupid. They weren't being selfish, either. They were just trying to find a way to stop the pain. Where Theresa had used her pain as a catalyst to empty her life, these young women used their pain as a way to try and fill theirs.

These girls came from homes that weren't that different from the one she lived in. Their families were just as broken, disconnected, and empty. Theresa had no longer felt superior to them. Instead, she felt compassion and empathy. She wasn't the one who should be a superhero, these girls were. The challenges that they faced were far greater than anything Theresa had. That night, Theresa had cried herself to sleep. This time, it wasn't from her own pain but because she had felt theirs.

For the next few days after that, all Theresa could think about was how she could help. Since she was just fifteen, too young to be trained as a counselor like Beth, she was limited in what she could do. She felt useless. That was a new feeling. She had felt alone, empty, and abandoned. But never useless. Disappearing didn't help with feeling useless. Instead of giving her a way to escape, she was left with nothing to do but face it. All because of the day she had met Beth.

And now, tonight, when she had finally felt life getting back to normal, Beth had called. Once more, Beth had found a way to force Theresa out of her comfort zone. This time she had been informed that, rather than spending a few hours helping clean out a storage closet at Project Rachel, she was going to Panama to help build a school! For two weeks she would be trudging around the jungle, strapped to Beth's side, along with a couple dozen other people, all of which would be counting on her to do her part. How the heck would she be able to disappear with that much attention?

When Beth informed her of the trip, Theresa was going to lie. She was going to pretend to ask her mom but not really do it since she could no longer trust her mom to be predictable. But Beth had interrupted, letting her know that her mom had already said yes. Somehow her mom — who for the past few years had done everything she could to insulate her daughter from the dangers of the world — had just agreed to send her precious child halfway across that same world! Seriously? What was happening? Her life had been so simple before that stupid retreat!

Theresa buried her face in an oversized, fuzzy purple pillow and screamed as loud as she could.

Chapter Seven
Sometimes It Hurts

"Well, Terence, my friend," Thomas said as he joined his roommate at their breakfast table, "it looks like you win this time."

"Uh…what are you talking about?" Terence questioned, a little gruffly.

"You know that friend of yours? The one who needs a ride to Houston? Looks like I'm going to be heading that way after all," Thomas replied.

Terence tilted his head, giving Thomas a look of incomprehension. His mouth was frozen mid-chew.

"Come again?"

"Oh, come on. You don't remember? You made such a big deal of it a month ago when you asked me," Thomas replied, looking a bit surprised.

"BroTom, have you've seen my grades?"

"What the heck does that have to do with me taking one of your friends to Houston?"

"Simple. Memory. If I can't remember what I just learned last week, how the heck can I recall something I did last month?"

Thomas met his roommate's smug expression with a look of resignation and defeat.

"You don't remember?" Thomas sighed deeply. "I think there's something seriously wrong with you."

Terence looked like he had something to say but instead just rolled his eyes and turned back to his cereal, aggressively chewing his food.

Thomas turned, opened the refrigerator and glanced inside. He sighed deeply to ensure Terence heard him, and then firmly shut the door.

"You finished all the milk, didn't you?" he growled at his roommate.

Terence didn't even look his way.

"Sorry, man. Early bird and all."

Thomas felt he was on the edge of launching into one of his rare but memorable tirades. He stared his roommate down, waiting for the anger to subside. Terence stared back, his eyes narrowing just slightly. Thomas could tell Terence was ready for a fight. They had only had one blowout since they had moved in together. A few small arguments, but only one true fight. While he stood there, an empty milk container in one hand and the handle to the refrigerator still gripped in the other, Thomas weighed his choices.

He knew where the underlying frustration and anger was really coming from. It had been a month since he had truly been able to relax. The curse that the Devil had put on him had made certain of that. The one thing that stopped him from acting on his anger was the knowledge of what had happened the last time he had felt like this—the day he had fought with the kids who had tried to steal his bike. And then, he remembered the words Father Dominic had shared with him.

"Making that choice, the one that didn't end up with you sitting in a jail cell, was by far the harder choice to make. You would have to swallow your anger, swallow your pride, and ignore your emotions. But in the end, how would the outcomes have been different if you had made a better choice?"

"Whatever…" Thomas said, sighing deeply once more, ready to make a better choice this time.

Unfortunately, Terence wasn't ready. Thomas jumped as porcelain, cereal, and milk crashed against the cabinets, just inches from his head. With fire in his eyes, Thomas spun around.

"What the hell is wrong with you?" Terence screamed at him.

"What the hell is wrong with me?" Thomas shouted back. "What the hell is wrong with you? You're the one who has been walking around here with a permanent scowl. You look like your best friend died."

"Well, that would be weird," Terence responded. "Because right now that best friend would be you. So, unless you're a zombie…"

Terence's statement hit Thomas hard. For what felt like a long time, he had no idea how to respond. As he waited, he felt his anger slowly ebb away, replaced by a strong desire to help his friend, if he only knew how.

"Then, talk to me, Terence! Let me in on whatever you're dealing with," Thomas finally said, his voice barely more than a whisper.

Terence's expression twisted, changing rapidly from one of fury to one of absolute despair. Thomas also saw the image above Terence's head dissolve and morph, changing from what had looked like orange and red flickering flames, to a thick, black, droopy cloud. Though his mind bounced back and forth between possible words he could say, his heart urged him to remain at peace. And so, he waited for Terence to release the pain he was carrying, giving him the space to let his despair flow until there was nothing left. Until he did, the pain that remained would prevent Terence from healing.

Slowly, his roommate regained control and the tears stopped flowing. The tension in his shoulders and neck faded away and the look of anguish and despair was replaced by a blank, empty gaze. Terence wiped the wet streaks from his cheeks and then slowly turned his eyes towards Thomas. The orbs looked empty and pleading. Thomas watched the image above Terence evolve again, now taking on a gossamer-like veil that spread until it was so thin that Thomas wasn't sure it was still there. He knew he was losing his friend. If he didn't do something soon to help, Terence would be lost, trapped in the downward spiral of despair.

Thomas knew that path led to a pain-filled life that would be so hard to climb back out of. One that the Devil could so easily gain power over, too. He had watched as the same thing had happened to his father. The once proud and confident man had simply washed away like a sandcastle dispersed by the incoming tide, leaving nothing but memories behind. His father had given up. Hope could be such a fragile thing. When it was gone it was almost impossible to find again. Thomas wasn't going to let that happen to Terence.

"Look, Tee, you don't have to tell me if you don't want to. I get it. Some things are just too hard to share. Just don't hold it inside. Find someone that you can talk to. A counselor, one of the friars, someone. Please."

Terence opened and closed his mouth three times, struggling to find the courage to speak. Again, Thomas waited. This time, he didn't have to wait long.

"I'm afraid, Thomas," Terence began.

Thomas could see his roommate struggling to continue, not because he couldn't find the words, but because of how hard it was going to be to admit whatever it was he held inside. Once he said it out loud, it would be real, leaving him with no choice but to deal with it. That, Thomas knew, would be the hardest part. For whatever reason, holding things inside, even though they hurt, always felt easier.

"Afraid of what?" Thomas asked quietly, hoping to break the spell that Terence's fear had cast.

Terence's mouth opened and closed again. Then, finally, the words leaked out. They were barely discernable, even in the quiet of the room.

"Of becoming my dad," he said, his head drooping low, his face devoid of expression.

Thomas nodded gently. He knew that feeling, having once admitted the same thing to Father Dominic. For the third time since the conversation started, he fought his desire to speak, allowing Terence to continue.

"Do you know what my dad told me the other day?" Terence asked quietly, his eyes locked on some random spot on the floor.

"No," Thomas said, moving closer to the table where Terence sat but not yet joining his friend.

"He said he wants me to come to his wedding, the weekend right after finals. And I didn't even know that he and his fourth wife had been divorced!"

Thomas moved a few steps closer, slowly pulling out the chair next to Terence. He gently sat down, never taking his eyes off his friend.

"I'm going to have to apply to take some of my tests early, just so I can fly down before the wedding, get my tux, meet the new Mrs. Portman, blah, blah blah…"

Terence gave Thomas a quick glance. Thomas noticed the empty glaze in Terence's eyes was gone, replaced by a deep look of resignation.

"And the worst part of it is, the more I think about my dad, how many times he's been married, and how many times he's had an affair, I can see me falling into the same patterns."

Terence took a deep breath, holding it for a long, long time. He sighed heavily.

"You know why I am never with one girlfriend for very long, Thomas?" he said, glancing back up with tear-filled eyes.

Thomas shook his head, "No, Terence, I don't."

"Because I'm afraid they'll get hurt. I'm afraid that things will get serious and I'll wind up doing something like my dad would. I'll end up hurting them and they'll hate me. Just like how my dad's ex-wives hate him."

Thomas watched as the tears began to fall again. This time, he felt like crying right along with his friend. He could feel his pain. Thomas blinked back the wetness that had begun to pool, sending one lonely tear trickling down his cheek.

"I don't want to be like him, Thomas. But I don't know how to change."

"Maybe you don't have to change, Terence," Thomas said quietly, drawing a look of confusion from his roommate.

"What do you mean? Just go ahead and be an asshole like him? Just treat women like they're possessions? Like I can just have whichever one I want regardless of any commitments I have made?"

"No, not that at all," Thomas began, "Look at it this way. Maybe you're already different than your dad. Maybe he doesn't think about trying to not hurt the women in his life and just does whatever he wants to do. Maybe he doesn't even care. But you do care, and you do worry about hurting others. That's why you don't let yourself get too close. That's why your relationships break off so soon. That's why you're afraid to make a commitment. Would your dad do the same? Would he think about the other person's feelings and do something to prevent the other person from getting hurt?"

"No," Terence said quietly, his eyes reflecting the deep questions that were racing through his mind. "He would just do whatever he wants, regardless."

"And that's completely opposite of what you're doing. Right now, you're so afraid of hurting someone, you're not even giving yourself the chance to try."

Terence looked away again, staring off into space, trying to make sense of what Thomas had just shared. Eventually he looked back, his eyes reflecting the empty resignation Thomas had earlier.

"Then, what do I do?" Terence inquired.

"Honestly? The first thing I would do is pray. I would pray for the strength to forgive your dad. As long as you continue to hate him for the man that he is, it will be harder for you to become the man you are meant to be. But if you can forgive him, truly forgive him, then the power his life has over yours will become less. Our fathers may have failed in different ways but I assure you, Terence, I've been where you are now.

"I learned that my fear of becoming my dad was keeping me from finding out who I was born to be. I mean, how will you ever know if you can be in a committed relationship until you are in one?"

"So, what, I should just run out there and find someone to marry? Just so I can see if I can be faithful?"

"Yeah, something like that. Just don't get anyone else involved."

"What the heck are you talking about? You want me to marry myself?"

Thomas laughed.

"In a way, yes. But not in a strange Dennis Rodman kind of way. I was thinking more along the lines of attending that *Freedom to Love* program. Maybe what you need isn't help making commitments to others. Maybe it would help to make a promise to yourself."

Thomas could tell that Terence was actively thinking about what he had just proposed.

"So, no relationships at all? Like, don't even date until I know I'm ready to get married? But, I don't get it. How will I know that I'm ready to marry someone if we don't date first?"

"Oh, you can date. Besides, you're right. That's the only way we can determine if we are ready or not. You just need to make sure the person you are dating knows about your promise, and is willing to support it."

"I'll have to think about it," Terence said quietly.

Thomas could tell Terence wasn't convinced. But at least he was no longer spiraling down in despair. When he looked in his friend's eyes now, he saw the smallest flicker of hope.

"Tell you what," Thomas said slowly, "there's a group starting this Friday night. Why don't we just go to the first meeting and see how things go from there?"

Terence nodded, looking up at Thomas again.

"Yeah, I guess. I mean, it couldn't hurt."

"Cool. Now, can you do me a favor?"

"What's that?"

"Can you run down to the store and get us some milk? I'll clean up this mess while you're gone. Deal?"

Terence flashed the smallest of grins.

"I got one even better. I'll clean up, you shower. Because, well, mostly, you stink. Then I'll take you out for breakfast. We can hit that waffle place, you know, the one where they always give us so much food that we come home and sleep for a week?"

Thomas extended his right hand to his friend.

"Deal."

Terence shook it, smiling warmly at him, and then got up to clean the kitchen. As Thomas started back down the hall to the get ready, Terence called out once more.

"Oh, Thomas?"

"Yeah?"

"What were you saying about Houston earlier?"

"Oh, nothing. Just that I'm going to be meeting a friend at the Houston airport, so I have no problems giving your friend a ride home."

"Oh, okay," Terence said, turning back to clean up the mess. "Wait...why Houston? Where are you going?"

"I'm going to be joining my friend, Father Dominic, at a mission project down in Panama. We're going to be building a school."

"Seriously? That sounds way better than what I have planned for summer right now."

"Oh, yeah? Why, what's that?"

"Dad wants me to spend the summer in the Hamptons with him and his new wife. You know, get to know my new stepmom, before he trades her in, I guess."

Thomas snickered. As he began to turn away, a thought flashed through his mind.

"Why don't you come along?"

"What, to Panama?"

"Yeah! Why not? Father Dominic said he could use a few more hands down there."

"Will there be any girls?"

Thomas gave Terence a look of shock.

"Oh my Lord, Terence! You're impossible."

Terence laughed out loud. It was good to hear his friend in a moment of joy.

"Just kidding, BroTom. But, seriously, yeah, I'd love to come along."

Thomas turned and headed back down the hall. The trip to Panama was gradually becoming something he would never forget.

CHAPTER EIGHT
THE PROMISE

Thomas walked into the small conference room, moving immediately to the back wall. He knew some of the students in the room, but not all, and felt more comfortable with a solid surface at his back and an eye on the door. Glancing at his watch, he saw there were still ten minutes until the meeting was set to begin. The room was set with two long tables against one wall. Each was stacked with books, DVDs, and a few snacks. There were two rows of chairs in an almost complete circle, with a lectern standing between the disconnected ends.

Digging his phone from his pocket, he sent Terence a text asking if he was on his way yet or not. Terence said he was, and that he was bringing his friend with him—the one Thomas would be driving to Houston. He thought it would be a good if the two met ahead of time and got to know each other better, seeing as how they would be spending over twenty hours on the road.

While he waited for Terence to arrive, he greeted the students he knew with a casual wave or head nod. He considered taking a look at the resources (and snacks) on the tables, but that would put the doorway, and most of the room, at his back. As long as he was seeing, feeling, and smelling the emotional states of those nearby, it was better to keep them where he could see them as well. Being surprised by a sudden influx of emotions from behind him had caused a few embarrassing moments already. He hoped to avoid any of those tonight.

After a few minutes of waiting, he felt a familiar presence and turned to see Terence walking into the room. With him was a young female student that Thomas knew he had seen somewhere, but couldn't place. It wasn't until the pair got closer that he recognized who she was. It was the young woman who had served him the two cups of coffee the day his visions became permanent. He tried jogging his memory to recall her name, but nothing came.

"Hey, there, Thomas!" Terence said, waving his hand as he recognized his roommate.

Thomas waved back, and then waited as the two made their way across the room to join him.

"Thomas, this is Gemma. She's the one who needs a ride to Houston," Terence informed him.

Thomas was a bit taken aback. All this time he had assumed that Terence had meant a male friend. He wasn't sure how he felt about being alone in a vehicle for twenty hours with a girl. Not that anything would happen, of course, but his social awkwardness around women would haunt him again.

It was weird, though, that this happened to be the person Terence meant. Thomas had felt a strong connection with Gemma even before Terence had brought the request to him. He had even gone back later that day and left his phone number for her. Realizing she was standing there with her hand extended looking more and more uncomfortable as time went on, Thomas quickly and awkwardly shook her hand.

"Sorry, I was thinking about something," he said as he shook her hand. "Glad to meet you, Gemma."

"Oh, we met once before, Thomas," she replied, smiling warmly. "Don't you remember?"

"Actually, I do. I just wasn't sure that you would and I didn't want to say anything if you didn't because that might embarrass you if you didn't remember me so I just decided to pretend I didn't remember."

Thomas felt his face flush.

"Oh my God, why am I such a dork around women?" he chastised himself silently.

Gemma smiled, blushing slightly as she did.

"Wow…that was a mouthful!" Gemma replied.

Thomas returned her smile with an awkward, embarrassed smile of his own. He liked Gemma. She had a positive feeling about her, and a relaxed and gentle spirit. Her emotional signature felt comfortable, too. It was warm and inviting. Like a hot cup of tea on a cold day. Tonight, her shape was a wave, flowing back and forth, migrating from a warm pink to strawberry red. It had the scent of mint and lavender, reminding him of his grandparents' garden, which he hadn't seen in too long.

Thomas was lost in thought. Since his grandparents lived in Arizona, he realized that he could swing by on his drive from Houston to California after he returned from the mission trip to Panama. Making a mental note to call them and make sure it was okay, he turned his attention back to the room. Terence and Gemma had already found seats and were engaged in quiet conversation. Thomas had been so preoccupied with his own thoughts that he hadn't even noticed that they had walked away.

Once more feeling the hot flash of embarrassment flush through him, he walked over and sheepishly sat down next to Gemma. He then began fiddling with his backpack, hoping they hadn't noticed how long it had taken him to come over.

"Well, thanks for finally joining us," Gemma teased, turning away from Terence and putting her full attention on Thomas.

Thomas blushed, looking up from his meaningless searching for the moment. Oh, how he wanted to get away from his own awkwardness. Instead, he gave Gemma a shy smile and then buried his eyes once more in the depths of his backpack. There was nothing in there that he needed, but it was better than doing something even more embarrassing. He could feel her eyes on him as he pretend-searched through the pack. His search went on for so long that he decided he had better pull something out just so it wasn't obvious that he was avoiding her. Finally, he settled on his pocket Bible, a small notepad, and a couple of pens.

Making an overly dramatic show of retrieving the items, Thomas blurted out, "Oh, thank goodness. I thought I forgot them."

Gemma burst out laughing.

"Oh, Thomas. You are just too precious," she said, then turned to Terence. "You were right, Terence. He does get absolutely embarrassed meeting new people."

"Just the girls," Terence whispered, winking.

Thomas knew they weren't trying to be hurtful or mean. The energy Thomas was receiving from Gemma still felt as warm and inviting as it had when she first walked in the room. And he was more than used to Terence teasing him about his awkwardness. Thomas decided to try and make the best of it.

"Yep. That's me," he said, laughing uncomfortably as he shook off the nervousness growing inside.

"You're going to have to get used to me if we're going to be spending two days together," Gemma joked.

Thomas thought about that. Two days…that meant one night, too! He had thought, had his passenger been a guy, that they could just sleep in his car at a rest stop, or perhaps share a cheap hotel room. But now, with a girl? Overnight? That brought up a whole new set of circumstances that he wasn't prepared to face.

"Uh, yeah," he stammered. "But I was thinking, we could get an early start and drive straight through."

Gemma gave him an incredulous look.

"You know how bad our butts would hurt sitting that long? Plus, this girl needs her sleep. I can't show up looking like I'm homeless! Not in my neighborhood!"

Thomas didn't know what to say. He wanted to call the whole thing off, say he couldn't do it anymore. But he didn't want to disappoint Gemma, or Terence for that matter. He had already made a promise, and it was one that he was going to have to stick with.

"Don't worry, Thomas," Terence interrupted. "Gemma said she'll pay for any expenses—gas, food, hotel—whatever you guys need."

"Uh…it's not that," Thomas began, "it's just, well…how should I put this…"

Thomas paused, searching for the right words. From the corner of his eye he saw Gemma turn to look at Terence. When she looked back, her face had a strained look, as if she was trying not to sneeze. Suddenly, she burst into laughter once more. Terence joined in.

"Oh, my God, Thomas. You should see your face right now!" Terence exclaimed.

Thomas shot Terence a hard look. He was getting tired of their jokes. And, he didn't see what was so funny about his discomfort at being alone with a young woman. Especially one that he had just met.

"Well, if you two are having so much fun," Thomas snarled at Terence, "then maybe you should be the one to drive Gemma home!"

"Woah, woah, settle down, BroTom," Terence said, extending his hands out in front of him as if warding off an attack.

"I'm sorry, Thomas," Gemma said between giggles. "We did this on purpose, as a joke. It was Terence's idea."

Terence mocked a look of innocence.

"What? Me? Never…" he said through his wide, toothy grin.

Thomas shook his head.

"Ha, ha. Okay, so you got me. What, now you're going to tell me that Gemma isn't really the person I'm driving to Houston?"

"Oh, no. She's definitely the one," Terence said.

"But don't worry, Thomas. I'll get us separate rooms if we decide to stop," Gemma promised.

"Naw. You don't have to do that. I don't want to be a burden. You can have the room. I'll sleep in the car."

"Wow…you were right, Terence. Thomas is a real gentleman," Gemma said, looking impressed comment. "But, seriously, Thomas, let's get to know each other before the drive. I have your number from the day you left it at the café. We can find a time to meet up soon, okay?"

"Yeah, sure. That sounds great."

Thomas was about to continue talking, but was cut off as the session leader announced they were about to begin, asking everyone to make sure they had copies of the resources from the side table. Terence jumped up, saying he would retrieve copies for Gemma and Thomas as well. Thomas and Gemma were alone.

"Look, Thomas," Gemma whispered, leaning in close, "I really am sorry about teasing you like that. It's just, well, you know how Terence can be. Sometimes I wonder if that guy is ever serious."

"Oh, you'd be surprised, Gemma. You'd be surprised," Thomas said, his eyes growing wide.

"Really? Pray, do tell!" Gemma said expectantly.

Thomas smiled, laughing and shaking his head.

"No way. I'm not violating the Bro Code."

"Phhhttt… Bro Code," Gemma sneered.

"Like you women don't have your own code?" Thomas prodded.

"No!" Gemma said, mocking a look of surprise. "We ladies have nothing to hide."

"Yeah, right!" Thomas huffed, feeling his nervousness start to fade.

The two sat in silence for a moment as Thomas tried to gather his courage and ask why she never called or texted him before. He had left his number for her about a month ago and had not heard back. As he was about to ask, Gemma interrupted him.

"So, you're probably wondering why I never replied to your note," she said.

Thomas nodded, "Yeah, I was actually."

She smiled at him.

"Well, I guess that's a good question. I really wanted to. I mean, I kept looking at your number, and I thought about texting you, but I guess I was kinda hoping you would stop by the café again. When you never did, I wondered why. Plus, I wasn't looking for a relationship at the time. I'm still not. That's why I'm here tonight."

"Oh, I'm definitely not looking for a relationship, either," Thomas interrupted.

"Yeah, I know that now. But your note didn't say either way. Plus, Bethany, the girl you gave the note to?"

"Yeah? What about her?"

"Well, she said it looked like that's what you wanted. I just didn't want to deal with all of that. I really haven't had much luck with boys. Again, that's why I'm here tonight."

"What do you mean?" Thomas asked, feeling himself slide into counselor mode.

"Terence told me about the fight you two had. And he told me about what you said. About how he needed to make a commitment to himself, first, how this program might help him figure out who he is, and help him get over his fear that he's like his dad.

"I really think this is something I need right now, too. I'll be honest, I'm not happy with some of the choices I've made in the past. I guess I'm ready to start over, to stop just giving my heart away to every boy that shows even just a little interest. So, I guess, in a way, I have you to thank for me being here tonight."

Thomas was about to respond when Terence returned, casually dropping copies of the resource material in both of their laps. He then leaped over the back of his chair, landing in a perfect seated position.

"Well, judging by the looks on your faces, I missed out on something good. Fill me in!" Terence said, jokingly.

Gemma and Thomas gave each other a knowing look, neither of them interested in sharing what they had just discussed. Finally, Gemma turned to Terence.

"I was just asking Thomas for some advice on some stuff. Nothing really interesting."

"Really?" Terence asked, doubtfully. "You don't think I'm going to believe that, do you?"

"Hey," Thomas interrupted, "it looks like the programs about to start. Let's talk about this later."

"Oh, I get it. I'm suddenly the third wheel here, right? You two want me to sit somewhere else?"

Gemma put her hand on Terence's knee.

"You're not going anywhere, Tee. I promise, I'll tell you later, okay?"

"Yeah, okay," Terence conceded.

Two hours later, the three were seated at an outdoor table of a local coffeehouse just off campus. Though it was a fairly warm evening, they were the only group sitting outside. Thomas was enjoying a dark chocolate and cherry mocha, his absolute favorite menu item. Terence had a coconut milk latte, and Gemma was drinking green tea. During the ride from campus to the coffeehouse, the three had mostly joked about complete nonsense stuff. But now that they were alone and had a moment to reflect on what they had learned at the conference, the evening took on a more serious tone.

"You know something, Thomas?" Terence said, when all three had gotten comfortable in their chairs.

"What's up, Terence?" Thomas replied.

"Well, I've been thinking about what that program was all about. I guess I see what you meant earlier this week, you know, when you said I needed to make a commitment to myself?"

"Yeah, I remember."

"Well, I guess my question is, how do I know if I'm ready for something like that?"

"I don't think you can know, Terence. I think this is something that you just take on faith. And definitely not something you want to do alone. Making a commitment like this is going to be hard. It's supposed to be. You're talking about making a lifestyle change, and one that doesn't really fit within the trends of the world. Most of the messages you will see and hear in the media won't support this decision, which is why you can't make this choice lightly."

"What do you mean?" Gemma questioned. "Aren't we talking about our own bodies and what we're comfortable with?"

"Yeah, we are. But the rest of the world doesn't get that. We live in a world that has a very aggressive, demanding, self-centered, 'just do it' theology. It's completely backward from making a commitment like this. I know. I've dealt with it for two years now. So, if either of you is going to do this, I would suggest that you do what they recommended tonight," Thomas proposed.

"You mean, start with going to reconciliation?" Terence inquired.

Thomas took a drink as he nodded his head.

"Exactly. After you get right with God, make a more formal commitment. Something that isn't just in your head. I think the point they made tonight about having an accountability partner was a good one. Find someone you can totally trust and can turn to when you're having a hard time. Someone who also understands the challenges of this type of commitment."

Terence turned to Gemma, giving her his trademark grin as he asked, "What do you think, Gem? You in this with me?"

Gemma brought her tea to her lips, blowing softly into the small hole in the white biodegradable top. Even without his usual visual aid, Thomas could see that she was deep in thought.

"I want to say yes, I really do. But I think Thomas is right. This isn't a decision that we can just make on the spot. It's a serious commitment. Just as serious as if we were thinking about getting married," Gemma said, her eyes focused somewhere in the distance.

"I'll tell you guys, when I made this commitment myself, I thought it was going to be really easy," Thomas shared. "But keep in mind, chastity isn't about just not having sex. It's much deeper than that. It's about becoming and remaining pure. Not just in our actions, but in our thoughts and especially in our words. It's not enough to just resist our desires. We have to find a way to go beyond those desires. And that's hard."

"Yeah, but you've done it," Terence mentioned.

"Trust me, Terence, there are days I struggle with staying true to my choice. It's hard. But then, nothing good is meant to be easy, right?" Thomas said.

"So, what do you do on those days, the ones that are harder than the rest?" Gemma inquired.

"First, I pray. If I can, I'll go to adoration, or say the rosary. And I get to reconciliation as often as possible," Thomas responded.

"You? But you're like a seriously committed Catholic. You're studying to be a priest! You really still struggle with desires like that?" Terence inquired, a bit surprised at what he was hearing.

"What do you think, Terence, that as soon as I made my profession to the Franciscan order, that it took away all my humanness? It's not that easy. But nothing worth doing should be easy. The things that matter in life are meant to be tough."

"You can say that again," Gemma interrupted, looking out towards the horizon.

Thomas set his coffee on the table, then reached out his hands, one to Gemma, who was on his left, and the other to Terence, who was on his right.

"Why don't we pray about it?" he suggested.

"What, here?" Terence asked, looking around to see if anyone was watching.

"Yes, here!" Thomas responded. "You think you're just making a commitment to be celibate, but what you don't understand is, this commitment is really a profession of faith. If you can't stand up for your faith by praying in public, how easy is it going to be to stand up for your faith the first time you're out on a date?"

Terence's expression suddenly became serious.

"Yeah, you're right, Thomas. Okay. Let's make a promise, the three of us," Terence said.

"What kind of promise?" Gemma asked as she set down her tea, taking Thomas' offered hand and reaching her other hand to Terence.

"You guys ever read those books about King Arthur?" Thomas said offhandedly.

Terence and Gemma glanced at each other briefly and then shook their heads.

"Can't say that I have, Thomas," Terence informed his friend. "But I know the story. That's the one with the sword in the stone, right?"

"Yeah, that's the one," Thomas said, nodding. "Well, in the story, when King Arthur starts to gather his Knights of the Round Table, he had them take a pledge. He called it the Code of Chivalry. If they don't take the pledge, or if they ever break it, they can be exiled from Camelot, or even killed."

"Huh, that sounds really interesting. So what's in this code?" Gemma asked.

"Simple stuff, like always fearing God, serving the Lord of the castle with valor, protecting the weak and defenseless, always speak the truth. Stuff like that."

"And you're thinking we should take an oath like that?" Gemma asked, very interested in where the conversation was going.

"Yeah. I think if we write down all the things we believe are part of living a moral, chaste life, then we have something to fall back on when we face a challenge."

"Oh, I get it," Terence said with a look of recognition and understanding. "It's like in that video game I play. If I let my character do something that might be considered wrong, like killing a townsperson or robbing someone, then he becomes more prone to evil and can become a Dark Knight. But if I choose to do what's right, then eventually he can become a Paladin."

"Yeah, kinda like that," Thomas agreed.

A hush fell over the trio as they became lost in thought for the moment. Gemma was the first one to break the silence.

"So, what kind of promises should be in our code?" she asked the others, pulling out her phone.

"I think the first one should definitely be that we will always treat ourselves and others with respect," Thomas offered.

"Should that be first? Or should remaining true to our faith be first?" Gemma wondered.

"Good point. Let's put God first," Thomas agreed.

"And then being faithful to ourselves, and finally being faithful to others. Is that all?" Gemma asked.

"What about standing up for those who can't stand up for themselves?" Terence suggested. "Like, I'm thinking we should always be an example for others to follow. And since we won't be walking around in suits of armor like they did in medieval times, we need some way of letting others know what we're doing."

"Okay, so the first code will be to remain faithful to God, the second code will be to remain faithful to ourselves, and the third code will be…how should I word it?" Thomas asked.

"What about 'to help anyone who is in need'?"

"Yeah, that works," Terence said. "Maybe we should add a fourth one, something about protecting the marginalized?"

"Yeah, that's perfect," Gemma said. "And don't forget the one about always speaking the truth."

"Okay, good. So that's basically five things for us to remember for our code. And they're fairly easy to keep in mind, too," Thomas said.

"Should we have a secret handshake or something?" Gemma asked as she finished typing a few notes on her phone.

"Ha ha! I don't think we need to go that far, Gem," Terence stated. "I think the promise is good enough."

"Yeah, but let's not just make this promise tonight and be done with it. Let's make sure whenever the three of us are together, that we always repeat our promise, okay?" Thomas suggested.

"Okay, yeah, I can commit to that," Terence stated. "Too bad we're going to be out of contact for a few weeks when I'm in Panama."

"Yeah," Gemma responded, her face twisting into an expression of disappointment. Then, suddenly, she brightened up, turning her entire body to face towards Terence. She grabbed his arm excitedly, exclaiming, "Why don't I come with you?"

Terence sat back in surprise, his eyes wide and his mouth agape.

"Can you do that?" he inquired. "I thought your parents had your entire summer planned out."

"They do. But it's nothing they can't cancel or do without me. Besides, if we're going to start down this road of chivalry, which would be better? Spending the summer flying to a remote, tropical island and wasting a fortune on materialistic junk, or spending the summer building a school for people in need?" she proposed, turning to face Thomas. "Can you squeeze in one more person?"

Thomas pulled out his phone and started typing a text to Father Dominic. As he did, he said, "I should get a reply sometime later tonight, but I'm sure it will be okay."

"Oh, this is going to be the best summer ever!" Gemma enthusiastically shared with a wide smile and bright twinkling eyes.

"Yeah, it will be," Terence agreed.

"Let's make our promise now. Let's repeat our code together, and then I'll say a quick prayer," Thomas suggested, once more extending his hands.

The three joined hands and together repeated their promise, not realizing the depth of the commitment they had just made or the size of the challenge that lay ahead.

PART TWO

If we are intended for great ends,
we are called to great hazards
                    — Cardinal John Henry Newman

INTERLUDE
GEMMA

"We need to stop for gas," Thomas said, finishing a yawn. "There's a town coming up. We can stop there."

Gemma was more than ready to stretch. Her legs had been in the same position for hours, having only stopped once during the eight long hours they had been on the road. Though she knew there was only an hour or two remaining until they reached Jackson, Tennessee where they planned to stop for the night (and would rather have just pushed through) an empty tank was an empty tank. There was nothing she could do to help with that. She gave Thomas a silent nod, then glanced out the window as the exit sign came into view.

"Bucksnort? You gotta be kidding me. We're going to stop for gas in Bucksnort, Tennessee?" she said incredulously.

Thomas laughed.

"Yeah, I thought you'd get a kick out of that. If there's a 'Welcome to Bucksnort' sign on the way in, we are totally grabbing a selfie," he said, smiling.

"Oh my God…" Gemma sighed.

Thomas eased the car off the freeway and into the small gas station. Unfortunately, there was no welcome sign in sight. Still, a selfie in front of the station with a geotag would work just as well.

"Hey, look, Gemma," he said, pointing to her right, "there's a hotel here. How'd you like to spend the night in Bucksnort instead of Jackson?"

Gemma looked out her window at the Travel Inn that Thomas was pointing to. Of all the hotels she had ever stayed in, this would be the absolute worst, and by far. Being the only heiress to an oil family fortune meant she had never had anything but the best growing up. Her parents would never have stuck her in a car for a twenty-hour drive. And they definitely wouldn't have dreamed of even stopping in a town like Bucksnort. Their idea of a family vacation meant a private jet to the Cayman Islands or a first-class flight to Paris. Gemma hadn't even had to carry her own luggage until the day she left for college.

According to her father, her four years in college would be spent living 'like the normal kids do'. He wanted his daughter to have an understanding of the privileges she had been given, and what it would be like without them. He said she needed to have an appreciation for the wealth her ancestors had accumulated, a small fortune that he had carefully turned into a much larger one since becoming executor of the family estate. Everything the family owned would one day be hers. He trusted this experience would ensure she never did anything frivolous.

Therefore, he had put his only child on a very modest weekly allowance just low enough so that, like most college students, she would understand what it was like to live off ramen and tuna for a while. It was a good plan, if she had stuck it through (which she hadn't). The moment she had moved into her first, tiny dorm room, Gemma had immediately gone to work crafting ways to earn a buck or two. Though her parents were not aware, Gemma wanted nothing to do with the family fortune. She didn't want to be a woman of wealth like her mother, and she definitely didn't want their circle of friends.

Everything was always such a huge ordeal. Nothing could just be simple with that crowd. Even the neighborhood barbecues were always more involved than most families would plan a wedding. Caterers and parking attendants, bartenders and waitresses, even live bands and entertainment for the kids. Their parents would spend tens of thousands of dollars, and all for a simple Fourth of July block party.

Gemma had no intention of living off family money either. Not in college, and definitely not after. The resume her folks cared about wasn't the type a young woman her age would use to apply for a job. The type they wanted her to have was the kind debutants used to attract a husband. Which, in her father's mind, meant the son of some rich cattle baron, or a family whose money had been made on the backs of slave labor. Even though she talked about that type of resume, Gemma never intended to use it. It was only her way of getting her father to give in and let her do some of the things she wanted without having to jump through hoops.

This trip to Panama had definitely included a few hoops. Her father had insisted he hire a private jet to pick her up in Steubenville. When she had refused that, saying she wouldn't even get on the plane if he did, he had offered the next best thing: a first-class ticket. Although Gemma had accepted, as soon as she had the ticket in hand, unbeknownst to him, she called the airline and switched it to a standard fare. She requested the remaining funds to be issued as a credit, which she had then used to purchase flights for Thomas and Terence. They, in turn, paid her for their tickets in cash, which she deposited in a private account—one that her parents knew nothing about.

This was how she made most of her extra money, by selling the overly expensive items her parents bought for her at discounted rates. She would then use the money she made to buy the same type of item at a regular store, like Target or Staples. The rest of the funds were placed in her secret account which she would then invest on her own instead of through her father's friend at the pretentious investment firm back home. After only two years at college she already had saved almost ten thousand dollars, an amount she intended to use to start her own charitable organization after graduation. She vowed that she would never accept a single dime of family money. Not even as donations.

Her attention was brought back to the present moment as Thomas hit the brakes a little hard, causing her to lurch forward.

"What the heck?" she said.

"Sorry, I think my leg fell asleep holding it on the gas for so long," Thomas muttered as the car slowed to a stop next to one of the pumps.

"I'm going to go see if they have a restroom. I'll be back," Gemma said as she climbed out of the car, pausing to stretch her back.

Glancing at the exterior condition of the gas-station-slash-general-store, Gemma didn't hold high hopes for finding anything clean. She didn't need five-star, resort-hotel clean. Serviceable would do. Hopefully she would at least find seat covers and a good supply of soap. Entering the gas station side of the building, she inquired if the restrooms were located indoors and if she would need a key. The heavy-set cashier with 1980s feathered hair and far too much eye shadow looked her up and down.

"Oh, honey," she said with a thick southern drawl, "you don't wanna go in there. Go over to the hotel across the way and tell Tammy-Lynne that Joanne at the Citgo sent you over. She'll let you use the employee restroom they have. That's the one all us girls use. This one here we save for truckers and such."

Gemma considered saying she was brave enough to use whatever facilities they had but the look on Joanne's face made her think otherwise. Pointing to the hotel, she asked, "You mean the Travel Inn?"

"Yep. That's the one. It's the only hotel 'round these parts for miles. It's a decent place, though."

Gemma smiled, "Thanks for the tip. Can you make sure my friend knows where I went, please?"

"Which one's yours?" Joanne asked, gazing out the window towards the gas pumps. "Oh, that cute one in the red shirt?"

"Yep. That's the one. His name is Thomas," Gemma informed her.

"Honey, you listen to Joanne here. That one's a keeper. He's cute."

"Thanks," Gemma said, laughing, "but we're just friends. He's going to be a priest."

Joanne looked out the window again, saying, "Now ain't that just a shame." She made a few 'tsk' sounds, then looked back at Gemma. Lowering her voice to a whisper, she winked, adding, "Maybe there's still time to change his mind, if you catch my drift."

"I'll keep that in mind," Gemma said as she moved towards the door.

"Pretty girl like you? It shouldn't be all that hard, sweetie. Men never know what it is they really want. That's what us girls are for."

Giggling to herself as she left the station, Gemma followed the road that led to the hotel. When she had made it about halfway, she slowed down, suddenly moving with caution. The smile she had worn since her conversation with Joanne quickly disappeared. Somewhere nearby, she just knew, someone or something was hurt. More than hurt, she realized. It felt like it was dying. She didn't have much time.

Stepping quickly off the road and into the thick woods that wound throughout this part of the state, Gemma began to follow the feeling. When she moved in the right direction, the feeling was strong, pulsating deep within her. When she shifted away, the sensation would fade. Like a homing beacon, Gemma felt her way towards the injured creature, unsure of what she might find.

Deeper into the woods she traveled, stopping periodically to look back, hoping she could find her way out again. She thought about going back and asking Thomas to come with her, but how could she? She couldn't let him see what she was about to do. No one could. It was something she still didn't understand herself. The first time this had happened was about five years ago when she had saved her father from his second heart attack, one that would have been fatal had she not been there to intervene.

Now, as she rushed through the woods, changing direction as her senses guided her, she wondered what lay ahead. Soon, she came to a thicket of bushes in a dense clump. In the center she saw a young doe on the ground, lying still. An arrow was sticking out of its side, just above the front leg. As she knelt down beside the deer, Gemma heard the hunters approaching. She hoped she would have enough time.

First, she grabbed the shaft of the arrow, holding it firmly with one hand while her other hand lay on the deer's side. She could feel the life energy ebbing away. Focusing her thoughts, Gemma let her own energy flow through her arms and into the animal. The doe flinched, trying to get back to its feet. Gemma made soft shushing sounds, coaxing the animal to relax. The terror she felt from the wounded deer was intense, but it slowly faded as the deer realized Gemma was there to help.

The blue, electric energy emanating from her hands pooled around the base of the arrow at the point where it penetrated the animal's thick hide. Slowly, the arrow dissolved and faded away. The feeling Gemma sensed changed as her focus switched to repair the damage the arrow had done. She felt the muscle fibers stitching back together, felt the ruptured organs as they, too, began to heal. Finally, she flooded the animal with healing energy, taking away the fear the doe carried and replacing it with the strength to run.

As the hunters grew close, she felt the animal was ready to bolt. Still, she held on, using every second she had to give a part of her life to the deer. At the last moment, she released her hold on the animal, leaning back as the doe leaped to her feet. The deer paused only a moment. Dark, black eyes gave her a look of thanks, and then it turned and bolted away, disappearing quickly as her natural camouflage melded in the woods.

As soon as the deer was gone, Gemma was on her feet as well, running back the way she had come. When she reached the trunk of a large tree, she stopped and looked back. A moment later, four boys between the ages of nine and eleven came into the clearing. They were wearing jeans that looked desperately in need of washing and flannel shirts of various colors beneath camouflage vests with bright orange piping. Three of the four carried composite bows. Two of the boys wore John Deere baseball caps, one was green and the other was brown. A third one wore a cowboy hat.

"I swear it came right through here," the boy with the green hat said. "Look! There's the trail of blood!"

The four began to follow the red stained path that led to where Gemma had healed the deer.

"The trail stops right here," the cowboy hat kid said. "It looks like it went down. The grass is all matted."

"Where did it go?" asked the boy with no hat.

The four began to search the surrounding area, looking for any sign of their wounded prey.

"There's a trail leading off this way," the boy with the brown cap said, "but there's no blood."

"Heck, I ain't seen nothing like this before," the cowboy hat kid said.

They continued to search for a few minutes more, then, scratching their heads, they started walking back the way they had come. The last thing Gemma heard was the boy with the cowboy hat saying, "I swear I saw the arrow hit it. I've never missed from that close."

Then, they were gone. Gemma stepped out from behind the tree and started heading out of the woods at a light jog. She absolutely hated hunters, and anyone else that would do an animal harm. She made a note to speak with Thomas and Terence about adding a line to their code about never intentionally injuring an animal. She smiled as she jogged, realizing she had just completed her first act of chivalry. Grinning brightly, she thought about how much fun she was going to have being a knight.

CHAPTER NINE

PANAMA

Before the flight touched down, Thomas could already feel the hot, sticky climate that would be his world for the next few weeks. Evidence of it was everywhere he had been able to see out the small window of the plane. The flight had passed over miles of jungle on their descent into Panama City. Still, he couldn't wait to disembark. Being trapped with two hundred passengers and crew in such a tight environment had meant he had been forced to see, feel, and smell every emotion for the four-hour flight. Fear, excitement, wonder, awe, and boredom all mixed together in an extremely unsatisfying cocktail.

He had tried sleeping but with the activity around him sleep was elusive. He had tried having a theological discussion with Father Dominic, but that was something he couldn't stay focused on either. He had tried thumbing through the travel magazines, watching the in-flight movie, even putting headphones on and trying to drown out the onslaught with music. Nothing worked.

Unfortunately, Gemma had been issued a seat near the back of the flight, whereas Thomas and Father Dominic's seats were near the front. They had tried to get a few passengers to switch places with Gemma but no one had been willing. Gemma was left flying alone. Thomas had walked back to check on her as soon as the captain had turned off the 'fasten seatbelts' light and had found her fast asleep with her head resting on the shoulder of the woman seated on her right. The woman had smiled at him, putting her finger to her lip, indicating she wanted Thomas to let Gemma sleep. Thomas had simply nodded and returned to his seat.

Throughout the flight, he had tried picking out her unique emotional signature from the pool of emotions clustered tightly together. Her energy was different than most others he had felt. It felt familiar somehow, as if they shared a similar past. Thomas looked forward to learning more about Gemma on this trip, and was genuinely excited that she had agreed to come along. Plus, the funds her father had donated to the project were going to go a long way in providing the resources required.

Now, as the passengers were beginning to depart, Thomas waited for Gemma. Father Dominic had already left the craft, leaving Thomas half-standing in the empty row. As the flight emptied out, the pressure from the cramped quarters slowly reduced. Thomas was now breathing more freely and less stressed. He watched the other passengers file out, occasionally glancing up.

One passenger in particular caught his attention; their eyes locked together for the briefest of moments. When they did, Thomas felt a twinge of energy flash between them as if they had connected at a deep, spiritual level. It was something he had never felt before. As he attempted to follow the connection in his mind, the man quickly looked away and the feeling disappeared. A moment later he caught sight of Gemma as she exited her row. Her eyes looked tired and she stifled a yawn. She smiled at him sleepily, giving him a playful wink. Thomas returned her smile.

Finally, Gemma reached the point where Thomas was able to step into the aisle beside her. She wrapped her arms around his neck, giving him a quick, friendly hug.

He returned her hug, feeling a sudden calm wash over him as their energies reconnected. Releasing his hold on her, Thomas stepped into the aisle behind her and offered to carry her bag.

"That's okay, Thomas," Gemma said, "It's not heavy. But I will let you carry my suitcase when we get to baggage claim. That one is overstuffed with clothes. I think I brought enough for the entire summer!"

"Yeah, I know what you mean. I did the same. I had no idea what I might need in this environment, so I pretty much packed it all. Minus the Ohio winter stuff. That I'm certain I won't need," Thomas replied.

"You got that right. I can already feel the heat and humidity and we're not even off the plane yet!" Gemma responded. "I hope there's someplace to take a shower when we get to the camp. I'm a mess."

"You look fine to me."

"Aww, Thomas. You're so sweet," Gemma said, reaching back and grabbing hold of his hand, giving it a tight squeeze.

Thomas felt his face flush as his heart was filled with a familiar warmth—the same sensation he had felt all those late nights he had spent with Lily. Once more, he began to feel torn between his two desires. One side of him wanted so much to become a priest, while the other side called him to a different life. One where he could experience the full dimension of a relationship.

Father Dominic had warned him there would be times like this, even after he had taken his vows.

"*Becoming a priest,*" he had said, "*doesn't turn off the way the heart works. It just means you need to channel those feelings in other ways. Perhaps learning to paint, sculpt, or write poetry.*"

His mentor was an avid landscape photographer, and had captured some amazing shots. Most of which had been taken in remote locations such as the small village the three companions were headed towards now.

Thomas knew he couldn't tell Gemma about the crush he felt developing. Not just due to his commitment to the priesthood, but also because of the promise they'd taken together only a short time ago. Thomas, Gemma, and Terence had all promised to support each other during times of emotional challenge as they worked towards a life of chastity and chivalry. He would simply have to forgo any feelings that might develop and constantly remind himself that they were just friends.

Finally stepping off the airplane and leaving the stale, air-conditioned cabin, Thomas took in a deep breath. Though the airport held far more than the two-hundred or so passengers of the plane, at least they were spread out with plenty of spaces between. For the first time since the doors had been locked and the plane pushed back from the gate in Houston, Thomas felt a small haven of peace.

Gemma excused herself to the restroom, giving Thomas the opportunity to do the same. On his way back out, he ran into the passenger he had locked eyes with on the plane. Once more, a spark of energy flashed between them. This time, with Thomas being more relaxed, it hit him much harder than before.

Thomas turned away quickly, breaking the connection. The brief taste that lingered in his mind told him more than he needed to know. Deep within this man with the terribly sad eyes, the darkness had found a home. Thomas could tell that the darkness didn't control the man—not as if he was possessed—but instead simply lingered within him. At some point in the past, the man had given up hope. That small crack was all the Devil needed to worm his way inside, filling the man with evil down to his very core.

"What's wrong?" Gemma asked as she returned. "You look like you've seen a ghost."

Thomas glanced at her, seeing that her eyes weren't as puffy and red. Her hair had that just-brushed look and her makeup looked fresh.

"Oh, it's nothing. Probably just this stuffy air," Thomas lied, hoping she wouldn't press the issue.

Gemma gave him a look that told him she knew there was more than he was saying. He shrugged.

"Sorry, Thomas, I'm calling the code on you. I know you aren't telling the truth," Gemma scolded him.

Thomas paused a moment. He knew she was right. They had made a promise to each other, and part of that promise said they would always tell the truth. But this was definitely not the right place for that conversation. Perhaps at some point during the next two weeks he might be able to find both the opportunity (and the courage) to let her into his world. Heaven knows he needed to tell someone what was going on—what was *really* going on—if only to give himself peace of mind.

"Come on, let's go find Father Dominic and get our bags," he said, turning as if to walk away.

Gemma grabbed his arm, held it firmly and locked her feet in place. Thomas stumbled.

"Ow!" he exclaimed, turning to face her.

"No," she said, adamantly.

"No?" Thomas questioned. "No, what?"

"No," Gemma repeated. "I'm not moving until you tell me what's going on."

Thomas took a deep breath, sighing audibly. He could see the determination with which she held her ground. When she wanted to, Gemma could be a force to be reckoned with.

"How about if I promise to find a time later. Just not now. And definitely not here."

Gemma held his gaze for a long moment and then gave him a long sigh in return.

"I'll hold you to that, Thomas. I won't forget," she said. "Remember our code. Always tell the truth."

"I swear. Hopefully later today when we get to the mission site, okay?"

Gemma nodded. "Lead on, then. Let's go find Father Dominic and claim our bags."

As they walked away, Thomas looked behind him. The man was standing with his back to the wall, absentmindedly scrolling on his phone. Thomas could tell the man had no interest in what he was looking at. His true attention was on Thomas and Gemma. At that moment, Thomas made a promise. Whatever happened, he would do everything he could to protect Gemma.

Pressing his hand against his chest, he felt his Miracle Medal under his shirt. Saying a silent prayer, he asked Our Lady of Graces for her help as well. Thomas took Gemma's hand, leading her forward through the crowded center aisle as they followed the signs to the baggage claim. Every fifteen seconds or so, Thomas glanced over his shoulder.

"What do you keep looking for?" Gemma asked after the fourth time Thomas glanced back.

"Uh…" Thomas stumbled to find something she might believe, "I just want to make sure we don't pass Father Dominic by mistake."

"Thomas, I can tell when you're lying. Your face has this look about it and your eyes get dark."

"Yeah? That's probably my 'tell'," Thomas said.

"Your 'tell'? What's that?"

"Something Lily once said I have. You know, like how a poker player can tell someone's bluffing?"

"Oh…so you were lying then."

"Gemma, please trust me. I can't tell you what's going on right now, but I will. Later. I promise."

Gemma didn't say anything at first and then simply nodded at him in silent agreement.

"Okay," she stated, "but, I won't give up on this."

The two walked for another minute or so, taking a left turn as directed by the signs overhead.

"By the way," Gemma asked, "who is Lily?"

"Just a friend I've known since high school. I had to live at her house for a while, back when my parents…" he paused, suddenly sensing the evil presence closing in from behind. "Look, now is really not the right time for this. We need to get out of this airport. Fast."

Gently guiding Gemma ahead, Thomas quickened his pace. As they reached the baggage claim area, he turned his attention to the displays, seeking the carousel which would correspond with their flight. Finding what he needed, Thomas began pushing his way through the crowd, Gemma following close behind. A minute later, he spotted Father Dominic having a conversation with a man Thomas didn't know. He guided Gemma to where Father Dominic was, trying to pick up as much as he could of the conversation, which was in Spanish.

The man speaking with Father Dominic was dressed in faded and heavily-stained cotton pants, dark brown leather hiking boots, and a lightweight, sky-blue shirt that was unbuttoned halfway down his chest. He wore dark sunglasses, the tops of which touched the bottom of a straw cowboy-style hat. On his back was a small pack stuffed to the point of bulging. As Thomas and Gemma drew near, the man stopped speaking. He nodded in their direction, causing Father Dominic to turn their way. The priest had a worried expression when he first turned, which grew a shade or two lighter when he recognized Thomas. Father Dominic waved at the pair, urging them over quickly.

When they reached Father Dominic, the other man wandered towards the exit. Thomas focused his eyes on the man as he left, trying to read his emotional aura. He could tell that the man was under a good amount of stress. Thomas turned his attention to his mentor.

"What's wrong, Father? You look worried. Who was that man?"

"That was Miguel, one of the leaders of the village where the mission is. He is here to fly us to El Real. From there he will drive us the rest of the way to Boca de Cupe," Father Dominic informed him, and then turned to Gemma. "But, forgive my manners. I haven't asked yet, how was your flight, young lady?"

"It was fine, Father. Thank you for asking. I actually slept most of the way. As you know, Thomas and I got a very early start this morning to make it to Houston on time."

"Well, you look none the worse for wear, dear," Father Dominic said, a warm and inviting smile spreading freely and his eyes flickering with warmth.

"It's a wonder what a splash of cold water and a little makeup can do, Father. Trust me, I feel a lot worse than I look," Gemma said, returning his smile.

"Well, let's get our things and get on the road. It's about a one-hour flight to El Real, and another hour's drive to the mission. We really should try to arrive before nightfall," Father Dominic explained, waving the two young adults back towards the carousels.

Thomas realized his mentor still hadn't answered the first question he had asked. He placed his hand lightly on the priest's arm.

"Father, I can tell you're stressed. What's going on? Maybe there's something I can do to help," Thomas said urgently.

Father Dominic sighed heavily.

"Yes, I should let you know—if only to ensure you are both on guard during our trip," the priest began, pausing a moment to ensure he had their attention. "It seems that there has been some smuggler activity near the mission. Though so far it has been several miles from our site. Still, Miguel would prefer it if we didn't draw any unnecessary attention."

"What do you mean?" Thomas asked nervously, his senses jumping to full alert.

"Not to worry, Thomas. Every few years the villagers near the mission see a higher level of activity like this. For the most part, so long as the villagers leave the smugglers alone, the smugglers leave the villagers alone, too. We just don't want to draw their attention. If they know that a group of Americans has arrived, well, they may take a more significant interest.

"Miguel has clothes for us to wear for the trip into El Real, items he borrowed from the villagers where he lives. The clothing should help us blend in. But, come, we can talk more on the flight down. We really should get our bags and be on our way."

Thomas nodded, turning to follow the priest as he weaved through the crowd. They reached the carousel just as a red light began to flash, followed shortly after by a brief alarm. With a heavy thud, the carousel began to move. Thomas watched as bags slowly began to appear, sliding down a small ramp to the now steadily moving carousel's treads. As he spotted the first of their bags, Thomas stepped forward to retrieve it, carrying it back to where Father Dominic and Gemma stood waiting. Depositing it at their feet, he turned to fetch the next.

Repeating this process three more times, Thomas returned to the carousel once more, waiting for the final bag. Glancing over his shoulder, he saw Father Dominic and Gemma working to secure the bags he had already retrieved into pairs, which would allow them to more easily navigate through the airport. Most of the crowd had already retrieved their bags, and had dispersed to car rental stations or ground transportation available outside. Thomas was alone in his corner of the baggage claim. As he turned to find their last bag, he found himself face to face with the man with the desperately sad eyes.

"He knows you're here," the man said.

Thomas jumped. Like a geyser erupting, he felt fear rush up from deep in his gut, leaving a sour taste at the back of his throat. His eyes locked on the expressionless face of the man before him.

"Who knows we're here?" Thomas demanded. "What are you talking about?"

"He knows you're here," the man repeated. "He will come for you. And for your friends, too."

"Leave me alone," Thomas said, an icy chill rushing down his spine, "I don't know what you're talking about."

Seeing the final bag sliding down the ramp, Thomas pushed past the man as he took a position to catch it. The man followed.

"He knows you're here. You shouldn't have come," the man said, a wicked sneer starting to spread.

"Thomas? Everything okay?" Father Dominic asked quietly from behind him.

Thomas could see the blank stare in the challenger's eyes quickly fade, replaced by a warmth that Thomas knew was as fake as the plants nearby.

"I was just asking the young man if he knew where I could catch the shuttle to the Intercontinental Hotel," the man said as he backed away from Thomas, a fake but convincing smile hiding his true nature.

Thomas looked at the man, wanting to tell Father Dominic the truth but afraid of where that might lead. Once his mentor knew the darkness had returned again, he would have to tell him the rest of what was going on, too. That meant disclosing his visits to the spiritual realm, the now constant visions, and the fact that he may have experienced a bilocation. He would even need to disclose what he carried in his heart. Father Dominic had a way of getting Thomas to share even his most guarded secrets.

"Thank you for your help, young sire. I'll bid you adieu," the man said. He then turned and walked away.

"What was all that?" Father Dominic wondered.

"It's nothing, Father. I'll tell you about it later. Let's just get out of here."

Thomas bent forward, grabbing the last bag as it began to sidle past. He pulled it off the carousel with a firmer yank than he had planned, sending the bag flying five feet away. The bag landed with a thump, slid for a bit, and then lay still.

"Sorry. I guess I don't know my own strength," Thomas said with a forced smile.

Grabbing the bag, he walked over to where Gemma stood guarding the rest of their luggage. He took the handle of one of the two pairs Gemma and Father Dominic had made, pulling it behind him as he headed in the direction he had seen Miguel exit earlier.

"Come on, let's get out of here. This airport stinks," he said, which was far truer than either Gemma or Father Dominic understood.

CHAPTER TEN
REUNION

As the dark gray Jeep came to a stop, tires spitting gravel and dust in the air, Thomas jumped out. His encounter at the airport, coupled with the worry and concern he was feeling from Miguel and Father Dominic, had put him in a foul mood. Lack of sleep and the hot, humid air of the jungle did nothing to stem the short-tempered feeling brewing deep in his core. All he wanted was to find a place to shower and get some rest. So far, neither Gemma nor Father Dominic had brought up his promise to share what he had been unwilling to share at the airport. Perhaps, he thought, neither of them wanted the other around when they pressed the issue. Or perhaps they could tell that Thomas needed some time alone.

Thomas wasn't worried whether the Devil really would come for him or not. He had faced him three times before, pushing him back each time. Though each new assault had left him feeling that the Devil's power was growing stronger. No, what worried him most was that he had possibly brought others with him into harm's way. Though he had a feeling that Gemma could handle herself against a threat like the man at the airport had posed, he didn't know how she would stand against the Prince of Darkness should he choose to challenge her directly. There was a quiet, inner strength in this new friend of his that drew his interest and left him guessing at the source of her confident ways. His biggest concerns were for Terence, Beth, and Theresa, all three of which he felt would be helpless to fend off even one of the Devil's minor demons. As far as he knew, Beth and Theresa had already arrived. Their flight was scheduled to land two days ago. Terence wasn't scheduled to arrive until tomorrow, having had to first return home to attend his father's fifth wedding.

And then there was the feeling that there was someone else down here. Someone far more familiar. Who it might be, Thomas couldn't place. He was sure it wasn't Lily, though he had asked her to come along. She had refused his offer, explaining that a group from her sorority had rented a beach house in Laguna for the summer and she didn't want to miss out. She had invited him to join her when he returned, which he had promised he would do.

He also considered it could be Amanda, since she had attended some of Father Dominic's missions in past years. But he didn't feel that he was as close to Amanda as he felt to this familiar energy. Shrugging it off for now, Thomas began to pull the luggage out of the back of the Jeep, setting each one down carefully. As he set the fourth bag down, he felt a sudden flicker of energy, a sensation of excitement and joy rushing towards him. Thomas had barely stood back up as a young woman he instantly recognized leaped into his arms, wrapping her legs around his waist, and burying her face in his neck. Thomas growled deeply as he gave her the biggest bear hug he could. The two laughed through tears of joy, hugging for a long moment before Thomas pulled away.

"Julianna?!? Where did you...? How did you...?" Thomas stammered. "How did you get here?"

Julianna loosened the grip she had around his neck and dropped back to the ground.

"Duh…on an airplane," she teased him. "Jeez. That college stuff isn't helping much, is it?"

"Duh!" he teased back, softly punching her on the shoulder. "That part I guessed, dork. But, you know what I mean. Why are you here?"

"What…you don't want to spend time with your sister?" she teased some more, giving him an overly exaggerated sad look.

"Oh, stop it. Of course I want to spend time with you. It's just, well, how did mom afford to send you?"

"Oh, that part. Well, I guess we'll have to fill you in on our little secret," she said, pointing to her right.

Thomas looked over to find Beth standing there, patiently waiting for her turn to say hello. He glanced back to Julianna, and then back to Beth. In the enthusiasm of the reunion, he suddenly had a brash and wild idea.

"Be right back," he told his sister, rushing over to where Beth stood before Julianna could respond.

Thomas wrapped his arms tightly around Beth, literally sweeping her off her feet. She yelped loudly, grasping him around the neck, her face a perfect display of surprise.

"How've you been? I've missed you!" Thomas said after a moment had passed.

"Put me back down and I'll let you know," Beth insisted, blushing with delight.

Laughing, Thomas set her down carefully, and then stepped back to give her some space.

Brushing her clothes to straighten them out, Beth shook her head playfully, smiling warmly at Thomas.

"Well, that was quite the greeting, Brother Thomas! If I didn't know better, I'd say you've had a few too many red vines again."

Thomas threw his head back, laughing loudly. These were the moments of life when he was most at peace, when the typical awkwardness that plagued him didn't surface, allowing allowed him to be open and free.

"I haven't had any since the retreat, actually," Thomas admitted. "But, I want to hear all about this little secret you have with my sister."

Beth blushed, then looked away, trying to appear innocent. "What secret?" she said in mock surprise.

Thomas crossed his arms, giving her one of his more serious looks.

"Okay. So we did something…a little…creative, you might say," Beth admitted.

Thomas turned back to Julianna.

"Sis? Spill the beans," he demanded.

Julianna appeared hesitant to speak, though once Thomas gave her the same serious look he had given Beth, she slowly began to share.

"Well, me and Lily were kinda talking one day. I know mom doesn't want me to talk to her, but that's only because she's embarrassed that the Thompson's have all this money and we don't. And, well, that's just her problem, not mine. I like Lily. I know you do too. She's a really good person," Julianna started to explain.

"So, what did you and Lily talk about?" Thomas interrupted impatiently.

"I was getting to that. Jeez! Anyway, I told Lily that you were coming here and how I really wished I could too. I need a service project for Confirmation anyway, right? All the other stuff Amanda has this summer is boring; working at homeless shelters, or spending time with old people," Juliana said with a look of complete disgust.

It was times like this that made Thomas wonder if he and his sister were really related. How could they be so different? It also made him realize how much growing up Julianna still had to do.

"Anyway, I got this plan. I talked to Lily about it, and then she told Amanda, so, we're like all in this together. Amanda told mom that there was this *anonymous donor* who gave a bunch of money so *some lucky kid* could come." Juliana pointed at herself, winking. "And then she told mom that my name was the one she picked out of a hat. Which she really did. We just didn't say that mine was the only name in the hat."

"And the anonymous donor?" Thomas asked, although he somehow already knew the answer.

"Oh, that. It was just Mr. Thompson. He dropped off an envelope full of cash at Amanda's office. So, technically, we didn't really lie!" she stated proudly, putting her hands on her hips as she stood up tall.

Thomas smiled at his little sister, and then turned to look back at Beth.

"And what part did you play in all this?" he asked, mocking an upset and serious tone.

Beth's face flushed even more. Her eyes opened wide and her jaw dropped.

"What? Who, me? I'm innocent here!" she pleaded in jest, her face turning pink.

"Sure you are," Thomas said, shaking his head.

"No. Really. I didn't find out until Amanda called me to make sure I was willing to be responsible for Julianna until you arrived."

"Okay, okay," Thomas said, turning back to face his sister. "So, you just hatched this little plan out all on your own, huh? And what if mom finds out?"

Thomas grabbed his sister in a headlock as he ruthlessly poked her in the ribs. She struggled to squirm out of his grasp, squealing louder with each poke. Twisting her head just enough to get her mouth near his arm, Julianna bit her brother gently. Thomas quickly let go, grabbing the spot where she bit him, his playful expression turning to one of surprise. Julianna straightened her ruffled shirt, giving her brother a vicious glare.

"She won't find out," she said smugly. "And if she does, well, too bad. It will all be over by then."

Thomas considered the situation. In the grand scheme of things, what his sister did would most likely fall under the category of a little white lie. He just didn't want her getting comfortable with little lies. He knew how quickly little lies added up, leading to bigger and bigger ones down the road.

"Okay, sis, I'll make you a deal. I won't say anything to mom if you find some time to go to reconciliation with Father Dominic while we're here. If it was this easy for you to lie to mom like you did, I'm worried there may be a few other things you need to confess."

Julianna's face went blank, her arms hanging limply at her sides. She stared at her brother as if she suddenly didn't recognize him.

"Oh my God! I don't believe it. You're really serious, aren't you?" she said, her voice as devoid of emotion as her face.

"Oh, you bet. Look. It'll probably be good for you. I'll bet you haven't been to confession since your eighth-grade retreat, if you even went then. You'll be fine. Deal?" Thomas asked, holding out his hand.

Julianna sighed heavily. She knew there was no way to twist out of *this* headlock.

"Whatever," she said as she turned her back on her brother and stomped away. "I'm going swimming. Who's going to *babysit* me?"

Thomas looked at Beth. She had an exaggerated smile, as if hoping she could get away unscathed. Thomas couldn't help but smile back.

"Swimming?" was all he said.

"Yeah. We've already gone twice since we arrived. You should come!" she said sheepishly, still unsure if he was angry with her or not. "Besides, it's our only escape from this afternoon heat."

"But, I didn't bring a suit," he informed her.

"Just swim in your shorts. Trust me. They'll dry off by the time we walk back."

"I'm up for a swim, too!" Gemma said.

Thomas suddenly remembered his manners, calling out, "Hey, Jules, come back for a second. There's someone I want you to meet."

Julianna turned around, reluctantly walking back towards him. Her shoulders were slumped forward, her arms hung limp, and her feet shuffled forward in short, loud, plodding steps which sent clouds of dust into the air with each thump. She groaned loudly, as if Thomas had just asked her to do the worst thing imaginable.

"Sorry," he whispered to Gemma, "she can be a bit dramatic at times."

"So, I see," Gemma whispered back with a smile.

When Julianna had made it back to the small circle, she stood with complete apathy, her body looking as if it had been carelessly placed there by some giant child who had grown bored playing with a doll.

"Julianna, this is Gemma. She's a friend of mine from school."

Julianna looked up briefly, gave her a weak wave, then let her arm and head fall back. Without hesitation, Gemma walked over and lifted Julianna's head so she could look her in the eye.

"It's nice to meet you, Julianna. I'm really glad you're here," she said, keeping her hold on the young girl's chin with one hand while she made her shake hands with the other.

Dropping her hold on Thomas' sister, Gemma turned and walked over to Beth, extending her hand to greet her in turn.

"Hello, Beth. I'll introduce myself, since Thomas seems to have forgotten."

Beth gave Gemma a smile, taking her hand and returning the greeting.

"Nice to meet you, Gemma. So, are you the one who has been looking after Brother Thomas while he's away at school?"

"Oh, no. Thomas and I just met, what, about two weeks back now?"

"Really? And yet he was already able to convince you to join him down here in paradise?" Beth said, waving her arms around in a slow circle. "Impressive!"

Gemma simply smiled and then turned around and walked back towards the Jeep. When no one but Thomas could hear her, Beth whispered, "I think she likes you," making Thomas blush.

"So, what was that about a swim?" he said nervously (and perhaps a bit loudly).

Beth's eyebrows raised as she realized the attraction between them was mutual.

"It's not far," Beth answered after a longer than normal pause. "About a ten-minute walk, I guess."

"What about our bags?" Thomas asked.

"Don't worry about those, Thomas," Father Dominic chimed in. "You young kids go have fun. You don't have much time left before it gets dark, so please, just a quick swim, and then right back here, okay?"

Thomas nodded his promise, turning to Beth.

"I guess I could just swim in what I have on now and change later," he said, then turned to Gemma. "Do you want to change first?"

"No. I didn't bring a suit either. Besides, in this heat, it might be good to be in wet clothes for a while."

"Not once the mosquitoes come out," Beth warned. "But we should be back here before then so you can dry off and change."

Beth paused for a moment, looking Gemma up and down, and then said, "Actually, I might have something that will fit you."

"Then, let's be off!" Gemma announced, moving to follow Julianna who was still lumbering with a zombie-like stride.

"Oh, wait," Thomas said as he began to follow behind, "what about Theresa? Is she here?"

"Yeah, she's been resting most of the day. She says this heat gives her headaches," Beth informed him. "We can stop by the tents and pick her up on the way."

"Okay then, Beth, I hereby dub you our official tour guide! Lead the way!" Thomas said, drawing a blush and a laugh from Beth.

Beth turned, walking quickly to catch up to the other two young women. Thomas followed close behind. As they made their way around the side of a cluster of trees, Thomas got his first look at the camp. The camp had been constructed from a series of old army tents set close together in a semi-circle. A longer, open-air tent was set where the circle split, creating what resembled a capital letter D. Inside this larger tent, Thomas could see tables and chairs, as well as what appeared to be a kitchen.

In the kitchen he saw a large metal table stacked with heads of lettuce, and mounds of tomatoes, onions and peppers, all of which were being chopped, sliced, or diced in preparation for the evening meal. As the piles of prepared ingredients grew large enough, one of the cooks would sweep them off the table into large, metal pots that sat waiting on the ground. The group of workers, including four women and two men, sang loudly as they worked. Thomas found the interplay of their mixed emotions to be wonderfully attractive, filling him with the desire to join in. Had he not already agreed to go for a swim, he would have been more than happy to.

As they crossed through the open-sided tent, the kitchen crew began singing even louder, their faces stretching into wide smiles. Thomas smiled back, then turned away as he exited the far side of the tent. Beth came to a stop in the center of the camp, which was marked by a large ring of stones surrounding a fire pit.

"Thomas," she said, pointing to her left, "those two tents with the blue tape on the doors are the men's dorms. You'll find a cot in there with your name on it. The women's dorms are on the other side, marked with red tape. Showers are in that gray building over there."

Thomas looked in the direction she was pointing, seeing a small concrete structure with three doors.

"There's no hot water, yet," Beth continued, "but in this heat, you don't really need it anyway."

"Ooh! All the luxuries of home," Gemma said jokingly, drawing a smile from Thomas.

"Come on, Gemma," Beth said as she headed for the women's tent, "let me show you where you'll be staying. Thomas, we'll meet you back here in five minutes, okay?"

"Sounds good. I'll check out my bunk and be right back out," Thomas replied as he walked towards the men's tent.

Entering through the flap, Thomas stood for a moment inside the doorway letting his eyes adjust to the darkness. The air felt heavy and dense, and there was a dusty, stale smell. Once his eyes adjusted, he took a look around. The tent had room for twelve cots, set in three rows of four. None of the cots appeared to have been used yet, which wasn't a surprise, since most of the volunteers were still arriving.

Walking in a clockwise circle around the center row of cots, Thomas found the one with his name on it in the back corner of the tent, furthest from the door. He sat on the bed, testing the firmness of the canvas, deciding it was definitely going to take a little getting used to. Turning on the lamp, which was the only item on the bedside table, he adjusted the small cone of illumination to shine on the portion of the cot where his head would be. The dim light that the lamp produced appeared to be just enough to read by, but not so bright it would bother those who would be sleeping in the neighboring cots.

Standing back up, Thomas switched off the lamp, and then searched the other cots to find Terence's name. He found it right next to his, one spot closer to the door. Suddenly, a sly and mischievous grin appeared on Thomas' face. He looked around the empty tent, just to be sure no one was watching, and then set to work. Flipping the cot over, and using the side of a quarter, Thomas began to loosen the screws that held the frame together. Each one was removed to the point just before falling out. Thomas then carefully flipped the cot back over, returning it to the place it had been before.

Laughing softly to himself, he put the quarter on the bedside table by his cot, and exited the tent, finding his sister waiting for him outside. She had changed into a bikini top and cut-off jean shorts that hung open at the flap. A matching bikini bottom peeked out.

"Modesty," Thomas thought as the smile faded from his face. *"That's another discussion we need to have."*

"What were you smiling about?" Julianna asked.

"Oh, I was just remembering something funny."

"Yeah, sure you were," Julianna responded with a look of distrust. "I know that face, big brother."

Thomas flashed her a shocked expression.

"Wow, Jules! And here all this time I thought I was your favorite brother."

"Uh...you're my only brother."

"Oh, yeah. I forgot," Thomas teased.

At that moment, Beth, Gemma, and Theresa came out of the women's tent. Beth and Gemma were wearing tennis shoes with no socks, and Theresa had on a pair of flat sandals. They all wore t-shirts and jean shorts similar to Julianna's, except their shorts were buttoned shut. Thomas thought about pointing that fact out to Julianna, but decided against it for now. He didn't want to upset or embarrass her in front of the others. Instead, he simply whispered to her as he walked past, "Remind me to tell you something later."

Julianna gave him a soft, friendly punch on the shoulder, and then started walking backward towards the jungle. She had a devious look.

"Last one there doesn't get to swim!" she shouted, spinning around and taking off at a sprint.

The rest of the group followed closely behind. As they cut through the dining tent once more, Theresa almost crashed into one of the volunteers who was carrying a pot full of water, garnering a few shouts from the kitchen crew. Thomas voiced an apology as he raced ahead, passing Julianna a few yards later.

Turning around and running backward, he said, "I don't know where I'm going!"

"I know where you're going. You're going to lose!" Julianna laughed as she ran past him again.

Thomas turned, hot on her heels, this time staying slightly behind, letting her lead for now.

"Can you guys slow down?" Theresa shouted. "I can't run in these sandals!"

"Do you know where we're going?" Thomas shouted back, turning around again as he did.

"Yeah." Theresa responded. "I just don't want to be the last one there!"

Thomas slowed, allowing Beth and Gemma to pass him by. Theresa caught up, then suddenly kicked off her sandals and surged ahead of Thomas, running far too easily in her bare feet.

"Chain up!" Theresa yelled, squeezing between the two older girls and locking arms at the elbows. "Jules, come join us! We'll block your brother out!"

Laughing, all four women, now linked together, spread out as wide as they could without breaking their link. They disappeared for a moment around a bend in the path. When Thomas made the same turn, he saw that the path quickly narrowed, allowing the young women to bunch even closer together. Thomas shook his head, knowing he had been played. They must have planned the whole thing while they were changing in their tent. Quickening his pace, he went from running to sprinting as fast as he could, hoping he could catch up.

Following the sound of laughter and taunts from up ahead, he dove through the jungle, chasing the girls down the well-marked trail. Rounding another corner he caught sight of his prey. They had stopped at a point where the path opened into a clearing, in the middle of which was a large pool of water. Beth and Gemma stood on the left of the path, and the other two were on the right. They had their backs facing Thomas as they removed their outer garments, hanging the clothes on the large ferns nearby. Thomas could hear Beth explaining to Gemma to make sure she placed her things as high as possible to avoid finding them full of ants on their return.

Thomas pushed himself even harder, his legs flying beneath him. The four women finished hanging their outer clothes and were slowly entering the water as Thomas exploded through the group, leaping high into the air and then tucking into a cannonball. He crashed into the water, sending up a fountain of spray. The water splashed the girls, drawing yelps and screams. They dove in after him, splashing even more.

Their laughter spread through the jungle, catching the attention of animals of every size. Luckily, the heavy, humid air and the thick undergrowth of the jungle deadened the sound from traveling too far. Where it did travel, the birds and animals fled, startled by the unfamiliar sounds. Unfortunately, the sound reached just far enough to be heard by one human as well. The man, dressed in full camouflage, his face wrapped in a green cloth, tensed at the sound of laughter.

Moving slowly and stealthily through the undergrowth, he inched his way closer to the sound. Staying deep in the shadows, his eyes peered between the branches of a thick fern as he watched the group at play. When he had seen enough, he backed away slowly and then stood, heading towards his camp at a run. The camp was located about five miles from the mission site, hidden in the deepest part of the jungle. The man, straining to catch his breath, reported what he had seen to the group leader. After a short conversation, a group of three men joined the scout as he retraced his steps, returning to the pool just in time to watch the five young adults disappearing down the trail.

Speaking in hushed tones and staying hidden from view, the rebels followed Thomas and his friends. When the jungle opened up into the clearing where the mission was located, the four camouflaged men retreated back into the trees, returning quickly to their camp once more. They arrived just as the sun dipped below the canopy of trees, casting eerie shadows through the jungle below. With excitement in their eyes, they shared with their leader what they had seen. The word, *Americanos*, was by far the word they used the most.

With brief commands, the rebel leader sent men into action, charging a team of four to return to the mission. He commanded them to stay out of sight, watch, wait, and to report back anything of significance that they might see. The four men gathered a few supplies and then headed out into the gloom, anxious to return to their post.

Nearby, outside of the view of any man or beast, a dark shadow stood where there was nothing solid to cast it. With a sinister laugh, the Devil laid out his plans.

CHAPTER ELEVEN
TACO TUESDAY

"Thomas!" Father Dominic called out from the far side of the camp. "Come have coffee with me."

Thomas waved his hand to let the priest know he had heard him, then ambled across the grounds towards the tent. He grabbed a white, porcelain mug and filled it with dark, thin liquid that the kitchen crew had tried to convince him was coffee, and then took a seat across the table from his mentor. Father Dominic pushed a small metal box closer to him and Thomas gratefully opened the lid, drawing out two bags of sugar which he added to his cup. He lazily stirred the mixture with his finger, and then put his finger into his mouth, closing his lips around it and pulling it out with a *pop*.

"I don't know how you do that," Father Dominic said, shaking his head.

"What, stir it with my finger? It's not that hot," Thomas replied.

"No, destroy a perfectly good cup of coffee with that dreaded white powder. I know it's not a sin, but it really should be."

"Trust me, Father," Thomas said as he raised his cup slightly, "this is anything but a perfectly good cup of coffee. The only way I can drink this stuff is by making it taste like candy."

Father Dominic smiled softly. "You young people. So spoiled with your gourmet coffee houses and drive-thru lattes."

"Hey, now…" Thomas chided. "You're not that much older than I am, Father. Starbucks has been around since you were my age!"

"True, true. But they didn't have one on every corner back then. We had to drive far more than just a few blocks to find one."

"And I'm sure your parents' generation thought you were spoiled because McDonald's were everywhere."

Father Dominic laughed.

"That is true! And their parents complained about something else. I guess that's just how things go."

"Yeah, I guess so. It makes me wonder what I'll think about the kids twenty years from now, what they will have that will make me think they're spoiled."

"We will have to wait and see."

Thomas took a drink from his cup.

"Ahh…" he sighed, flashing an obviously fake smile. "That's good."

"Well, now that you've had some caffeine, let's talk about your mission," Father Dominic said, giving Thomas a sly smile.

Thomas froze. Did he mean *the quest*? He was certain he hadn't told anyone about that. How could Father Dominic have found out? Not wanting to give anything away, he decided to play dumb.

"What mission?" Thomas asked hesitantly.

"The one I have planned for you tonight," Father Dominic informed him.

Relief washed over Thomas as he breathed a quiet sigh. Then, suddenly curious what Father Dominic had in mind, he said, "Go on. I'm listening."

"Well, the last of your friends will arrive before dinner tonight, correct?"

"Yeah," Thomas nodded, finishing his coffee and setting the empty cup aside. "His flight lands in about an hour, so he should be here by lunch, I would imagine."

"Good. Then it's time you established yourself as the leader of your group."

"And just how am I supposed to do that?"

"Simple. Meet me where we park the vehicles tonight at around five-thirty. Make sure you have all the volunteers with you who are your age or younger. Have you met the rest yet?"

'The rest', as Father Dominic had referred to them, was a group of young adults who had come from the priest's home parish in the Los Angeles area. There were six of them, four boys and two girls, all between the ages of seventeen and twenty. He had met the young men the evening they had arrived since they were housed in the same tent. The first to enter had been Francis, a seventeen-year-old math wizard who was already in his first year of college. He seemed like a nice kid, though he was painfully quiet and shy.

Next to enter the tent that night had been Brendan, a nineteen-year-old student-athlete who had lettered in five different sports during his high school career. With his chiseled physique, perfect tan, and radiant green eyes flashing beneath jet-black hair, he looked like he had just walked in from a photo shoot.

Behind him had come Jeremiah, a seventeen-year-old church history buff who carried a Bible everywhere he went. Everywhere. This made sense since he was on a similar path as Thomas, having also declared his intention to become a priest. The two priests-in-training had already spent time doing what Thomas had dubbed *back pocket theology*, an activity where one person would come up with a random word, and the other had to create a five-minute sermon about that topic, including at least two scripture references.

Finally, there was Sam, an eighteen-year-old video game prodigy who, according to legend, had once played *Fury of the Storm* by Dragonforce on GuitarHero, with his back to the TV, on expert level. His other talent was the ability to provide a list of the five best mods for every upgradable weapon in every first-person-shooter game ever released. Sam was always in a good mood, a trait that Thomas found endearing.

The two women, Jennifer and Adriana, were quite the pair. They had been best friends since preschool. Jennifer, who was nineteen, was dark-haired, tall and thin, with a picture-perfect smile highlighted on each side by deep dimples. Though she dressed modestly, her clothes all had a 'designer store' look to them, and she changed outfits often, as if she was at some remote tropical fashion show.

Jennifer's friend, Adriana, also nineteen, couldn't have been more down to earth, wearing outfits she had pieced together from second-hand stores. She rarely wore shoes, or makeup for that matter. Though, Thomas had to admit, she didn't need it. Her light brown hair, hazel eyes and perfectly placed freckles gave her a healthy, natural beauty which was highlighted even more by the warm, welcoming personality she shared.

For once, Thomas found he was comfortable around both women even though he barely knew them. They had a way of breaking through his usual awkwardness, leaving him feeling comfortable, accepted, and at peace. Thomas wasn't the only one who had been captivated by their charm and good looks.

With a slight smile, Thomas brought his attention back to Father Dominic, responding, "Yeah, I've had a chance to meet them. It will be interesting what happens when Terence gets here this afternoon. You haven't met him yet. He has a very strong presence, and a quick wit, too. Plus, he's a consummate flirt."

Father Dominic glanced at his watch.

"Well, I've got to get going. Final pre-construction planning meeting. I will see you later today, yes?"

Thomas nodded his consent. As Father Dominic walked away, he got up from the table to see what was for breakfast and then filled his plate with scrambled eggs, bacon, fried plantains, and a biscuit with fresh papaya jam. He also drank three more cups of coffee. After breakfast, he returned to the men's tent, ensuring that the guys were awake. He let them know they had only a few minutes left for breakfast before the morning's work schedule would begin. Though the primary construction hadn't started yet, there was still plenty of work to be done. Flatbed trucks filled with supplies would be arriving in less than an hour, and the young adults were tasked with helping to offload, sort, and stack the items.

Placing Brendan in charge of the other three, Thomas went to check on the women's tent. By the sound of laughter he heard as he walked across the camp, he could tell the girls were already up.

"Beth? Gemma?" he called out. "You guys up?"

The tent grew suddenly quiet, and then burst into laughter as the six young women inside shared a private joke. Thomas wondered if perhaps he may have been the subject of their laughter.

"Yeah! We're up." Beth responded after the laughter had died down.

"Okay. You have about an hour before everyone needs to be ready. We're going to be unloading trucks today, so make sure you're wearing clothes you don't mind getting dirty."

Their response was another brief moment of silence, followed by even stronger laughs. Thomas was more than curious to find out what was so amusing but decided to take the safer route and not ask. If they wanted to tell him, Beth or Julianna probably would.

The rest of the morning passed uneventfully. Every time there appeared to be a break in the steady flow of arriving supplies, another truck would rumble and cough its way into camp. The youth, for the most part, kept their spirits high, laughing and joking or challenging each other to made-up games. Even though the day moved quickly from the cooler temperatures of the morning to the oppressive, sweat-gland-activating sauna of midday, the mood stayed light and jovial. Terence arrived just before lunch, as planned. As lunch was ending, Thomas approached Father Dominic.

"So, I was thinking..." Thomas began.

"That's the first sign of insanity, you know," Father Dominic replied, chuckling softly at his humor.

"Oh, really? Then we should probably have you committed once we get back to the States."

Father Dominic laughed even harder at the reply.

"Very good, Thomas. You win this round," the priest said through a wide smile. "What can I do for you?"

"As I said," Thomas began again, "I was thinking that it might be good to give the group a break. They've been going at it since breakfast. I thought maybe I could take them swimming. It would give Terence a chance to get to know everyone."

"From what I see, the young man is doing a fine job of mingling on his own," Father Dominic said, lowering his voice as he used his eyes to point Thomas' attention to a table in the back of the dining tent.

Thomas casually looked over his shoulder, trying not to draw attention to his action. Terence was sitting at the table, surrounded by a harem of females. Beth and Gemma were standing on the side of the table opposite Terence, with Theresa sitting just below them. Adrianna and Jennifer were sitting on Terence's left side, and Julianna was on his right. From what Thomas could tell, the collective attention of the group was focused on his roommate, which he held captive with the occasional flash of his perfect grin.

"Do you want me to talk to him?" Thomas asked as he turned back around.

"No, no. It's harmless at this point," Father Dominic said. "But, to your earlier question, we don't expect another truck for about an hour or so, but we still have the materials from the last truck waiting to be moved. And it all has to be staged by tonight."

Thomas' face scrunched as he pondered.

"Let me talk to my group. I'll give them the options to push through until dinner, or to complete a little work tonight after it gets dark. I'll be back."

With that, Thomas spun around and headed towards the table where Terence was. As he approached, he saw Francis and Brendan seated at a table nearby.

"Brendan, can you go find Sam and Jeremiah, please? We need to have a quick meeting."

Brendan jumped up and jogged off in the direction of the tents, while Francis stood up and made his way to the table where Terence and the women were. Thomas joined the group, taking a seat next to Theresa, who turned and gave him a pensive smile. He made a mental note to check in with her, just to be sure she was okay.

The conversation at the table continued, with the younger girls asking Terence a series of questions about what it was like living away at college, if he missed anything about being at home, and other related queries. A few minutes later, Brendan arrived with the other two young men in tow. When they were all settled in, Thomas cleared his throat.

"I hate to break this up, but I need to talk to you all," he said loud enough to capture their attention.

Terence was the first to turn towards him, asking, "What's going on, Thomas?"

"Well, basically, we have two choices that I want your opinions on. There is still a bit of work left ahead of us today, and it will probably take us up until dinner time to get it done. Which means we may not have time for our usual late afternoon swim."

A collective sigh sounded around the table, coupled with a few boos.

"I'm going to give you guys the option. We have to be ready for dinner by five thirty. Father Dominic has something special planned. Which means we can take a quick swim now for about an hour, and then finish the work after dinner in the dark, or we can push through now and see if we can complete everything and still have time to swim before dinner. What do you all want to do?"

"I say we swim now, and then push through to try and finish before dinner anyway," Brendan said.

"That's easy for you to say," Jennifer chimed in. "You don't have to shower or get ready before dinner. Us ladies need time to clean up."

"Do we have to stick together?" Sam asked, "Or can some of us swim now, while the others work?"

"Oh, no. That's not going to work," Francis replied. "That might mean the people who work now don't get a chance to swim later. No, we need to stay together as a group."

"I agree with Francis," Thomas added in. "This may be our last day working as a team, too. After tonight we will be split into different work groups. We should take advantage of this chance to be together."

"I vote we swim now," Theresa said quietly.

Thomas watched her from the corner of his eye. He knew there was something bothering her. Her emotional energy had a reserved, self-protective feel.

"I'll second that," Brendan shared.

"I'd rather push through and get all this work done. That way, we might be able to cut off earlier than anticipated, which could give us a little more time before dinner," Terence shared.

"Okay, let's put it to a vote. Who wants to swim now?" Thomas asked.

Four hands went up around the table: Theresa, Brendan, Sam and Adriana.

"Who wants to push through?"

The rest of the group, except for Beth, raised their hands. Thomas turned and gave her a questioning look.

"I can go either way," she said. "It really doesn't matter. Besides, with only four votes for swimming now, it seemed a moot point."

"Okay, work first it is! Everyone make sure you get something to drink first. I'll ask the kitchen crew to bring over some cold bottles of water a little later, too. Let's make sure we're all staying hydrated."

The group began to break up, some heading towards the tents and the rest heading towards the area where they had been working most of the day. Thomas caught Theresa as she was about to walk out.

"Hey, Theresa, hold up a sec," he called softly.

"Yeah, sure," she said, not looking at him.

When the rest of the team had wandered a fair distance from where Thomas and Theresa stood, he turned to her again.

"I'm just checking in on you. You seem awfully quiet today. Is everything okay?"

Theresa, her eyes fixed on some random spot on the ground, shuffled her feet and shrugged.

"Yeah, I guess. I just can't get this feeling out of my mind that something bad is going to happen," she finally said, her voice barely above a whisper.

"Like what? What do you think might happen?" he asked, looking suddenly concerned.

"I really don't know, Brother Thomas. The last time I felt this way, my little brother got hurt in a pretty bad bike crash."

"Oh my goodness!" Thomas exclaimed. "When was that? Is he okay?"

Theresa finally brought her eyes up to meet his.

"It was like a month ago, maybe more. And, yeah, he's okay now," she said, her face devoid of emotion.

"What happened?" Thomas inquired.

"He was riding too fast down a hill and couldn't get the bike to turn the corner. He hit the gutter and flew over the handlebars. Broke both his legs, his right arm, and a couple of ribs."

"Oh, wow. That was pretty serious. But he's okay you said, right?"

"Yeah, he still has to use crutches, and he goes to physical therapy twice a week. But he's been back home for a couple weeks now. My mom took some time off work to stay home and take care of him until he can manage stuff by himself."

"I'll make sure to pray for him this afternoon. And I'll ask Father Dominic to pray as well. In fact, maybe we should have the group pray together tonight after dinner. Would that be okay?"

Theresa looked back down again, shuffling her feet once more.

"You don't need to do that. I'm sure he's fine, especially with me gone." Her head popped up suddenly, her eyes locking with Thomas. "But this feeling I have is far worse than what I felt back then. I think that's why I wanted to go swimming now. I think whatever is going to happen, it will be tonight. I don't know how I know. I can just feel it."

"Does this have anything to do with your Endlessly Dying Girl powers? Is it part of being invisible like you told me on the retreat?"

Theresa looked away. Thomas could tell by the way her emotional energy changed that she didn't think he believed her invisibility was real. He was about to share his story with her, to tell her about the visions he had with Saint Thérèse and Saint Maximillian, but something stopped him. Turning around, he saw Father Dominic walking up from behind.

"Can we talk about this later?" Theresa asked, her face pleading with him to accept.

"Yeah, that's fine. But if you see anything strange, or if you think you know what it is that might happen, come get me right away, okay?"

Theresa paused, her eyes peering deep into his, as if she was trying to draw out the reason behind his request. Again, he wanted to tell her everything he knew, but not with other ears within range. Finally, she nodded her head, satisfied that he was sincere.

"Okay, Brother Thomas, I will," she said quietly. "And thank you for being here and caring about me."

Thomas could see she had let down her guard. He could tell it was hard for her to trust. And now, with her fears on high alert, it must be even harder. As he watched her leave, he promised himself that the conversation they needed to have would not wait another day.

"So, what was the verdict?" Father Dominic inquired when the two men were alone.

"Work now, swim later if there's still time," Thomas informed him.

"Good. And I'll make sure they have time. The sun sets early here, but perhaps a night swim this evening would be a perfect way to kick off the start of construction tomorrow. What do you think?"

"Yeah. That would be fun. I think the group would enjoy that. Maybe if it works out we can do it more often. I have this feeling that it's going to be very important for us to bring this group together, although, to be honest, I don't know why."

"Ah, the Holy Spirit is at work in you!"

"In what way, Father?" Thomas inquired.

"Most people call it intuition, which is what it is, if you know the origin of that word. But we as Christians understand that it is God working through the Holy Spirit, hoping we move in the direction of what He has planned. Heed those feelings, Thomas. They may one day save your life!"

Before Thomas could inquire more about what Father Dominic had just shared, the priest turned quickly on his heels and strode off. Shrugging his shoulders, Thomas went to talk to the kitchen team, ensuring they would deliver water for his team every hour or so. He then downed four cups of cold water, feeling the fluid wash away the weariness from carrying the emotional baggage of so many restless hearts.

Joining his team, he pulled out the list of instructions the foreman for the construction crew had given him that morning. It detailed each of the work party locations, what they would be working on, what day each phase of the project would start, as well as a list of materials required and where the foreman wanted them stacked. Thomas passed along this information to the team and then broke them into four groups of three. He placed himself in a group with Terence and Brendan, giving most of the heavy lifting to his group.

For the next several hours, the youth and young adults worked tirelessly, taking breaks in the shade every hour to rehydrate and making sure everyone kept a close watch on the others in their group. Eventually, the trucks stopped arriving, and the work wound down to one final pile of supplies.

Thomas and his team sat in the shade one last time, greedily draining bottles of water and tossing the empty bottles into a box that was already half full. They were dusty, sweaty, and sticky. Their faces were red from exhaustion and exposure to the sun and their eyes had a distant, tired look, as if they could fall asleep right where they were. Still, the conversation was buoyant, and the mood was bright. The laughter, though somewhat reserved from exhaustion, was still as lively as before.

Ten minutes later, as the conversation was dwindling, and two of the teens were fast asleep in the shade, the sound of an automobile engine caught the attention of the group. Turning, they watched as Father Dominic drove up in an old, dusty, gray hatchback spotted with rust. The windows were down and the radio was playing loudly. Sam, who was one of those who had fallen asleep, sat up at the sound, glancing around as if unaware where he was.

Father Dominic parked the car nearby, turned off the radio, and shut down the engine. A thick black cloud of exhaust exploded out of the tailpipe with a thunderous bang, raising a few screams of surprise. As he got out of the car, a few of the young adults waved hello. Father Dominic returned the greetings, shaking the hands of the teens that were closest to him. He spoke briefly to a few of them, polite conversation mostly: how they were doing, if they had remembered to send a postcard home yet, how they were liking working on the mission project. Finally, he turned to face the group.

"Well, my young friends, I have some good news for you," he announced.

The side conversations ceased as eleven faces turned to hear what the priest was about to say. Thomas tapped Adriana on the shoulder.

"Can you wake Jennifer up?" he requested, surprised that the car backfire and the surprised yelps hadn't already done the trick.

Adriana leaned forward, shaking Jennifer aggressively until she finally began to stir. Sitting up, she rubbed her eyes with the palms of her hands, and then, blinking her eyes several times and yawning wide, she sat still for a moment, letting her mind catch up.

"Oh, hey guys. What time is it?" Jennifer asked, drawing a round of laughter from the group. "No, seriously, what's going on?"

"I was just about to fill you all in. Thank you so much for joining us, Jennifer," Father Dominic said teasing the young woman.

"Oh, Father Dominic is here, too. Great," Jennifer said uncertainly, then turned to Adriana. "I don't have drool on my face or anything, do I?"

This raised another round of soft laughter.

"You're good, Jen. You're good," Adriana replied, grinning broadly.

Father Dominic cleared his throat, finally getting Jennifer's attention.

"Are you ready, yet?" he asked.

Jennifer blushed slightly, and then nodded.

"Oh, good," the priest teased, smiling playfully at her. "Anyone else? No? Okay, then let me continue. As I said, I have some wonderful news for you all. Brother Thomas has volunteered to take you into town for dinner tonight. A little place called Cocina Urbina. After all, it is Taco Tuesday."

CHAPTER TWELVE
DINNER AND A SHOW

"Ah, Thomas?' Gemma whispered quietly. "Where's the other car?"

Thomas shook his head and shrugged his shoulders letting her know he had no idea. A moment ago, Father Dominic had tossed the set of keys for the dusty hatchback to him, told the group to enjoy their dinner, and began to walk away.

"Father Dominic?" Thomas called after him.

"Yes, Thomas?" Father Dominic responded without turning around.

"I have a question. Well, two actually. The first is, where is this restaurant you're talking about?"

"And the second question?"

Thomas looked around at the group. Every head was turned towards him, every eye held the same question he was about to ask.

"How are all of us supposed to fit in that?" he asked, pointing at the car.

Father Dominic turned around with a sly grin, saying, "To answer your first question, there is a map on the dashboard. And don't worry, dinner is already paid for. I set that up in advance. As for your second question, you're an intelligent, creative guy. I'm sure you will be able to figure something out."

Thomas gulped as eleven faces turned his way.

"Can I ask how far it is to the restaurant? Maybe we can take two trips."

"Oh, it's not that far. About thirty minutes or so, I imagine," Father Dominic replied.

"I'm starving," Brendan said in a hushed voice. "No way I'm going to be in the second car. That's a half-hour to drop off, then a half-hour back, and another half-hour to take the second group."

"Yeah, that seems like a long time to wait. Plus, another hour-and-a-half round trip coming home, too." Adrianna complained.

Father Dominic smiled, chuckling softly.

"I have an idea," he said casually. "Why don't you draw straws? The five lucky winners can go to the restaurant. The rest, well, you can join me for dinner."

Father Dominic turned and walked away again.

"This is crazy," Jeremiah said, shaking his head.

"I'm going to make a nice, healthy salad!" Father Dominic called out as he continued to cross the camp.

Suddenly, Brendan jumped up, racing towards the car, shouting, "Oh, hell no. I'm not eating salad!"

Francis and Sam were next, racing behind him, followed closely by Adrianna and Jennifer.

"There's no way the boys are going to beat us out," Adrianna said in a low, growling voice.

The three young men took up the available seats in the back, quickly buckling themselves in, leaving only the front seat open. Adrianna and Jennifer climbed in together, sitting closely side by side.

"Well, crap," Gemma complained, "that's five already, which doesn't leave any seats for the rest of us. This isn't very fair. Or fun."

"I don't need my own seat," Julianna informed her as she stood up and followed the others to the car. "Brendan, can I sit on your lap?"

"Yeah, sure. There's room," he replied.

"Maybe I can fit, too," Theresa said, scrambling to her feet and racing to the car.

"There's room for one more on my lap," Francis said from the center seat in the back.

"Mine!" shouted Jeremiah as he too raced towards the car.

Beth, Gemma, and Terence all turned to Thomas at the same time.

"Well, mister intelligent, creative guy," Terence began, "any suggestions?"

Thomas looked long and hard at the car, his hand coming to rest on his chin. His eyebrows furrowed as he contemplated what to do.

"Well, I'm not waiting for you to come up with a plan," Gemma announced, walking to the vehicle and tapping on the back door. "Make room back here!"

She then climbed through the opened window, laying down across the group of six already crammed into the back row. Her feet were dangling out the window, but she was mostly inside.

Beth turned to Terence.

"How do you feel about salad?" she inquired.

"It's okay, I guess. But I'd rather have tacos."

"Me too," Beth admitted.

Thomas tapped Terence on the shoulder, drawing his attention.

"Hatchback," he whispered.

Terence's face lit up, his eyes growing wide. He turned back to Beth, but she was already halfway to the car, dancing all the way. Terence walked slowly behind her, imitating her dance. The noise level inside the car grew higher as the young adults laughed, joked, and laughed some more. Thomas watched as their individual emotional displays blended into one large bright star, riding just above the hatchback's roof. Tossing the keys in his hand, he walked towards the driver's door, pausing before opening it. He glanced in the direction Father Dominic had walked, seeing his mentor standing by the dining tent holding his hands in front of him with both thumbs raised. The smile on the priest's face made him feel proud. Thomas smiled back, then opened the door.

Climbing in, he adjusted the mirrors and then announced, "I think I should check the engine first. Maybe change the oil? And it looks like it needs to be washed, too. Are you guys all good waiting for a bit?"

A chorus of responses flooded the interior of the car, eleven voices in unison urging him to start their drive. Laughing, Thomas put the key in the ignition and started the engine. He hit the power button for the radio, the music blasting loud enough to drown out the voices of the group. Half of the teens yelped in shock at the sudden onrush of sound. Thomas laughed again, then, turning the music down, he put the car in gear and started to drive.

The tires spit gravel and dust in a huge, gray cloud as Thomas pressed the accelerator, letting the wheels spin. Sudden shrieks of fear drowned out the flamenco music blasting from the speakers. Thomas spun the car in a circle, the passengers grabbing each other tightly as their screams echoed through the dust-filled air. Then, pointing the car towards town, their adventure began.

At every corner, Thomas went just a little too fast. At every cliff edge, he hugged the car close to the looming void. They splashed through every puddle, hit every pothole, and scared every animal that had been resting near the road.

Twenty minutes later, Thomas came to the fork in the road that Father Dominic's directions told him to watch for. He spun the wheels, letting the car drift to the right as they entered the paved road that would take them the rest of the way to town. Thankful for finally being on a more reliable surface, and for the fact that Thomas was now driving sensibly, the young adults began to relax. As the noise level subsided, Gemma suddenly screeched, bouncing as best as she could, still stretched out across the six others' in the back seat.

"Oh my God!" she shouted, "I know this song!"

Though the song was in Spanish, most of the group recognized the tune. The car again erupted in joyful sound as first Gemma and then Brendan, Jeremiah, and Julianna all started singing along. Eventually, the rest of the passengers did, too. Thomas turned the music up even louder as the car became more than just a means of transportation. It became a vehicle of transformation, forever etching in the memory of those inside the feeling of ecstatic joy they shared.

The final ten minutes passed quickly as the loud, jubilant hatchback sped into town, garnering strange looks from pedestrians along the way. Pulling into the mostly gravel parking lot, Thomas hit the brakes a little too hard, purposefully letting the car skid to a stop. Those not holding on at the time lurched forward, grabbing anything within range. Gemma and Theresa knocked heads, and Jeremiah bit his tongue. But they didn't care. They just laughed that much more.

All five doors opened simultaneously as the car emptied out passengers like oatmeal boiling over. The group, arms wrapped around each other, holding hands, or riding piggyback, made their way to the restaurant's front door. The short, stocky woman was already holding the door open, having heard their approach from a few blocks away. Her dark eyes twinkled with delight as she offered greetings, both in Spanish and English. Several of the group answered back. Jennifer, who spoke fluent Spanish, informed the hostess that their group was the one sent by Father Dominic.

"Ah, ¡Padre Domingo! ¿Dónde está mi amigo?" she inquired.

Jennifer explained that Father Dominic was not with them, but that he had told the group he had arranged everything in advance.

"Sí, sí. Venga, seguir Marisol. He aquí a tu mesa," she said, her smile as wide and as bright as her eyes.

Thomas, who was just learning the language, caught only bits and pieces. From what he understood, the hostess, whose name was Marisol, had a table set up for the group. Following behind the joyful woman, a parade of smiling, laughing, shoulder-punching young adults weaved their way through the restaurant. Thomas could tell that the few guests seated indoors were greatly relieved that his group was not being seated inside. Marisol waved them through a final doorway, beyond which they found an enormous wooden table with a turntable of almost equal girth covering most of the center. As the young adults began to take their seats, Marisol spoke once more in Spanish to Jennifer.

After a brief conversation, Jennifer turned to Thomas, saying, "She wants to know if we want regular or virgin margaritas with our meal."

Thomas knew the drinking age in Panama was only eighteen. Which meant, legally, everyone except Francis, Julianna, Theresa, and Jeremiah could drink. Yet, he knew this wasn't a question of legality, but one of logistics. If he opened the door to allowing alcohol, wouldn't the church then become responsible for anything that might happen? He also didn't know how Father Dominic would feel about it if Thomas brought a car full of inebriated young adults back to camp. They would all need to be in top form when the construction crews arrived tomorrow morning. He knew they would be far less capable if they were hung over.

"Do you really have to ask?" Thomas said with a teasing smile, raising one eyebrow in reply. "Non-alcoholic drinks, please!"

A chorus of boos and hisses sounded from those who had heard the conversation. Jennifer flashed a mischievous smile, then turned to Marisol.

"Nos traen los regulares, a excepción de Thomas," Jennifer said. "Asegúrese de que es virgen."

Marisol gasped, putting her hand against her forehead. "Oh, querida! ¡Vas a meterme en problemas!"

"What did you tell her?" Thomas asked Jennifer, again having only made out part of the conversation.

"I told her that you said they all need to be virgin drinks," Jennifer lied.

Thomas tilted his head to one side, giving Jennifer a peculiar, doubting look.

"Then why did she say she was going to get in trouble?" he asked, having made out at least that much.

Jennifer's jaw dropped and her face flushed bright red. Thomas chuckled as he watched her emotional display change from one that had looked devious, to one that resembled embarrassment, and a little bit of shock.

"¡Sin alcohol! ¡Sin alcohol!" Jennifer blurted out. "Solo trae té helado!"

"Oh, ice tea!" Marisol replied, speaking English as she gave Jennifer a knowing look. "With the lemon?"

"¡Sí! ¡Sí! Con el limón," Jennifer said as her face flushed even more.

Adrianna, who was sitting next to her, was blushing as well, though not from embarrassment but from the recognition that her friend had just been caught. Though she spoke even less Spanish than Thomas, Adrianna still understood what happened.

"Oh, God, Jen. You didn't just do that, did you?"

"What?" Jennifer replied. "It was worth a shot!"

Thomas flashed a broad smile, and then, when Jennifer looked his way, he gave her a wink to let her know he wasn't upset, just amused. She shrugged her shoulders and then shook her head at her own youthful imprudence. Slowly the story of what happened made its way around the table. Jennifer's face grew even darker.

Marisol, still smiling, mumbled to herself in rapid Spanish as she exited the patio. A minute later, a group of men entered in. One carried a stack of glazed terracotta dinner plates etched with an elaborate design. The other three held platters and large tureens filled with a variety of local cuisine. When the food was set, one of the chefs asked if anyone spoke Spanish. Half the table laughingly pointed to Jennifer, whose face flushed once more.

"He said don't touch the metal platters or you'll get burned!" she said a bit hotly after her brief conversation with the chef.

"You mean like you just did?" Sam teased her loudly, drawing a chorus of "Ooh!"

Jennifer shot him an incredulous look, which quickly turned into a sharp, dagger-like stare, after which she slunk back in her chair, dejected.

"Okay, okay," Thomas said. "Leave the poor girl alone. She's embarrassed enough as it is."

As her features and emotional display softened a little, Thomas had a wicked thought.

"Jennifer?" he asked sullenly, waiting until she turned her attention his way. "You look awful. Can I get you a drink?"

Though she gave him a wide-eyed, jaw-dropping stare, he could tell his joke broke through her gloominess. Shaking her head and smiling wickedly, she replied, "Esperen. Conseguiré mi venganza."

Though he could understand none of what he just heard, from the display above her he could tell she was quietly plotting revenge. Jennifer flashed him one last sassy sneer, then let herself be drawn back into the vibrant, boisterous conversation with her friends.

Marisol returned a few minutes later with three large pitchers filled with ice tea. As she set about pouring the drinks, she informed the group that this first round of dishes was just the appetizers. She then explained what each dish was and what was in it and then left the patio, promising to return soon.

For the next two hours, Thomas and his friends ate, and drank, and ate some more. Their plates were never empty for long, nor did their glasses run dry, as Marisol and her team of waiters kept the turntable filled with fresh platters. The appetizers and soups were replaced with main dishes and the ice tea was replaced with pitchers of *chicheme*, a traditional drink made with boiled corn, almond milk, vanilla, cinnamon, and nutmeg. Most of the group had never eaten so many different flavors or so much food at the same time. By the time dessert was served, the once eager, hungry faces now responded lethargically. Though, once they began tasting the sweet treats, the sound of forks scraping plates could be heard once more.

At the end of the meal the young men and women, exhausted from the day's work and bloated from the enormity of their meal, sat slouched in their seats. Their dreary, tired eyes blinked slowly, but they were beyond happy. Looking around the room, Thomas no longer saw a group of eleven individual lives, but a cohesive, blended, unified team.

"*Mission accomplished,*" he thought to himself as he watched faces struggling to hold smiles, their cheeks as weary as the rest of their bodies.

Marisol returned one last time, letting Thomas know that the bill had already been settled before they arrived, and that they owed nothing else for the meal. She then circled the patio, saying farewell to each of the teens in turn, specifically stopping by Jennifer's chair, giving the young woman a pinch on the cheek.

"¿Ahora, prometen comportarse bien?"

"Sí, lo prometo," Jennifer replied wearily. "Estoy demasiado cansado para conseguir en apuro ya."

This time, Thomas didn't even ask what the two had said to each other. The smile on Marisol's face as she leaned down and gave Jennifer a huge hug told him all he needed to know.

CHAPTER THIRTEEN
A SHOT IN THE DARK

Thomas blinked several times, and then stretched his eyes open as wide as he could. Around him, eleven young adults were once more squeezed into the dusty hatchback, though no one but Thomas moved. The events of the day had taken over, and tired bodies and weary minds had given way to slumber. Thomas knew that he, too, would soon be asleep, just not yet. He still had a few miles to drive before he could succumb. In more ways than he realized, the safety of the group was on his shoulders tonight.

With the bright light of the moon aiding him, Thomas drove on. He carefully guided the car along the winding dirt road, though this time at a far more reasonable pace. Within the small halo cast by the headlights, Thomas watched as shadows became shapes and then passed back into shadow again. Though he saw nothing that raised suspicion, he still had a feeling that something was wrong. Using what little control he had over his strange ability, he placed his attention on the emotional energy of each person in the vehicle with him. Though he felt a minor twinge of distress from Sam, the energy of the remaining passengers felt quiet, peaceful, and at rest.

Perhaps it was simply the nervousness he felt driving a road he hadn't navigated in the dark before. Or it could just be that they were out in the middle of nowhere, still quite a ways from camp. Besides, he considered, the jungle could be a dangerous place. Snakes and spiders the size that were only seen in horror movies, jungle cats that hunted with a silent and deadly precision, and plants that could inflict terrible pain (or outright kill someone) could all be found within a short distance of where he was.

And then there had been the conversation he had had with Theresa earlier in the day and her confession that she, too, had a feeling that something bad was going to happen, perhaps even tonight. He tried to not think too much about it, focusing instead on his drive. Which was why when he came across a fallen tree blocking the road, he simply slowed the car to a stop, put it in park, and shut off the engine.

"Are we there?" Terence, the first one to stir, asked quietly as he tried to stretch, which was more than difficult given the cramped quarters of the back seat.

"Not yet. There's something blocking the road," Thomas informed him. "Wanna get out and help me move it?"

"Yeah, sure," Terence agreed through a yawn.

Thomas removed his seatbelt and opened his door, pausing for a moment as the feeling of danger rose precipitously.

"That tree fell just like that?" Terence asked.

"It looks that way," Thomas said, cautiously. "The trunk looks like it exploded, not like it was cut."

"Yeah, it's weird," Terence admitted as he woke Julianna, who was asleep in his lap. "If this was a movie, this would be the part with some kind of trap."

Thomas remained silent, his senses reaching out in every direction trying to find the source of the danger. Though, try as he might, nothing responded.

"Maybe Terence is right," Thomas thought, *"Maybe this just feels like what would happen in a movie."*

Getting out of the vehicle, Thomas walked slowly to where the tree lay, his senses on alert. Turning back, he saw Terence had freed himself from the intertwined, sleeping teens in the back and had stepped out of the car.

"Better wake Brendan, too. This looks too heavy for just the two of us," Thomas requested as he tried shifting the weight of the tree on his own.

Terence leaned back into the car, reaching over Julianna to shake Brendan's shoulder. When the young man didn't respond, he shook him again, and finally a more aggressive third time before Brendan flinched.

"What?" Brendan growled.

"We need your help out here," Terence informed him. "Come on, get up."

Brendan stretched as he yawned deeply.

"Help with what?" he asked.

"Just get out here," Terence growled, growing tired of asking.

"Okay, okay. Let me get Adrianna off my lap," Brendan grumbled back as he tried to wake Adrianna.

By now, a few of the other passengers had woken as well, curious as to what was going on.

"Everything okay, Thomas?" Beth yawned.

"Yeah, just a minor delay I think."

"Need any help?" she inquired.

"I think three should be enough, but if you want to get out, that would be fine."

"Yeah, I think I will. My left leg feels like it's fallen asleep. I could use a quick stretch," Beth announced as she opened the door and climbed out, leaving Gemma sitting by herself in the front of the car.

Beth's departure from the vehicle was followed soon after by Julianna and Adrianna, who both had to move before Brendan could get out. The hatchback door also opened, releasing Francis and Jeremiah who had taken refuge in the back.

"Oh, man," Francis said, bending at the waist, "that is not a comfortable place to ride."

Next to depart the vehicle was Sam, exiting the vehicle from the back door on the passenger side. As he exited, he woke Jennifer, whose lap he had been sitting on, since she was far taller than him.

"Why are we here?" he asked, suddenly realizing they weren't back at camp as he had assumed.

Jennifer yawned, and then announced, "Well, if everyone else is getting out, I might as well, too!"

Taking positions on either side of the tree, Brendan, Terence and Thomas began to move the large impediment. When it barely budged, Terence called for more help. Francis, Jeremiah and Adrianna joined in the endeavor, which split the group in half. Six of them were at the tree, and the others were near the vehicle, with Gemma and Theresa being the only two still left inside. As the group at the tree made ready for another attempt, Thomas suddenly collapsed. The impending danger he had been feeling exploded into reality.

Four armed men dressed in camouflage and wearing black bandanas across their faces emerged from the jungle. Two of them came from the shadows behind the car, and the other two from near the tree. Their weapons were raised, muzzles leaping from one member of Thomas' group to another as they barked out commands in both English and Spanish, demanding everyone lay down with their hands behind their backs.

"What's going on? What are you doing?" Terence demanded of the bandit closest to him, receiving a blow to the head from the butt of the man's rifle in reply, sending him crashing unconscious to the ground.

"Do what they say!" Thomas yelled to the group. "They probably just want our money or our car."

Slowly, the young adults got down on their knees, and then carefully lowered themselves to the ground, lying on their stomachs and reaching their hands behind their backs. As three of the bandits kept watch, their rifles still raised, the fourth went from one prostrate youth to the next, strapping their wrists together tightly with large, black zip-ties. When he got to Terence, he roughly rolled the unconscious body over, and then aggressively dragged the young man's arms into position.

Thomas was the last one to be secured. His muscles tensed as he expected to be treated as roughly as the others, causing him to be surprised when the man instead dragged him to his feet, placing the barrel of his rifle against Thomas' temple, pressing hard.

"You! Pick him up!" one of the bandits, obviously the leader, shouted at Thomas.

"What is it you want?" Thomas asked, nervously. "We don't have any money."

The bandit leader laughed.

"Trust me, niño, we don't want any of your American dollars."

"Then, what do you want?" Thomas pleaded.

The bandit leader sighed. Lowering his rifle to his side, he removed a pistol from the holster at his hip. He pointed the weapon at Thomas, and pulled the trigger. The sound of gunpowder exploding as the firing pin struck the casing was followed just moments after by a mixture of screams and cries. Thomas, his face suddenly without expression, felt the world drift into slow motion as the round slammed into his chest.

"No, not like this…" he thought as he collapsed. *"The mission! What about the mission…?"*

※

Gemma lay perfectly still, hugging the floor of the hatchback, praying it would open up and swallow her in, at least until the armed men left. Then perhaps she could do something to help. She didn't see who had been shot. She only heard the unmistakable sound followed by the feeling she always had when something alive was broken or damaged. That was followed by the feeling of terror pouring out of her friends as they screamed. She didn't dare look. So far, none of the bandits seemed to know she was in the car. They were too busy dealing with the group outside the car. They hadn't had time yet to check the vehicle. Hopefully, they wouldn't. Hopefully, they would complete whatever devious task they were here for and then go away. Maybe they would each assume someone else checked the car, and no one actually would.

She knew it didn't matter what they did, as long as she could get to whoever it was that had been shot in time. She could fix it. It's what she did. As long as they didn't find her, she could fix whatever they did. With nothing else to do, Gemma prayed.

※

The moment Theresa saw the men in camouflage coming out of the shadows, she disappeared. Moving quietly, she eased out of the car, grateful that the door had been left open. She was also grateful that Thomas had stopped the car on a dirt road. If she walked lightly, no one would see the footprints she would leave behind in the darkness. Carefully, she retreated into the shadows, tucking behind the fronds of a large palm.

Squatting down, she found a comfortable position where she could see her friends through the fronds. She watched as the men forced her friends to lie down. She watched as Terence was struck unconscious. She watched as the bandits bound everyone's hands. She watched as the man closest to her set down his rifle, pulled out a pistol, and fired. Holding her hand over her mouth and biting her lip to keep herself from screaming, Theresa looked away. She couldn't believe what she had just seen.

"Oh, Thomas!" she screamed in the silence of her mind, her heart racing with fear.

With tears streaming freely, Theresa listened to the screams of her friends, the angry commands of the camouflaged men, and the terror in her heart. Hesitantly, she turned her eyes back to her friends. She had to know. Moving slowly, she adjusted her position until she was lying on the ground. She could just see Thomas, lying motionless in the dust. She couldn't tell if he was breathing or not, as his face was turned away. All she could do was watch, pray, and hope.

One of the men walked over to Brendan, pulling out a knife. He knelt down beside him, cutting him loose from his bonds. Then, grabbing him by the arm, he pulled Brendan to his feet, pushing him in the direction of where Terence lay. He told Brendan to pick Terence up. Brendan responded, kneeling down and cradling Terence over his shoulder. The man then went to each of the others on the ground, violently pulling them to their feet.

The four armed men spoke in harsh tones, though Theresa couldn't understand most of what they said. They pushed and tugged and dragged her friends into a line, and then looped a rope from one neck to the next. They made them kneel, leaving one of his men to watch them while the other three searched. The leader came close to where Theresa was hiding but only casually looked around. Finding nothing, he returned to the group.

"There are two missing. Where are they?" he asked in a gruff, raspy voice.

When no one responded, the man grabbed Julianna and roughly pulled her to her feet. He pressed the barrel of his pistol against her head.

"Where are the other two?" he asked again. "There are only ten here. We saw twelve get in the car when you left camp. Where are the other two?"

Theresa could feel the fear flooding through her friends. She was terrified as well. She watched as one of the men searched through the car, wondering if Gemma was still in there, or if she, too, had escaped. The man looked in the front, then the back, and finally, lifted the rear hatch to look inside. He then stood back up, shrugging his shoulders. The man with the pistol shook Julianna violently, driving her back to her knees. He stood behind her, his pistol locked on the back of her head.

"I will ask one more time…" he growled.

"They went home," Beth shouted.

Theresa could hear the nervousness in her voice. The man pushed Julianna, sending her falling to the ground. With her hands tied behind her back, she had no way of stopping her fall. Her face struck the ground, hard. He then walked over to Beth and pulled her to her feet, placing the pistol against her head.

"You lie," he said.

"No…no, I don't. It's true. They had to leave. They had an emergency at home," she said, her voice shaking as much as she was. "We dropped them off at the airport."

The man put his face just inches from hers, the gun still pressed against her temple. He stared into her eyes, looking for any reason to distrust her. After what felt like forever, he pulled the gun away.

"You," he said, grabbing Sam's arms and pulling him to his feet. He cut the bond strapping Sam's hands, then pushed him towards where Julianna lay crying and bleeding in the dirt. "Help that one," he growled.

Sam knelt by Julianna's side, taking off his shirt and wiping the blood from her face. From what Theresa could see, Julianna appeared to be okay, other than being shaken up. She watched as Sam helped Julianna to her feet, putting his arm around her to support her. He whispered something to her, but Theresa was too far away to make out what was said. She watched as the men dragged the rest of the group to their feet, herding them in the direction of the jungle. As they passed where Theresa lay, two of her friends nearly stepped on her legs. Had one of them tripped, or stepped on her, she didn't know what would have happened. She prayed they would all be okay.

Crying silently, Theresa waited until the group passed, and then waited a few minutes more. When she could no longer hear the sounds of the group crashing through the jungle, she got to her feet, cautiously looking around. Carefully, one tentative step after the next, she began moving towards where Thomas' body lay. Suddenly, she froze, her ears pricked back and her senses on alert. Something moved inside the car.

※

Gemma raised her head slowly, worried that one of the men might have stayed behind. She glanced over the headrest of the front seat. No one was behind the car. Moving carefully to the side window, she raised her head just enough to peek out. She saw no one there, either. Knowing that time was against her, she knew she had to take a risk. She had waited long enough. Gemma got up off the floor, turning so she could sit on the front seat, and then slide her feet out of the car. Slowly, she pulled her body out and then stood up, once more listening to the sounds of the night. Satisfied that she was alone, she rushed over to Thomas' side, sliding on her knees.

"Oh, my God, Thomas," she breathed. "Oh my God. What did they do?"

Thomas was on his back. His face was turned towards her, and his eyes were open. Gemma lay her right hand on his chest, feeling for a heartbeat. She felt nothing. Burying her face in her hands, she silently screamed, wishing she could voice her anguish aloud but worried the bandits would hear her and return. Calming herself, she knew she had to try and save him. She had never done anything like this before, not with someone who had died, but she had to try. Shaking her hands rapidly, Gemma breathed deeply, blowing the air through pursed lips.

"Okay, okay, okay…" she repeated tersely. "This has to work. This has to work."

Placing her right hand on Thomas' chest, just over his heart, Gemma slid her other hand under the back of his neck. She lifted him just slightly off the ground. Closing her eyes and letting her head hang loosely, her chin swaying against her chest, she began making a soft humming sound. The air around her began to sparkle and dance, and a whispery blue light formed around her. Her hair began to stand up, strands pointing in all directions. The humming grew louder, though not all of it was coming from her. The air hummed, the dirt road hummed, even Thomas' body began to hum. Continuing to lift Thomas' neck, his head hanging limply in her hand, Gemma began to speak.

"Rise, Thomas," she whispered, "Rise, and live."

Again and again she repeated the phrase, the humming sound growing louder, and the air around her starting to sizzle and spark. Thomas' body lifted off the ground, her hands no longer holding his weight. Gemma raised her head quickly, throwing back her hair and casting her eyes to the heavens.

"Rise, Thomas," she said, her words pleading, and desperate. "Rise!"

With her face now pointed to the heavens, and her body aglow with electric, blue light, Gemma opened her eyes. Two bolts of white light shot into the sky, shattering in a shower of tiny stars that twinkled as they fell back to earth. Fading quickly, the shower of stars disappeared, taking with them the humming, blue, radiant glow. Thomas' body slumped back to the ground, and then lay motionless. Gemma leaned over him, pressing her ear to his chest. No sound responded. He was gone.

Softly at first, she began to cry, then louder still, no longer worried who might hear. Suddenly, the sound of her sorrow stopped short, and her entire body tensed. Someone was near.

"Gemma?" a soft, quiet voice whispered from just behind her. Gemma lurched to her side, landing in a crouched position, ready to bolt away.

"Who's there?" she asked fearfully.

"It's Theresa," the voice replied.

"Where are you?" Gemma questioned.

"Oh, sorry, I forgot," Theresa's voice echoed.

Suddenly, where nothing was before, Theresa now stood. Her clothes were dusty, and her face was wet. Gemma could tell that she, too, had shed tears for the fate of their friends.

"What? How?" Gemma stammered as her mind tried to grasp what she saw.

"I was about to ask you the same thing. What was that you just did?" Theresa inquired.

Both girls froze, staring at each other, waiting for the other to speak.

"You first," Gemma finally whispered.

"It's nothing," Theresa admitted reluctantly. "I just disappear sometimes."

"Oh no, that's not enough. How do you do it? Is that how you escaped?" she demanded.

"Yeah, I guess so. As soon as I saw those men coming out of the jungle, I just disappeared. Then I hid in the shadows until they left. I can't believe they killed him. I can't believe Thomas is gone!"

"I know," Gemma said softly. "I tried to help him. That's what I was doing."

Theresa choked back her tears.

"Can you? Do you think you can save him?"

"I don't know. I've never tried anything this big before. Fixing things, broken things, like a bird's wings or like my dog's leg when it was hit by a car, that I can do," she informed Theresa.

"How do you do it?" Theresa asked, her eyes wide with wonder.

"I don't know. I just see a picture in my head, like how they were before they were injured. Then I just see them like that again, but now. I don't know how it all works, it just happens."

"Why didn't it work?" Theresa asked.

"Like I said," Gemma repeated, "I think this is bigger than what I can do."

The two women paused for a moment, holding each other's eyes. Then, slowly, Theresa knelt down beside Thomas. She turned her head down to look at him, then looked back to Gemma.

"Try again. I think I can help."

"How?" Gemma asked, her eyes filled with hope.

"I'll explain later. Right now, we need to focus on Thomas," Theresa said, holding her hand out to Gemma.

Gemma grasped the outstretched hand, allowing Theresa to assist as she moved to kneel beside her friend.

"Okay, tell me what to do," Gemma said.

"Just do what you did before, and I'll add my power to yours."

Gemma took her position, sliding her hand under Thomas' neck, and placing the other hand on his chest. She calmed her nerves by breathing deeply once more, and then let her head hang low, starting to hum. Slowly, the blue electricity returned, the air humming like before. Humming louder, Gemma lifted Thomas' neck, raising his upper body off the ground. She felt a soft touch as Theresa's hands came to rest on hers. She could hear Theresa humming in harmony as well.

And then, she felt something she hadn't felt before. The electric humming didn't just buzz, it began to flow. The sensation came from Thomas' chest, up her right arm, across her own chest, and then down her left arm, back into Thomas' neck. Gemma had never felt power this strong. It surprised her a bit, but also gave her courage. Welcoming this new sensation, she raised Thomas up further, feeling his body growing light.

"Rise, Thomas," she began, softly at first, "Rise and return."

Gemma didn't know what Theresa was doing, but she knew it would work. She had faith, and that was all she needed. All of the other times she had used her power, she had had to control it. Now, it flowed through her without any effort on her part at all. Rather than creating and sending out the energy, Gemma just had to let it flow. It was a part of her now, and she, a part of it. Opening her eyes, she saw a vortex of energy spinning before her. It surrounded Thomas' limp body as it pulsed and flashed. It was beautiful, and Gemma was in awe.

Turning her head up to the heavens, Gemma whispered three words.

"By your grace…"

The vortex began to spin faster, growing larger and larger until it surrounded all three of the young adults. The center burned with white-hot light, chasing the shadows of night away. Louder and louder the vortex hummed, the power flowing through her begging for release. As it coursed through every vein, Gemma felt giddy and bright. Squeezing her eyes tight to keep them from opening too soon, she laughed out loud.

"Rise, Thomas! Rise!" she shouted, aware that the power to return life was now hers. All she had left to do was open her eyes.

With a howl, Gemma's eyelids flashed open, releasing the power inside. This time, instead of two small bolts, the light came forth in continuous rays. The rays shot through the heavens, exploding with a thunderous roar, and then rained back down to earth as a curtain of light. The light continued to fall until it reached where they sat. As it washed over her, Gemma felt its warmth. The light soaked into the vortex, the cyclone readily sucking it in. It coalesced at the center and then poured into Thomas' chest where the bullet had struck. And then, with a tremendous *whoosh*, the vortex drank the last of the light and closed.

Afraid what she might see, Gemma closed her eyes. Her ears, though, were wide open, listening for sounds that what they had done had worked. Any sounds at all. She heard someone gasp.

"Gemma," Theresa whispered. "Look!"

CHAPTER FOURTEEN
GUARDIAN, ARISE!

For some time now, Thomas floated in the void, aware only that he was no longer aware. Though it was peaceful here, it was not comforting. It felt as if he didn't belong. Though, try as he might, he couldn't remember where it was that he *did* belong. He had no memory. Nor sensation, emotion, or understanding. There was only an endless, permeating emptiness. After some time, (how much, he didn't know) the emptiness became lighter. It was as if one moment he was peacefully non-existent, and then the next moment his non-existence was even less. Awareness didn't return so much as unawareness no longer was. No veil was removed, no revelation exposed. Thomas simply became.

The first sensation to return was sound. Faintly at first, as if silence itself was whispering, a word formed in his mind.

"Rise!"

The word called to him, flooding his spirit with an urgency to move, to reach forward and hold on. It was there, just within his grasp. And then, it was gone. Thomas returned to the void, once more aware that he was no longer aware. Time passed, one moment folding into the next. Countless creases blending in a fabric with no seam. And then, suddenly, awareness was there once more. Again, the voice called.

"Rise!"

This time, Thomas did. Reaching out, he held the word tightly as it pulled him along, the void threatening to pull him back. But the voice was strong. It, too, pulled, temporarily trapping him between two worlds. With awareness returning, Thomas understood where he was. Purgatory. Limbo. The space between. Neither heaven nor hell. Not life nor death. This was why he had felt like he didn't belong. Nothing *belongs* in the void, it simply is.

As he focused more intently on the sound of the voice, he realized he knew its' source. Gemma. She was the one who called to him. He tried to call back, feeling the words forming in his mind, but when he spoke them they turned to vapor and faded away. Twice more he struggled to speak, watching the words flow away like smoke. It was then that he had a realization. He couldn't create physical sound because he was no longer in his physical form. He was spirit, ethereal. The question was, how to return.

As he searched for a solution, a memory came to light. He recalled his recent conversation with Saint Maximillian, and the gift he was carrying in his heart. Thomas realized that if he could find the gift, he would find his heart. And when he found his heart, he would be reborn. Since the gift was spiritual, not physical, it should exist here, too. If only he could remember the words Saint Maximillian had used when he had secured the gift within him.

All he could remember was that it was one of the famous teachings of Jesus, one of the most quoted and memorable. It was the basis of the Christian relationship, how the faithful were meant to act. Yet, it was more than just action. It was a set of principles behind the actions, an underlying attitude that inspired the beliefs.

That was it. Attitude. The attitudes of being. The beatitudes. Slowly, Thomas began to recall each one, letting the memory of the words unveil his heart.

"Blessed are the poor in spirit, for theirs is the kingdom of God. Blessed are the meek, for they shall inherit the earth. Blessed are they who mourn, for they shall be comforted. Blessed are they that hunger and thirst for justice, for they shall have their fill. Blessed are the merciful, for they shall obtain mercy. Blessed are the clean of heart, for they shall see God. Blessed are the peacemakers, for they shall be called the children of God. Blessed are they that suffer persecution for justice' sake, for theirs is the kingdom of heaven."

And then, there it was. Thomas found his heart. This was the moment Saint Maximillian had told him about, the moment when he would know what to do. He knew now not only who the gift was meant for. He knew in that moment that there was someone he loved. Not with a physical, emotional love born from desire, but a spiritual love born from a place deep within the foundation of truth. It was a love that gave itself away, expecting nothing in return. The feeling saturated his soul, spreading like wildfire through his core. Thomas knew all he had left to do was to find the one for whom he held this love. And then, he heard her call.

"Rise, Thomas! Rise!"

Thomas' blinked, trying to clear the dryness of his eyes. At first all he saw was black, though no longer the same black emptiness of the void. He blinked again, finding the black curtain suddenly dotted with small white halos that overlapped in a confusing array. After several more blinks, the halos began to coalesce, shrinking down to single points of light. The black he was seeing, Thomas realized, was the night sky, and the points of light were stars. He was lying down, on his back, looking up to the heavens. He felt at peace, though something didn't feel quite right.

He could feel the presence of others nearby and he tried to turn to see who they were, but other than his eyelids nothing else would move. The return from death, Thomas considered, must be a slow thing. Regardless how long it took, he knew it would be far less time than the eternity he had just been about to spend. And so, when his nose twitched and his ears wiggled just a bit, he knew he would be okay.

The next of his senses to recover was sound. Strange, muffled, imperceptible noises pushed their way in. Thomas waited, allowing time to heal, as it did all wounds. As he mended, he began to make out words.

"Gemma, look!" a quiet, sweet, female voice broke through.

Thomas immediately recognized Theresa's voice. Her words had an excited feel to them. From the direction the words came from, he knew she was the presence he felt at his left.

"Oh, my God! Theresa! His eyes blinked!"

That, Thomas knew, was Gemma. A rush of emotions poured through him. Excitement. Joy. Elation. Delight. It reminded him of waking early on Christmas morning when he was young, the lights of the tree reflecting off the brightly wrapped packages stacked underneath. He knew the strange and yet sometimes wonderful ability that allowed him to feel what others felt had awakened once more. But why didn't these emotions have a scent? They were so powerful, they must have a smell, too.

And then, Thomas took a breath. The first breath he had taken since the bullet had crashed into his chest, shredding his heart and lungs. He could still feel the echo left behind from the pain, could still taste the bitterness of the terror he felt as he had faded away. But, now, there was no pain. Just a peaceful warmth that caressed him, coaxing him back to life.

Above him appeared the faces of the two angels who had saved him, looking down. Their expressions were perfect images of wonder and awe, and their eyes leaked tears of joy, which splashed his face as they fell.

With effort and more than a little concentration, Thomas smiled. Theresa raised her hand to her mouth as she fought back the tears. Gemma, however, just let them fall. The look in her eyes told Thomas what he already knew. She was the one the armor was meant for.

"Gemma," Thomas said, his voice cracking.

He swallowed, trying to moisten his throat.

"Don't speak, Thomas," Gemma said, her face blushing with a warm glow. "Take your time. It's okay. It's going to be okay."

Her head tilting slightly, Gemma blinked away a few final joyful tears.

"I just can't believe you're alive!" she told him. "Even though I'm here right now, looking at you, hearing you breathe, I still can't believe it's real."

"What happened?" Thomas croaked the question, then coughed twice, trying to clear his throat. He tried again to swallow.

"I'll tell you all about it. I promise. Just not yet. Do you need anything?"

"Water," he mouthed.

Theresa jumped to her feet, saying, "I'll get it. There's got to be some in the car."

When she was gone, Thomas whispered to Gemma, "There's something I need to tell you."

"I know," Gemma said. "I felt it while we were healing you."

"Does Theresa know?" Thomas asked.

"I don't think so."

"How did you…" Thomas said, pausing as his throat tightened once more.

"Here," Theresa said as she returned, kneeling back down at his side and holding a plastic bottle against his lips. "Drink this."

As the warm liquid poured into his mouth, Thomas drank it greedily, his body demanding the moisture faster than Theresa poured. Suddenly, some of the water went down the wrong pipe, and Thomas coughed, sending a cloud of water into the air, the spray dousing Theresa's face. As he coughed, Gemma helped him roll onto his side. When the spasm subsided, Thomas motioned for help sitting up. Theresa knelt behind him and leaned against his back, giving him support.

"I'm okay," Thomas said, reaching his left hand over his right shoulder and giving Theresa's arm a gentle squeeze.

Theresa moved back to his side, taking a seat on the dirt road next to him. Thomas turned to face his younger friend, seeing within her eyes a strong desire to do whatever she could to help.

"Do you need any more?" Theresa asked.

"Yeah, but not yet. What I want most is for you two to start telling me what happened. Start from the moment I was shot," Thomas requested. "How did you avoid being captured or killed?"

His face suddenly turned an ashen white, his eyes filling with fear.

"Where are the others? Where is my sister? What happened to Julianna?" he said, his voice rising in proportion to his concern.

"They took them," Theresa said, pointing into the jungle. "That way."

"Are they okay? Did they hurt anyone else?"

"Terence was unconscious when they left," Theresa informed him, "and they pushed Julianna down. I think she split her lip. But, yeah, they were alive."

"How did you escape?" Thomas asked again.

Theresa was the first to respond, shrugging her shoulders slightly as she said, "I used my power. I went invisible. They didn't know I was even there."

"And you?" Thomas asked after a short pause, looking at Gemma.

"I don't know, really. I was in the car when they came. I got down on the floor and just tried to blend in, hoping they would forget to search."

"Hmmm…" Thomas voiced his curiosity. "And what about how I came back to life?"

"Well," Gemma began, and then paused for a long moment. "I guess it doesn't matter anymore, since Theresa saw me do it, and you know it happened."

Clearing her throat and changing her position so she was more comfortable, Gemma began to fill Thomas in on the details.

"I have…" she said, pausing for a moment.

"An ability, or a power, like a superhero, right?" Thomas asked, hoping his admission of what he knew would ease her concerns about sharing.

"So, you know?" Gemma asked, looking at him with surprise.

"Not before tonight, but it's pretty obvious now. I'll fill you in on my story after I hear the rest of yours. And, yes, I have an ability, too. Still not sure what it's for yet, but it's there."

"What is yours?" Gemma inquired.

"Oh, no, ladies first," Thomas pushed back.

Gemma sighed.

"Okay, I guess it all started about four or five years ago, back when I was just starting to drive. I was out late one night, driving on the back country roads near my parents' home. Out of nowhere this fox darted across the road. I couldn't stop in time. The car slammed into him.

"I was horrified. I'm a huge animal lover. I've had more pets than I can remember. Plus we had a large property, almost like a small farm, I guess. My parents had a couple cows, some goats, chickens, a horse…"

"I thought you said your family was wealthy, that your great-grandparents had made a fortune in the oil industry," Thomas interrupted.

"Oh, that's true," Gemma allowed. "But, I mean, come on, we're from Texas. Every rich family in Texas owns some kind of ranch."

Thomas nodded in understanding, waving his hand for her to continue.

"Anyway, after I moved the car to the side of the road, I got out and went to see if I could help the fox. He was pretty banged up, but I could tell he was breathing. I wanted to take him home, or get him to a vet or something, but I didn't know if I should move him. Plus, I didn't think I had much time. So I prayed."

"And that worked?" Theresa asked.

"Not at first, but I kept doing it. And then, I laid my hands on him, and I felt something. Like, you know how the air feels in summer before a lighting storm? Like how it has that electric feel?"

"We didn't have many summer thunderstorms where I grew up, but I think I know what you mean," Thomas admitted.

"Well, that's what I felt, so I kept praying. Then, when that buzzy feeling went away, I stopped and looked down. The fox was gone. I guess at some point whatever it was that I did healed him enough that he took off. He must have been so scared."

"So, that's your power? That you can heal broken things?" Theresa asked.

"Yeah, I guess so," Gemma replied.

"Any idea how it works?" Thomas asked her. "I have a feeling we may need to use it again soon."

"It's kinda like this," Gemma said, looking away as she searched for the right words to explain. "I don't think I do anything, not like I actually fix whatever's broken. It's more like, well, like with that fox, I just saw him in my mind the way he was before my car hit him. It's the same thing I did with you. I just focused on what you were like before you got shot, though the first time I tried, it didn't work. Somehow Theresa was able to help focus my energy or something."

Thomas turned to Theresa.

"I guess it's your turn now," Thomas prodded. "You already told me about your invisibility, though I don't see how that helped Gemma save me."

Theresa blushed slightly, giving off an aura that told him she wasn't comfortable discussing what she was about to share.

"You remember back on the retreat," she asked after taking a few deep breaths, "when I told you about The Endlessly Dying Girl?"

"The Endlessly Dying Girl? What's that?" Gemma interrupted.

"Just a name, I guess. I figure, since I have a power, I guess I needed a superhero name."

"Ooh, I like it," Gemma said. "I'm going to have to think of one for myself, too!"

"Go on, Theresa," Thomas said, bringing the conversation back to how he had been healed. "Yes, I remember what happened on the retreat."

"Well, after we talked, you remember how I said that I found my next superpower?" Theresa continued.

"Yeah, is that what you used tonight?"

"Yeah. You see, I was thinking that night, like, if I'm endlessly dying, but yet I never die, then I must also be endlessly living, too, right?"

"Yeah, sure, that makes sense," Thomas said, nodding with understanding. "Saint Maximillian told me pretty much the same thing."

"Who?" Gemma asked.

"I'll explain in a minute," Thomas stated. "Let Theresa finish her story. Go on Theresa, I'm really interested in what you discovered."

Theresa shrugged her shoulders, saying, "Well, so that's what I did tonight. When I helped Gemma, I became The Endlessly Living Girl. I shared my energy with her, gave her all of my power so she was strong enough to bring you back to life."

"Oh, that's what that was I felt," Gemma said with a look of recognition. "I'll be honest, I've never brought anything back to life before. Healed some things, animals and plants mostly. Never a person, and never dead."

"Well, I'm definitely glad you tried," Thomas told her, holding her gaze for a moment. He then turned to face Theresa again. "And thank you, too, Theresa. For whatever it was you did that helped. I am forever grateful for the two of you."

"There was no way I was going to lose you, Brother Thomas. Not if I could help it," Theresa said, breaking down in tears again.

She leaned forward, wrapping her arms around him and hugging him tight. Thomas returned the hug, comforting her as she let her fear and sadness go. A minute or so later, Theresa pulled away and Thomas loosened his embrace. She wiped her wet eyes with the sleeve of her shirt, and then shook her head.

"I'm such an Emo," she said, embarrassed at her emotional display.

"Oh, heck, girl," Gemma said, leaning over to hug Theresa, "I'm there with you."

The two hugged, and sighed, and squeezed each other even more. Then, as they separated, Gemma turned towards Thomas.

"Okay, Thomas, your turn to share," she said, mocking a stern look. "What is your power? Let's hear it. The whole story. And don't leave anything out. If we're going to go save our friends, we need to know what powers you have that will help."

Thomas sighed heavily, and then began. He told the two women about his visions, how he could see the emotions and feelings of other people. He told them how the emotions look, and how they sometimes come with a scent. When they asked, he explained the shapes and smells they were each currently displaying. He also shared the dream he had where he had met Saint Thérèse, and the experience with Saint Maximillian.

"That's when I entered into this...alternate reality, I guess. Inside your picture, Theresa," he said.

"What picture?" she asked.

"The one you drew with the demon and the dark forest on one side, and the monk with the crystal cathedral on the other."

Theresa's face went blank.

"How did you know about that?" she asked.

Thomas froze, realizing he would have to share one more thing. Luckily, Theresa put the pieces together before he began to explain.

"So, that *was* you!" she exclaimed.

Thomas grinned sheepishly.

"Yeah, I guess it was..." he said, a bit flushed with embarrassment.

"That was you...what?" Gemma asked, watching the exchange of embarrassed glances between the two. "What are you two talking about?"

"Well, I guess I kinda showed up one night at Theresa's house," Thomas said, glancing at the ground.

"Yeah..." Theresa huffed. "Right in my room!"

"What?" Gemma said, her mouth agape.

"It wasn't like I wanted to appear there. I didn't even know how it happened!" Thomas said. "You guys get that, right? It's like with your powers, how you didn't know how they worked at first. I didn't even know I was going to travel like that. I was just in one place one moment, and in another the next."

"Yeah, sure," Theresa teased him.

The trio sat in silence for a moment, sharing a combined feeling that the new level their friendship had just reached was going to be with them for a long while.

"So, now what do we do?" Gemma questioned, breaking the silence.

"Like you said earlier," Thomas said, rising to his feet. "We need to save our friends. But, first, I have something for you, Gemma."

CHAPTER FIFTEEN
HOME IS WHERE THE HEART LIES

"Theresa, can you take another look for more water bottles, please? Even empty ones. Anything we can fill if we find a water source along the way. I know we're going to need it."

Theresa gave Thomas a curious look, as if she knew there was another reason he was asking her to step away. Thomas could see both by the look on her face and the emotional signature floating in the air that she wasn't happy being excused like this.

"Please, Theresa? I just need to talk to Gemma for a moment alone."

Theresa stood, harshly wiping the dust off her knees, and then turned and walked away, her feet stomping firmly with each step.

"Let me know when I'm welcome back!" she said over her shoulder.

"She'll be fine," Gemma whispered. "It's the age she's at right now. Everything is drama."

Thomas turned to look at Gemma, giving her a slight frown as he said, "Yeah, I hope so."

A moment of silence passed, approaching the uncomfortable.

"So, was there something you wanted to tell me?" Gemma asked, breaking the silence.

"Yes, there is," Thomas replied after a moment. "I'm just not sure how."

Gemma reached out and took his hand, holding it gently as her eyes poured into his. Thomas felt a warmth flow through his hand as she held it, spreading slowly up his arm. He wondered if she could feel it, too. The smile in her eyes and the tender way her thumb stroked the back of his hand told him that, most likely, she did. What Thomas didn't know, was that Gemma was healing him. In her mind, worry, concern, doubt, and fear were only present when trust or faith was broken. Like any other broken thing, Gemma knew how to put it back together.

Thomas gave Gemma a sweet, innocent smile, and then, trusting fully in the warm glow flowing through him, he began.

"When I told you and Theresa about my experience with Saint Maximillian, I held something back," Thomas said in a whisper. "I didn't tell you, because I wasn't sure if you would understand. And, to be honest, I'm still not sure that I fully do."

Gemma squeezed his hand.

"Why don't you start from the beginning, and just trust that I won't judge, or criticize, or condemn you for what you need to say," she whispered.

Thomas sighed. He knew she was right. The best thing to do right now was to just open up and share what he needed her to know. Still, that didn't take away the nervousness he felt. He knew if she hadn't been holding his hand right now, it would be shaking.

"When I was with Saint Maximillian, he gave me something, a gift that I was told to keep safe until the time was right to give it away. I wasn't told who it was for. If I knew, then there would have been a chance that the Devil would find out and do something to prevent me from giving to them. He wants what I have."

He paused, gazing into Gemma's eyes for a moment, trying to discern her reaction so far. The orbs that looked back were filled with compassion and a desire to know more. As promised, there was no judgment, no condemnation. Just a willingness to hear what he had to say. Clearing his throat, Thomas continued.

"What he gave me was the Armor of God. It's been worn by various men, and women, too, ever since Old Testament times. Like me, you probably never thought it was real. Heck, you might not have even heard of it before, I don't know. But what I do know is that this armor is meant for you. You are the one who is supposed to wear it. You are a Knight of the Immaculate, a Holy Paladin."

Gemma said nothing at first. She simply held his gaze, waiting for him to say something more. Thomas noticed that her thumb had stopped stroking the back of his hand and wondered what that might mean. Though he couldn't read her thoughts, the chaos of wildly changing shapes and colors floating above her head was enough to tell him that her mind, and her heart, were working hard to understand.

"How do you know? I mean, how do you know it's meant for me?" Gemma inquired.

"Saint Maximillian told me I would know, that I would feel it when the time was right. When you were bringing me back to life, that's when I knew."

"That sounds like an awfully big commitment, Thomas," Gemma admitted after another silent few moments of contemplation. "I don't know if I'm ready."

"Gemma," Thomas whispered, turning his hand so he was now holding hers, "we're never ready to be who God needs us to be, who we were created to be. There is always a challenge in taking on our purpose. Which is why there is nothing you need to do to prepare for this. All it will take is to surrender to God's plan for your life, to give yourself fully and completely to His divine will."

"But, what if I can't? What if what God wants is too big for me?" Gemma pleaded.

Thomas breathed in deeply. As he did, he caught a slight tinge of metal at the back of his throat. There was also just the slightest scent of sulfur and charcoal in the air. The darkness was here, hiding nearby, somewhere in the shadows. It was the Devil that was responsible for the fear and worry filling Gemma's mind. It was working with great subtlety. Rather than attack her directly, which would be something Thomas would have easily sensed, it was slowly guiding Gemma's thoughts, drawing her away from the path she had been chosen to walk.

Thomas would have to act quickly, and yet, with the same subtlety the Devil was using. Tensing slightly, he turned his eyes away, preparing what he would say and do next. He knew the only way the darkness could be stopped was for Gemma to take on the Armor of God, to become the Holy Paladin she was meant to be. Then she would be strong enough to withstand the gentle words the Devil was whispering in her subconscious mind. Right now she wasn't aware of how the darkness was turning her away from God. Thomas wondered how long the Devil had been casting his evil spells on her. He couldn't have known the armor was meant for her, not until Thomas knew it himself.

He also knew there was no way he could expose the armor, not with the Devil so close by. Since he couldn't wear the armor himself, he couldn't just release it from inside his heart. That would give the Devil the opportunity he needed to steal it away. Thomas knew there was only one way he could pass the armor to Gemma. They would have to join together somehow, heart to heart.

"Gemma," he said softly, drawing her attention. "Do you believe in love?"

A look of surprise flashed across Gemma's face, momentarily releasing her from the fear that the Devil was creating inside her.

"What?" she said, a bit shocked. "Why bring something like that up now?"

Thomas simply reached his empty hand for her free one. Holding both of her hands in his, he whispered again, "Do you believe in love?"

Still unsure where he was going with the questions, Gemma's head tilted slightly to one side, her jaw dropped slightly and her eyebrows bunched.

"What do you mean, believe in love? Like, do I believe love is real? Or do you mean, do I believe I'm *in* love?" she questioned.

"Let me ask this way. What do you think love is?"

Thomas knew the darkness was listening, biding its' time, looking for the perfect moment to strike.

"Well, I know what it's not," Gemma said. "It's not passion, or desire, or physical contact. It's not anything like the fairy tales, and it has nothing to do with whether you're attracted to the other person. This world has distorted the concept of love, making it something it was never meant to be."

"I believe every word you just said," Thomas shared with her. "But that doesn't answer the question. What do you believe love is?"

Gemma's eyes closed slightly and her lips pursed just a bit. Thomas could tell she was lost in thought.

"I guess, if I had to describe it, I would say it's a willingness to give yourself fully to someone else, without expecting anything in return. If you were willing to do whatever you had to do, take on any sacrifice necessary, so that someone else was able to be who they were born to be, and you didn't expect or need anything in return...that, I believe, would be love."

She turned her eyes back to Thomas, giving him a questioning look. Thomas could see the nervousness and fear that had been evident in her soft, dark brown eyes were gone. In their place he could see a deep sense of confident curiosity, as if she was suddenly willing to search for a love like she had just described.

Thomas knew that Gemma had carried some guilt about her past—she had told him so the night they had been introduced. What it was in her past that had filled her with guilt was not something she had explained. Yet, somehow, Thomas didn't need her to. The look in her eyes told him she would never go back to being the person she had been back then. She was ready to be loved. If only she could find someone who loved her like she just described.

"This is what I've been struggling to tell you, Gemma. That type of love, that willingness to sacrifice oneself for another, is the purest and truest form of love. It doesn't demand anything in return, it exists only to give. That is the love that I believe is behind our powers. The love that comes from the Holy Spirit, which gives us the ability to do things no one else can.

"When you brought me back to life, we shared a deep and spiritual connection. In that moment, you were willing to sacrifice everything to help me. Isn't that right?"

Gemma nodded gently, recognition slowly brightening her eyes.

"Yeah, you're right. But, I don't understand. Are you trying to tell me that we are in love?"

"No, not like the way the world would choose to describe it, anyway. But your willingness to sacrifice whatever you needed, while getting nothing in return, just so I could be whole again, is that not love?"

Her eyes squinting once more, Gemma simply gazed at him, unsure of what to say.

"Why?" she finally said, her voice cracking. "Why tell me this now?"

"Because there is only one way I can pass along the gift I have for you. It's not something physical, so I can't just hand it to you. The only way it can become yours requires two things. The first is for you to willingly want to accept it. Though it is destined for you to become a Holy Paladin, you hold the right to refuse it. Yes, there is danger in taking it on, but if you fully trust its power, the danger will never overcome you."

"And the second thing you need?" Gemma inquired after Thomas had gone silent for a moment.

"For you to open your heart. For us to share a pure and true love. I know you would sacrifice yourself for me, you've already proven that tonight. Trust now that I would do the same for you. Open your heart to me, Gemma. Will you let me love you in the way that Jesus asks us to love one another?"

Thomas watched as Gemma considered everything he had said. He could see the darkness working behind the scenes trying to fill her with doubt and fear. He could also see that every time the darkness tried to move her away, something in Gemma reached out. The emotions she wore gyrated with such speed that Thomas was unable to discern what her true feelings were.

As he watched, the object folded in on itself, becoming dense and heavy. Flashes of light burst within, testimony to the storm that seethed in Gemma's heart. Thomas could feel her muscles tense as the battle raged on. He wished there was something more he could do to help her. But this was her decision now. She would have to face her fears, fight back whatever doubt still lingered, and accept the path she was born to tread.

Suddenly, just when Thomas felt that she was about to refuse, a small tear fell from her eye. At the same time, above her head, the dancing chaos froze. As he turned his attention to the frozen form, Thomas could see it begin to vibrate slightly. The vibration increased in both speed and intensity, shaking violently now. Gemma breathed deeply, unaware that the turmoil raging inside was being observed. Faster and more violently the shape shook, small cracks forming on the sides that let tiny rays of light shoot out in all directions. The cracks grew wider, longer, and deeper, until the dark, frozen shape exploded in a burst of white light. Thomas flinched slightly and closed his eyes as he both heard and felt the cloud explode. When he opened his eyes once more, the shape was gone, replaced by a new shape that looked very much like a door. As Thomas watched, the shape swung open, inviting him within.

Acting with haste now, as he could sense the Devil preparing to respond, Thomas let go of his connection to this reality, and stepped inside.

CHAPTER SIXTEEN
THE PALADIN

Gold. It was everywhere. Everything Thomas saw was made of gold. From deep, tiger-stripe orange to brilliant, platinum white, the landscape of Gemma's heart twinkled and flickered. Rainbows danced and chased each other across glittering fields. Canary yellow flowers bent gently against the warm breeze while shimmering lemony butterflies played games of tag. As he took in the dazzling view, Thomas saw a lone figure standing on the crest of a hill. The figure, like everything else, was clothed in gold. Thomas walked to where the figure stood. As he ascended the hill, the figure slowly turned his way.

"Oh my, Thomas," Gemma said, her eyes wide with wonder and awe. "Where are we?"

"We're inside your heart," he replied.

Gemma's arms dropped, hanging motionless at her side. Her jaw dropped as well, while her eyes darted rapidly in every direction.

"Oh, trust me. There's no way my heart is this beautiful," she whispered.

Thomas, now standing beside her on the crest of the hill, reached out and took her hand.

"Well, this is how it looks to me. As for how we got here? That's another one of those things I don't yet fully understand. Like the spiritual superpowers we have, I don't get how it works, I just trust it's true."

"You really see me this way? You honestly think my heart is this magic?"

"Gemma, no one sees themselves as they truly are. Instead, we focus on our flaws, when, all along, those are our smallest parts. You are a child of God, created to bring light and peace into the world. So, yes, to answer your question, this is how I see you. As the beautiful, caring, wonderful person that you are."

Thomas watched as a single tear fell from Gemma's eye, flowing gently across her cheek, which blushed the fairest shade of pink.

"Oh, Thomas," Gemma sighed. "You are the absolute best person I could have ever met."

Thomas let go of her hands, wrapping his arms around her shoulders, pulling her in close. She, in turn, wrapped her arms around his waist, squeezing him so tight he could hardly breathe. Thomas wanted to stay in this place forever but he knew that wasn't possible. Not for now. There was work to be done, and friends who needed their help.

Pulling away, he looked deep into Gemma's eyes as he placed one hand gently on her face, wiping away the trail her tear had left behind. Then, giving her one last powerful hug, he let go.

"Come, we don't have much time. I can already sense the darkness closing in."

As if on cue, an icy breeze brushed over his skin, causing him to shiver. Looking up, Thomas saw a black cloud building on the horizon. The cloud grew rapidly, chewing away the platinum white sky. As it grew, the air became hauntingly still. Thomas turned, reaching for Gemma's hand and pulled her close beside him.

"The darkness? What's that?" Gemma asked.

"It's everything that's wrong with our world. It's the worst kind of evil, and it wants us dead."

"What should we do?" she asked, her eyes growing wide with fear.

"We need to find someplace safe, Gemma. A secret place the darkness can't get in. Tell me, where do you keep your dreams? Where do you store your hope?"

"I don't know what you mean. Where I store my hope?" she replied, giving him a confused look. "What's going on? Why is it so cold all of a sudden?"

"The darkness has found us and is preparing to attack. We have to find safety. I know you don't fully understand what's going on, where we are, or how we got here, but you have to trust me. This place we're in isn't real, not in the way the world we live in is real. It's a form of reality, an alternate realm. I created it when you opened your heart to me. It's something one of my powers does, though I don't know how.

"I need you to believe one thing. I need you to believe that you are a Paladin, a Knight of the Immaculate, God's Champion. Have faith. Trust that you are who I say you have been called to be. My power allows me to create this realm in any way I believe it to be. If you can describe it to me, I can change the landscape to match. We cannot defeat the darkness, not alone. We will need some help. As a Paladin you must have a fortress or a castle? A place you call home, that you are sworn to protect. Tell me about it. What does it look like? Just pretend, like back when you were a child. Remember, Jesus said *'Unless you change and become like little children, you will never enter the kingdom of heaven.'* So let your imagination run free. Let's have a little fun!"

"A castle, huh? Okay, I'll try," Gemma said, closing her eyes. "It's not a large castle, but it's beautiful. The stones used to build it are brilliant white, and the gables are made from the purest gold. There are flags of every color flying from the tops of the towers, too. What else should I say?"

"Where is it located? In the mountains? In a forest? Is there a drawbridge…or a moat?" Thomas encouraged as he began walking, drawing Gemma behind him.

"It's on a hilltop, surrounded by trees. There are flowers everywhere. And animals, too. They have no fear and will come right up to you if you stand still and call them. There isn't a moat, but there is a crystal blue river that flows at the bottom of the hill."

"Like that one?" Thomas asked, pointing.

Gemma looked where he pointed, seeing a brilliant, sapphire-blue river flowing about a hundred yards away.

"How'd you do that?" she inquired. "That river wasn't there a moment ago."

"Like I said, I'm creating it as we go. Tell me more, what kind of trees are they?"

"Maples and ash mostly. A few fruit trees as well. Apples and pomegranates. The trees are amazingly tall, with branches that intertwine. There's a bird's nest on every branch, and dozens of birds singing in every tree."

As she continued describing her fortress, the landscape around them began to change. The yellow and white-gold flora showed speckles of green and brown, and the hills around them became less steep. They passed a few trees, spread far apart, and then more, growing closer together. They followed the crystal blue river as it twisted through the ever changing countryside.

"Are there any buildings nearby? Or other structures? Like a town, or a village? Fill in as many details as you can."

"Oh, yes!" Gemma said with excitement. "There is a town, filled with the friendliest people you've ever met. They live in the cutest little houses, with thatched roofs and gilded paths between."

"Anything like that?" Thomas asked as they rounded a bend between two hills.

Ahead of them, about half of a mile away, Gemma saw one, then two, and then a whole cluster of houses, all with thatched roofs.

"That's it!" she shouted. "That's exactly what I imagined! How is this even possible?"

"Well…they say that faith is believing without seeing. As you are telling me what this place looks like, I simply have faith that it really exists. Faith is a powerful thing. It really can move mountains. Watch."

Thomas pointed off in the distance. Behind the trees, a mountain peak suddenly appeared, growing taller as they walked. Next to the first one, another appeared, and then another, until a whole range filled the sky.

"I hope you don't mind if I use just a bit of artistic freedom," Thomas said playfully.

"Oh, not at all. Besides, it's perfect. But, I still don't see the castle."

"You will. It's just past that group of trees."

The two sped on, walking even faster now. Behind them, the dark cloud had swallowed almost half of the sky. Lightning bolts reached down and scorched the earth while thunder rolled so loud it shook the land.

"Come on. We're almost out of time," Thomas pleaded, pulling Gemma along as they broke into a jog.

As they came around another bend in the path, the trees, which had become quite dense by now, suddenly opened up. There in the center of the forest, sitting on the top of a small hill, the castle Gemma had imagined came into view. They slowed their pace as they began to ascend the hillside, allowing one of the townspeople to catch them from behind.

"Milady!" the townsman called. "You look worried. Is everything okay?"

Gemma didn't answer at first, looking to see who the man might be speaking to.

"He's talking to you, Gemma. That is your castle, and this is your town. You are the Lady he is speaking of. Tell him to have the town prepare. Darkness is coming. They need to be ready."

Gemma shook her hand from Thomas' grasp as she stopped and turned to face the man.

"What's his name?" she whispered to Thomas.

"I don't know. This is your town. You decide."

Gemma nodded with an excited and playful look.

"Gerald, call the town council together. The darkness is coming and we must be prepared. I'm going to the castle to…" she paused, unsure what to say next.

"Don your armor," Thomas whispered.

"What?" Gemma questioned.

"Tell him you're going to get your armor."

"I'm going to the castle to get my armor. There's a battle ahead of us. Make sure the children are safe!"

"Yes, milady. Of course! At once!" Gerald said as he turned and rushed back to town.

Now it was Gemma's turn to reach out and grab Thomas' hand.

"Thomas, this is so amazingly cool. I've always dreamed of living in medieval times," she admitted, her eyes twinkling with joy. "Come on, follow me. If I'm the Lady of this castle, then I better lead."

"Yes, milady!" Thomas said through a wide and laughing grin. "As you command!"

Together the two ran up the hill, through the raised portcullis and into the castle's front door.

"Summon the army! Archers to the rooftops! Prepare for battle!" Gemma shouted as she raced through the halls.

Around her the castle responded as men and women broke away from their tasks, scurrying off in every direction. Thomas could hear the sound of their preparations down every corridor as they continued on.

"Do you know where you're going?" he asked Gemma as she sped down one hallway after another.

"Of course. This is my castle, isn't it?"

Turning another corner, they came to a large, ornate hallway with dozens of flags adorning the walls. At the end of the hall stood two enormous, elaborately decorated doors made of dark ebony and trimmed in gold. Gemma headed straight for the doors, extending her hands out in front of her. Without slowing down, she simply pushed the doors inward and burst into the room.

As Thomas entered, he knew this was her private room. In the center was an over-sized bed covered with a crimson and gold comforter and matching pillows. A warm fire blazed in the fireplace. The walls held paintings and sculptures mixed between rows of windows that reached to the ceiling. In the furthest corner stood a tall folding screen with a clothing rack on one side.

Gemma turned suddenly, catching Thomas by surprise, his attention still focused on the elaborate décor. Stepping out of the way at the last moment, his right leg caught the corner of a table, sending him toppling to the floor in a heap.

"How are you supposed to help me if you can't even walk?" Gemma teased him.

Thomas carefully gathered himself and then stood up, brushing his clothes back into place.

"I'm going to step behind the screen to change. Can you lay my armor out on the bed? I'll ring for my maids to come help. And then you should probably go and get ready, too. Your room is back down the hall, second door on the left."

Thomas walked over to the bed, pausing a moment to watch Gemma pull a velvet cord that hung on the wall. When she finished, she walked to the corner and stepped behind the screen. Thomas noticed there was an outfit hanging on the clothes rack, one that wasn't there a moment ago. He knew Gemma had placed it there, using the same imaginative power to create that he had used to build the castle and town.

Turning back to face the bed, he raised his arms slightly, then closed his eyes. Softly, he whispered the Beatitudes as Saint Maximillian had done. When he finished, he opened his eyes once more and lowered his arms. As he had imagined, the armor he had been carrying in his heart was now laid out in perfect fashion at the foot of the bed. Satisfied that his work was complete, Thomas smiled briefly and then turned towards the door. As he left, three young women walked in, dressed in the finery of medieval handmaidens. One of the three ladies stopped, turned, and closed the door. The last sound he heard was giggling laughter from the four women inside the room.

Smiling to himself, Thomas walked back down the hallway until he reached the second door on the left. Opening it, he found a small, parochial bedroom with sparse furnishings. Only one item hung upon the walls: a small, wooden cross. The bed in this room looked barely large enough to fit him and was covered in a simple, plain, brown blanket. There were no pillows that he could see.

A small wardrobe was in one corner, with one of the doors standing ajar. Inside the wardrobe Thomas could see only a few items hanging on hooks or folded on the shelves. He took a moment to survey the items, selecting a pair of black cloth pants and a matching shirt. He also pulled out a pair of well-worn sandals and a dusty gray-white friar's robe as well.

Stripping off the clothes he had been wearing when he had been shot, a moment in time that suddenly felt like years ago, he put on his new attire. He tossed his cargo shorts and blood-stained shirt on a small wooden stool, and then pulled the friar's robe over his head. Reaching into the wardrobe once more, Thomas removed a white corded belt, wrapping it tightly around his waist.

As he was about to leave, he spotted an ordinary walking staff leaning against the side of the wardrobe. Feeling that the staff was more than it appeared, he reached for it, holding it aloft as he measured its weight in his hands. Satisfied he had all he would need, Thomas closed the wardrobe door, placed the staff on the bed, and then knelt down in front of the wall where the cross was hanging. Blessing himself, he began to pray.

"Father, I still am not aware of all that you have blessed me with, or what it is meant for. I can only trust that, as I need to know, your grace will fill me with the knowledge I need. Protect us in our coming battle, as you watch over us every day. Give us the strength to stand for what is right. And please, while we are here in this place, watch over my sister, Julianna, my friend, Terrance, and all the young people who were captured tonight. Fill their hearts with peace, and grant them the courage to endure until we can free them once more."

Blessing himself once more, Thomas stood back up, dusting off his robe. A knock came to the door.

"Come in," he called.

The door opened slowly inward. Thomas froze. There standing in the doorway, was Gemma. She, too, had changed her attire, now wearing dark leggings and shirt that covered her from her ankles to her neck and down to her wrists—though the outfit was barely discernable through the shimmering, ethereal, blue-white glow of the Armor of God. She looked absolutely radiant; with the soft glow from the armor giving her features a warm, peaceful look.

"Wow, Gemma," Thomas said after a moment of silence. "You look amazing."

Gemma smiled, turning her body as she posed.

"You really think so?" she blushed.

"Yeah. I do."

"Well, then, so do you, Brother Thomas. I hope you like what I picked out for you."

Thomas spun in a slow circle.

"I'm the best-dressed friar in town!" he said.

Gemma laughed, the sound like crystal raindrops on a metal roof. Her laugh was infectious, causing Thomas to join along. After a moment or two, the pair faced each other.

"So, what now?" Gemma asked, always the one to break the silence.

"Now, we fight back."

CHAPTER SEVENTEEN
HERE BE DRAGONS

Thomas stood at the parapet overlooking the courtyard below. Before him, stretching all the way back to the castle walls, more than two thousand soldiers stood in squads of forty men each. On both sides of the soldiers stood another one thousand archers, five hundred on each flank. Closest to the castle, just beneath where Thomas and Gemma were, stood three hundred knights on horseback. Their mighty steeds stamped and pawed at the ground in anticipation of the upcoming battle.

Gemma, resplendent in her otherworldly armor, was a wonder to behold. Rays of the setting sun splintered into rainbows as they reflected off the Armor of God. Thomas sensed excitement and anticipation from her, and he didn't need to read her emotional display to know she was nervous as well. She had never been through anything like this. Then again, neither had he. This challenge would his greatest and most important yet.

Though he had faced a few encounters with the darkness before, he had never confronted it directly. Still, he braced himself knowing that so far his faith had never let him down. Reaching out to Gemma, he touched the top of her left hand, drawing a slight smile from her. She turned her head just slightly to face him, whispering quietly, "How much longer do you think?"

Thomas looked out into the distance, over the forces gathered below, beyond the castle walls and past the forest to the black cloud.

"I'm not sure, but it won't be long now," he informed her, casting his eyes back to the ground below. "You know, I really hated to leave Theresa behind."

Gemma nodded curtly, responding, "I know. What do you think she did when she realized that we were gone?"

"Time doesn't flow here like it does in the real world. When we get back, even if we spend days in this realm, barely a moment will have passed there. I doubt she will even know."

"Well, that's something positive, then."

"I agree. The downside is, even if we win the battle today, the effect in the real world will be diminished too."

Thomas sensed a shift in Gemma's aura. Her confidence of a moment ago drooped like an unwatered flower and her shoulders slumped.

"Then, what's the use? Why do we even fight?"

"First, because it's the right thing to do. We've been given special powers, Gemma. When God grants someone power, like with us, it comes with great responsibility. Though we could use it to just do our little magic tricks, that's not what our powers are for.

"And second, because this is the only place we *can* defeat the darkness; here in the spiritual realm. Though what we do here won't do much to change the balance of power between dark and light in the real world, it will dampen the darkness' ability to affect us there. It will create a period where the Devil will be weaker, unable to exert his power. Then, what happens in the real world *will* have an effect."

Thomas placed his hand on Gemma's shoulder and gave it a soft squeeze. She smiled weakly, reaching up to take hold of his hand.

"You see, to defeat the clouds of evil in our world, we must first do battle in the spiritual realm. Prayer, fasting, studying scripture, those are the weapons of the spiritual war."

"I think I understand. By defeating the darkness here, where Spirit lives, we create a period of inactivity in the real world, giving God's soldiers the opportunity to swing the balance of power from evil to good. Is that what you're saying?"

"Exactly. The last time something this major happened was World War II. Then, the balance of power had swung far to the side of evil. But it was because of that evil that so many good people, so many soldiers of Christ, began to do the works they did. Mother Theresa, for example, first heard the call of God in 1946. World War II ended in 1945. And the man who would later become Pope John Paul II entered a secret seminary in Poland in 1942, right in the middle of the war!

"When humanity becomes numb to the cry of the poor, that's when evil begins to rise again, waking us back up. The human race becomes more charitable, more spiritually centered, and that's when people like Saint Theresa of Calcutta or Saint Pope John Paul are born into their spiritual roles. That's what our world is facing right now, an imbalance of power. We're living in an age of shadows."

"Wow. I never thought of it like that. How do you know all of this?" Gemma asked.

"Mostly through conversations I've had with Father Dominic," Thomas replied. "And, well, because of my ability—the one that lets me see people's emotions—I witness it on a much smaller scale every day. I can see the battle between doing what is right, and what is easy or expedient. Students who are struggling in their studies, torn between asking their professors for help or cheating the system in some way. Mothers and fathers in grocery stores, torn because they can't afford the things their families need, and yet their shopping carts are full of alcohol or other items to help them deaden their emotional pain. Entire communities failing to respond to the demands of the poor in their own backyards."

"And you can see all of that?" Gemma inquired, giving Thomas a look of concern and shock.

"Some days I wish I couldn't, Gemma. But this is why I was called. I can only pray that I'm strong enough to respond," Thomas said softly, his eyes moist with tears.

Gemma squeezed his hand, silently letting him know she was there for him. They both turned to face the other, sharing the last quiet moment before facing the oncoming storm.

"It's time," Thomas said, watching as the darkness began to gather, the cloud no longer spreading outward but instead coalescing, growing thick and dense. The cloud began to unite into one large, dark cluster. Lighting flashed and flickered. Thomas felt the air around him become heavy and thick with electricity. On the ground below, the horses grew restless, tossing their heads restlessly and whinnying nervously as they pawed and stamped their hooves.

He could feel fear growing stronger in the soldiers. Though they stood tall with brave faces, Thomas could see their secret. He knew the battle would need to swing quickly in their favor or some of those bravely standing might flee. He didn't blame them. For all they knew their lives were as real as Thomas' was back in his world. To them, there was no other reality. This was their home, and it was all they had. Even if he could explain it to them, he knew that the pain they were about to endure would still feel the same.

"There, Thomas! Look! Over in the trees!"

Thomas looked where Gemma was pointing, at first seeing nothing but trees. And then, through the small breaks between the tightly intertwined branches, he saw it. Within the trees, shadows moved. These weren't normal shadows like those cast by the bright summer sun. These shadows moved of their own accord. Where they went, death followed. He could see a wave of decay behind them turning the landscape black.

"Be ready!" Gemma shouted out. "Archers, nock your arrows! Soldiers, draw your swords! Stand the gates open! March forward, men!"

Thomas gripped the staff in his right hand a bit tighter as he listened to the drummers sounding out the march. The squads of soldiers began to flow outward slowly, moving with grim determination towards the forest beyond. On either side the archers stood waiting, their arrows nocked, bows raised high. As long as the enemy stayed within the trees, their arrows would be useless. The canopy was too thick. Far too few arrows would find their way through.

Behind the soldiers, the cavalry closed ranks. As they waited, the knights tugged at their swords, ensuring the blades would draw easily when needed. Their first weapon would be the long, heavy lances they held resting across their mounts. These would be used in the charge, spearing as many shadow forms as they could.

Above and behind the forest, the dark cloud was becoming solid in places and a shape was beginning to form. At first, Thomas thought it looked like a bird, but the tail was too long and the neck was stretched too far forward. The wings, too, weren't the right shape, looking more like those of a bat than a bird.

"Oh, no," Thomas whispered as recognition came over his face.

"What? What is it?" Gemma pleaded, glancing about to see what had startled Thomas.

"That's not just a cloud, Gemma," he said pointing where he wanted her to look.

"Is that…is that what I think it is?" Gemma asked incredulously.

"I'm afraid so," Thomas sighed.

Just then, a horrifying scream shattered the sky. Thomas could see pockets of pure terror spreading among the troops. There was no doubt now, evil was coming. Its wings beat powerfully, each stroke creating a tornado of wind as the obsidian dragon climbed high into the air. Its eyes burned like fire, and its scales shone like dark, tainted diamonds. Higher and higher the dragon climbed, stretching its neck as it surveyed the battlefield below.

"My God, Thomas," Gemma sighed. "It's huge!"

"Trust me, Gemma, our faith will prevail."

The dragon, now at the peak of its climb, paused for a moment, hanging as if suspended in time. And then, it began to circle the castle walls, far out of the reach of the archers. At the same time, at the edge of the forest, the shadow creatures began to wail. The sound they made was beyond anything Thomas had heard before. It froze his blood, made his bones feel like they were cracking, and filled his mind with pain.

"Stay strong, Gemma," he whispered, feeling her fear start to climb. "Trust in your powers, trust in the armor, and trust your faith."

"I wish Theresa was here," she replied. "I wish she was beside me right now, filling me with her power, like she did when we saved your life."

"It's about time you said you wanted me," a soft female voice said from somewhere close by.

"Theresa?" Thomas gasped, turning towards the sound of the voice. "Is that you?"

A slight shimmer appeared before him, and then, slowly, Theresa appeared. She, too, had taken the time to change her attire, and was now dressed in a black leather skinsuit with silver décor. The suit covered everything but her face. On her feet she wore supple leather boots and the same type of leather gloves were on her hands. On each arm, just above the wrist, were strapped two daggers, the silver handles all that showed. She also had twin katana swords crossed behind her back, and several throwing stars were clipped to her chest. The bottom half of her face was covered in a thick black fabric mask. The only flesh that showed was what surrounded her eyes.

"How did you get here?" Thomas demanded.

"You really think I walked away when you asked me to? Those are my friends that got captured too. I want to help," she replied.

"So, what, you eavesdropped on our conversation? And then just followed us here?"

"Yeah, I did. Go ahead and punish me for it if you want. But the truth is, you both know you need my help. If we're going to rescue our friends, you're going to need my help. I've got powers, too, just like yours."

"Okay, okay. However you got here, you can explain it later. Right now, we've got bigger problems," Thomas said, pointing his finger towards the forest where the shadow creatures continued to wail.

Theresa looked in the direction he pointed, her eyes filling with a strange hue.

"I'm ready," she growled.

"Before we start, I have just one question for you," Gemma said quietly.

"You need me to help you increase your power again?" Theresa asked, assuming that was what Gemma was about to ask.

"That, too. But first, where did you get that awesome skin suit?!"

Theresa turned to look at her in surprise. Although Thomas couldn't see any part of her face other than her eyes, he could tell she was smiling broadly.

"Why? Do you like it?" Theresa replied, twisting her stance slightly.

"Um, yeah! I want one!" Gemma said, giving Theresa a high five.

"Just have Thomas create one. He said he can change this world however he wants," Theresa replied.

Gemma looked over at Thomas, who simply shook his head in reply.

"Oh, and, by the way," Theresa said, "The Paladin is a super cool hero name."

"You think so?" Gemma replied, blushing slightly.

"Oh, for sure. Now we just need a name for Brother Thomas."

"Ladies," Thomas sighed, "I hate to break up your fun, but please, we have work to do."

Gemma blushed again, and, though Thomas couldn't see it, he could feel that Theresa did as well.

"Work?" Theresa questioned. "With the three of us here, this is going to be fun! Besides, I have a plan."

CHAPTER EIGHTEEN
WHERE DARK AND LIGHT COLLIDE

With a sudden, ear-shattering wail, the shadows burst from the protection of the forest, oozing into the open like spilled oil. Gemma's army stood fast, though Thomas could tell their courage was fading. With a raise of her arm, Gemma signaled the archers to begin. Thomas could hear the captains bellow out the commands.

"Nock! Draw! Loose!"

The air became thick with brilliant flares as arrows of light launched into the sky. As the bolts arched upward, the dragon clapped its mighty wings, sending a vortex of air spinning towards the ground. The vortex met the arrows at their apex, crashing into the rays of light and sending arrows spinning off in every direction. Though some struck true, most fell harmlessly to the ground.

"I didn't anticipate that," Gemma said, grimacing.

"It's okay, just keep them firing. Look, where they are hitting true, the shadows are breaking apart," Thomas shared, encouraging his friend.

Gemma looked where he pointed, watching as one of the arrows struck and made a wide hole, the shadows dispersing away from the light. Slowly, the shadows reformed, filling the hole once more.

"The shadows are just gathering back together, Thomas! What now!" she cried.

"Keep firing. They may be recovering, but that means they are spreading thinner in other areas. Signal the knights to prepare the charge."

Gemma waved her right hand above her head. On the ground below, two of the knights signaled back, and then, splitting into two groups, the cavalry slowly made their way to the each side of the soldiers. When the groups were established, the knights lowered their visors, raised their javelins, and prepared to charge. Their horses stood unnervingly still.

Thomas watched as the shadows continued to pour forward, quickly closing the gap to the soldiers standing ready below. Another round of arrows launched into the air, creating a rainbow of light. Once more the dragon responded with a vicious beat of its wings, sending the arrows scattering again. And once more, only a handful of arrows struck true.

"Oh, come on!" Theresa moaned. "This is going to take too long."

"What, did you think it was going to be easy?" Thomas inquired. "We're fighting an enemy who has been around since the dawn of creation. He's been on this battlefield a thousand, thousand times before! He's seen every trick in the book. Heck, he probably invented most of them! Our only hope is to persevere."

"I'm sure he hasn't seen this trick before," Theresa said, leaping over the parapet four stories to the battlefield below. She turned invisible halfway down.

Thomas watched as a puff of dust billowed, indicating the point where Theresa had landed.

"I wonder what she's up to," Thomas whispered to Gemma, who gave him a sideways glance.

"Who knows? You know what it's like at that age. One day you're indestructible, and the next, you want to stay in bed watching cartoons and eating sugary cereal."

"Ain't that the truth!" Thomas smiled slyly.

Another round of arrows arched into the air, and once more the dragon slapped most of them aside. Now, only a few hundred yards separated the two armies. The knights bellowed fiercely as they drove their mounts forward. A sound like thunder rose from the cavalcade of hooves. As the cavalry rounded the corners of the soldiers, the lead horse on each side turned towards the center. When the two groups met in the middle, the horses all turned at once, creating a line that stretched across the battlefield from end to end. Still surging forward, the mounts in the center began to pull ahead faster than those at the ends, creating a wedge.

Behind the horses, the soldiers began to advance, first at a fast march, then at a jog, and, finally, screaming loudly, they charged. The archers pulled another arrow from the supply stuck in the ground before them, preparing to send another round high into the air. At the last moment, just as their commanders yelled 'loose!' the archers changed their aim, sending this round just inches over their own armies' heads.

This change caught the dragon off guard, preventing it from sending another vortex in time. The volley, no longer scattered, struck hard and true, and the entire front line of shadows vaporized in a ray of light. A few heartbeats later, the point of the cavalry's wedge struck, their lances beaming like sabers of light, cutting a wide swath through the midst of the foe.

Above them, high in the air, the dragon screamed as it watched the tide began to turn. And then it dove, aiming towards the front of the battle, its eyes burning with red hot rage. The dragon tucked its wings against its side, creating a streamline shape that easily cut through the air, picking up speed as it fell. Faster and faster the dragon raced towards the ground while the soldiers fighting on the ground below, their attention fixed on the foe before them, stood unaware.

"Do something, Thomas!" Gemma begged.

"Like what? We didn't plan for this."

Suddenly, just as the dragon was moments away from striking, another volley of arrows shot into the sky. This time, however, rather than being fired in a wide arc, the arrows were all aimed at a single point. Closer and closer the arrows grouped, their light shining brighter with each passing moment. Glowing as brightly as the sun, the combined force of one thousand bolts of light crashed together. The dragon tried to swoop to the side, but for a two-ton beast at break-neck speed, directions don't easily change.

With a painful howl, the dragon crashed through the ball of light, slamming into the battlefield below. Another explosion sounded as a shower of dirt, grass, horses, shadows, and men were launched into the air. As the debris rained down, a hush came over the battlefield. All fighting stopped as man and shadow turned together to see if the dragon still lived.

Those closest to the edge of the massive crater moved cautiously towards the rim, their necks stretched as they tried to peer down inside. The silence lingered, feeling more unwelcome the longer it endured. After the chaotic sounds of battle, the hushed landscape felt strange indeed. Thomas turned to look at Gemma, her eyes were as wide as his, her face expressionless.

"You think Theresa did that? Changed where the archers were going to aim?" she whispered.

"It's quite possible," Thomas admitted, turning his attention back to the field.

"If she can have an effect on the outcome of this battle, then so can I," Gemma said confidently. "When I signal you, Thomas, raise your staff."

Gemma turned to face him, her eyes burning with a strange passion, her lips curled into a snarl. Giving him a playful wink, Gemma turned, placed her hands on the parapet, and then, as she had seen Theresa do, vaulted over the top. Thomas gasped.

"Gemma!" he called out in shock.

Rushing to the edge of the parapet, Thomas looked down to the ground below. He watched as Gemma fell to the earth, tumbling at the last moment and somersaulting across the field. After only a brief pause, she stood up, dusted herself off, and then raced towards the crater. Thomas watched as Gemma closed the distance, her feet moving quick and sure, leaving a trail of grass swaying behind her. And then, suddenly, he saw a second trail coming up quickly from behind her. Though he couldn't see what made the trail, Thomas already knew. As the second wake caught Gemma, he saw Theresa come back into view. Gemma turned her head towards her companion. Thomas swore he could hear them laugh.

As the champions reached the edge of the field, the combatants from both armies stepped aside, granting them a path to the crater's rim. When they were within a few dozen yards, a terrifying howl rose from deep within the crater. The two Guardians skidded to a stop. A moment later, a heavily armored hand grasped the top of the basin. A second hand appeared just a few feet away.

Thomas watched in horror as the darkness pulled itself out from the depths below, no longer in the form of a dragon. After crashing to the ground, the darkness had transformed, taking the shape of a Black Knight. The obsidian scales of the dragon had become its armor. The dragon's tail was now its sword. The only thing that remained from its previous incarnation were the blood red eyes. Heaving itself upright, the Black Knight raised both hands above his head and howled. The shadow creatures answered with howls of their own as they waved their weapons in challenge.

When the tumult died down, the air again felt heavy and still. Nothing moved, not even the wind. Slowly, Gemma raised her sword above her head, answering the Black Knight's challenge with her own primal scream. Standing at her side, Theresa drew both of her katana swords, slicing menacingly through the air, adding a primal scream of her own. Inspired by their show of bravado, Gemma's army joined in as well. The battle was on.

Thomas could hear the clash of metal against metal as the combatants resumed their attack. He watched as the Black Knight began to cut a path through Gemma's army, crushing men and shadow both. Giving no regard to who or what he killed, the champion of evil continued on. Reaching the Armor of God was his only goal. In response, Gemma swung her blade viciously, though with much greater care. Her blade only struck shadow, creating a shower of sparks with each strike. At her side, using speed and dexterity over power and strength, Theresa's twin blades flashed wildly as she, too, cut a path through the foe.

For how long the battle continued, and which side held the advantage, Thomas could no longer tell. His eyes were fixed on his companions, his lips barely moving as he sent whispered prayers into the air. A few tense moments later, the three champions came together. Pausing for just a moment, Gemma and Theresa sized up their adversary. He, in turn, stared back. All at once, the three attacked.

Thomas saw that the Black Knight quickly gained the advantage as both Guardians moved quickly to defend. The great, obsidian blade swung almost constantly, slashing and hammering with abandon. Gemma blocked and parried deftly, making Thomas wonder where she had learned such skill. Theresa, too, wielded her blades as if she had done so before, dancing away from the larger assailants attacks. Around them, men and shadow fought valiantly, yet, Thomas could tell, more men than shadow fell. The battle was not going well. There was a strong chance they would lose.

"Archers!" Thomas yelled to the men gathered below. "Move forward! Pick your targets. Aim true!"

The bowmen started forward, spreading into a half-circle, no longer standing man by man. When they were close enough, bolts of light began flying, each one striking true. Thomas watched as shadows began to fall. Yet, where one fell, another took its' place, and more still poured forth from the trees. How large an army the darkness commanded was something yet to be seen. Thomas had to do something to turn the tide.

And then, he saw Gemma take a moment between defending blows to quickly turn his way, waving her sword in a wide arc above her head. Thomas realized that was her signal. She may have planned something more elaborate at first, but in the heat of the battle, this was all she could do. Tightening his grasp on the twisted, wooden staff, he raised his hand upward, holding the staff high above his head. Nothing changed.

Wondering what he did wrong, Thomas tried holding the staff in his other hand, and then again in both. Still nothing. He tried shaking the rod, pointing it, and striking the base on the ground. The feeling of fear flowing up to him from the men on the battlefield below was gaining in strength, becoming so thick he could taste it. Shadows had broken through the main line of Gemma's army, causing the bowmen to rout. What had started as a well-trained, disciplined army battling according to a strategic plan was now small clusters of desperate men fighting to stay alive.

Thomas searched through the chaos for signs of his friends, finally spotting them in the middle of a circle of shadows. They looked weary, their blades dropping after every parry, neither Guardian able to press the attack. Towering above them the Black Knight continued to hammer blow after blow, at times driving one or the other to their knees. With tears in his eyes and despair in his heart, Thomas, too, fell to his knees, a sad and lonely cry escaping his lungs. With no other option, he began to pray. As he did, his hands started to vibrate, and the staff began to warm. Thomas opened his eyes, seeing the tip of the staff glowing brightly in a halo of pure white light. Slowly standing back to his feet, Thomas lifted the staff high, raising his voice, he continued to pray.

"Our Father…"

A beam of light shot outward, blasting a group of shadow creatures at least a dozen strong. The shadows splintered, bursting into thousands of smaller shadows which the light then devoured.

"Who art in Heaven…"

Another ray shot outward, striking more shadows, consuming this group whole.

"Hallowed be thy name…"

Another blast, this one streaking directly towards the circle of shadows surrounding Gemma and Theresa. Half of the circle vanished, causing the other half to flee. Stopping a downward strike that had been aimed at Theresa's head, the Black Knight let his blade rest motionless as his eyes turned towards the castle, seeking the source of the light.

"Thy kingdom come…"

Thomas was now in tears, pouring his emotion into the words. A group of fifty or more shadows fell as three bolts fired at once. The Black Knight, his attention now focused on Thomas, left Gemma and Theresa where they had fallen. Striding with confidence, the demon headed towards the castle, slapping away any resistance he met along the way. Where his obsidian boots trod, the ground became trampled and black with decay.

Thomas continued his prayers, gaining confidence as the staff he held fired bolt after bolt of pure white light at the battlefield below. With each strike, dozens of shadows fell. Once more the tide began to turn. Soldiers who had begun to flee turned back to the field, pairing together and fighting side by side. The archer's bolts, which had become erratic and ineffective, began to fly with confidence, once more striking true.

Slowly standing to her feet, Gemma turned to assist Theresa. Together, the two began to stumble after the Black Knight, supporting each other as they walked. From where he stood, Thomas could see a faint glow form around them as the two wrapped their arms across one another. Immediately he knew where the aura came from: they were sharing powers. Theresa, using her power of Endless Life, strengthened Gemma, who in turn used her power to heal. They created an endless loop of energy—a halo of life. The more power they shared, the larger and brighter the halo grew. Where the halo touched the ground, the once trampled and damaged earth sprung back, glowing with new life. Strengthened now, the two women strode with purpose, following the dark swath the Black Knight had tread.

Thomas watched the demon move purposefully towards the castle walls, his only focus was on ending the constant barrage of white light. The Black Knight was unaware the two Guardians had closed the gap. The women now stood just a few feet behind him, their swords once more held high. Just then, as the edge of their halo touched his back, the demon turned their way, facing an opponent he thought he had beat. Though he was unable to read the emotions of the creature, Thomas could guess at the confusion going through its mind.

Gemma, her sword pointed at the beast, bellowed out loudly, "Demon, drop your sword! Look around you. Even now your own army retreats!"

Thomas glanced around the battlefield, seeing that Gemma's words were true. The shadows no longer flowed out from the trees but instead had started to flow back in. The small pockets that remained grew smaller and more spread out as Gemma's army picked them apart. The battle hadn't ended yet, but Thomas was no longer fearful of which side would win. The soldiers he could see, though exhausted from the conflict, fought with grim resolve. They, like Thomas, could tell the tide had turned back their way.

Shaking mightily, the demon began to emit a sound that made Thomas think it was choking, until he realized that that was how it laughed.

"Stand aside, little girl," the demon challenged. "You are no match for me! If I choose, I could crush you with one blow."

"Your threats won't work on me. Nor will your tricks. I can feel you at the edge of my thoughts, trying to choke my resolve. As long as I wear this armor, you will not prevail!" Gemma shouted back, suddenly raising her sword high and charging boldly at the beast.

Beside her, Theresa began slashing wickedly with both swords once more, forcing the demon to turn, driving him back towards the pit. No longer the aggressor, the demon wailed angrily as he parried blow after blow, only to step backward time and again, drawing ever closer to the crater's edge. As the battle continued, Thomas again raised his staff, his words bringing forth shafts of white light once more.

The rays cut through the remaining shadows, drawing more and more cheers from the soldiers below. As the soldiers found themselves with no more foes, their attention was drawn to the trio now positioned at the edge of the bowl. Raising their voices, the men began shouting encouragement to the Lady they served. Gemma answered back not with words but with her sword, slicing the blade in violent arcs aimed at the demon's head.

Just then, three things happened at once. The first was a solid ray of light flashed forth from Thomas' staff, striking the demon right near its heart. The second was Gemma's sword striking true just above the demon's knee. As the blade cut deep, a spray of jet black blood darkened the ground. And finally, Theresa's twin blades found themselves deep within the Black Knight's side, buried all the way to the hilt. The beast cried in agony, knowing his end had come.

Theresa stepped back, leaving her weapons embedded in the creature as the demon began to stumble and then fall. Its armored hands dropped both sword and shield, flailing aimlessly at the air. With both feet on the lip of the crater, the demon began to slide, toppling backward. Without warning, his right arm shot out, grasping Theresa by the arm. As he began to fall backward, the demon held tight, threatening to pull Theresa down too. But just as Theresa lost her footing and started to fall, Gemma screamed loudly, bringing her blade down hard. She cut through both armor and shadow with a single, powerful blow, severing the demon's hand. With a final, painful scream, the beast fell into the blackness below.

Theresa reached to remove the severed hand that still grasped her wrist. As she did, the hand dissolved and faded away. A hushed silence hung in the air as the two women locked eyes, sharing a moment of shocked recognition of what they had just done. And then, with a wide smile, Gemma raised her sword in triumph. Around her, her army raised their voices in cheer. They had done it. Once more, goodness had prevailed.

CHAPTER NINETEEN
WE'RE BEING CHASTE

"Theresa," Gemma said as she finished cleaning her weapon, sliding it back into the scabbard, "how much energy do you have left?"

Theresa shrugged.

"I don't know. Enough, I guess. Plus, I'm the Endlessly Living Girl now, remember? I never really run out. What do you need?"

Gemma paused, gazing across the battlefield at the hundreds of dead and wounded men.

"It's not what I need," she gestured around her, "but what they do."

Theresa turned in the direction indicated, recognizing what Gemma had in mind.

"You think you can heal all of them? That's going to take hours!" Theresa whispered.

"Not if we do it all at once," Gemma told her, turning to face the castle. "Thomas! We're going to need you down here. Bring your staff!"

Thomas waved his hand and then disappeared from view, choosing to take the stairs rather than vault over the wall as his friends had done.

"Come on," Gemma said, offering her hand to help Theresa stand, "let's get ready."

The two warriors stood facing each other, adjusting their armor and brushing back stray strands of hair. They said nothing, for no words were needed now. A few moments later, Thomas joined the group.

"You know, Brother Thomas," Theresa said wistfully, "I still don't understand why we were chosen, or what the purpose is for these powers of ours, but I doubt I could have picked a better group to be included in. That…was…epic!"

Thomas smirked slightly.

"I know what you mean," he said, pensively, "but you have to understand this. What we're doing here isn't just a dream, and it definitely isn't a game. There is a deeper reality here. Everything we do in the real world affects what happens here in the spiritual realm. And everything we do in the spiritual realm will create ripples of change within the physical world. We may have defeated this one demon today, but just look what it cost!"

Thomas waved his arm at the destruction and death surrounding them.

"That," Gemma mentioned, "is why I asked you to join us down here. It's time for us to fix the damage the darkness caused."

"And just how do you intend to do that?"

"By joining our powers together, the three of us, as one," Gemma announced.

"I'm not sure I understand," Thomas admitted.

"Don't worry. Theresa and I have done this once already. We know what to do," Gemma reassured him.

"Okay, so what do you need from me?"

"Here's what I'm thinking…" Gemma began.

※

Five minutes later the three Guardians stood in a circle, their hands on each other's shoulders. Thomas' staff was in the center of the group, one end sticking partially in the ground. Thomas glanced from side to side, giving each of his companions a nervous but confident nod. They had never tried anything like they were about to attempt and yet, given their experiences of the past few hours, there was nothing to indicate it wouldn't work.

"Okay, I'm going to start imagining my army the way it was before the battle, before any of this happened," Gemma stated, taking a deep breath. "I'll let you know when I've got the image in my mind."

"We can do this, Gemma," Theresa said, hoping her words would inspire a greater confidence than she actually felt.

"Remember," Thomas reminded his friends, "the key here is to have faith. Believe it before you see it. I know that might be hard, but it will help."

Gemma nodded, and then closed her eyes. Almost a full minute passed before she nodded her head once more, letting the others know she had the image she needed in her mind. Thomas closed his eyes, opening his heart as he began to pray. Like before, he could feel the staff start to vibrate and warm, even though he wasn't holding it this time. As he raised the volume of his voice, the vibration grew stronger, as did the warmth. In the essence of time, they had decided against a test run. All three wanted to return to the physical realm—and their friends—as quickly as possible, whether time was moving forward there or not.

Suddenly Thomas felt a different kind of warmth flow through him, like the warmth a child felt being held in its mother's arms. It was soothing, relaxing, and had a protective feel. He had never felt warmth like this, and silently hoped it would linger long after their task was complete. Thomas let his mind drift on the feeling.

The sensation provided Thomas with the poised and self-assured knowledge that he could stretch his powers far beyond what he had tried so far. And so, he did. Although the reality they were in currently existed within Gemma's heart, and this spiritual realm belonged to her, Thomas imagined himself going even deeper still. He knew that if he went deep enough he could help her find her hope.

Letting his own heart lead the way, Thomas imagined he was standing on the top of a giant cliff. The ground below was so far down that he couldn't even begin to make out the details. Though his knees began to wobble and his palms started to sweat, he still found the strength to edge closer to the cliff. Inch by inch he approached the drop until his toes were right at the edge. Then, with courage and trust, he stretched his arms out wide, leaned forward, and fell.

The air that rushed up to meet him was heavy with fog, soaking him through to the bone. Faster and faster he fell, each moment finding him closer to the ground below. Somewhere down there he knew he would find what he was searching for. Though he couldn't see the place he was aiming for, he knew he wouldn't miss.

Thomas shared a deep connection with Gemma. Theresa, too. It was the same connection he would someday feel with all of the Guardians of Zion, whenever and wherever he would meet the rest. It allowed him to see what even Gemma and Theresa themselves could not. Thomas could see their purpose, the reason they were created, their true self. This was the spot he was aiming for, the tiny point that was, as Jesus taught, as small as a mustard seed. Yet that same seed had the power to grow thousands of times its size.

To Thomas, it didn't matter if Gemma was aware of her faith because he was. He knew her faith was far greater than she realized, which meant that the target he aimed for would be of great size indeed. And so, he fell with quiet conviction, secure in the knowledge that he had already arrived where he was headed, long before he and Gemma had even met. This was all part of God's plan. All Thomas had to do was believe.

As the ground rose up to meet him, Thomas closed his eyes. No sense watching when he already knew the outcome. A moment later, he felt something had changed, as if he was no longer falling as fast as before. Opening his eyes, Thomas saw that he was no longer falling downward but was now flying across the sky!

Smiling broadly, Thomas laughed out loud. Stretching his arms out before him, he leaned his body to the left, willing his flight path to change. Laughing loudly one more, Thomas twisted and curved his torso, his path through the air changing in sync with his moves. He dipped, soared, and swooped and then rocketed back towards the ground, pulling up at the last moment. His feet landed softly on the dark, rich soil. Instantly he knew where he was.

Thomas knew she had dreamed all her life of living on a farm, a quiet place where she could raise a family. Which is why it made sense that the place where she held her deepest secrets, the place where she had planted her faith, would be the same place she hoped she would one day find herself calling home. Thomas turned, already knowing what he would see when he did. A quaint little farmhouse, with chickens strutting on the driveway and two sheep grazing on the front lawn. There was a corral that held horses, and several cows in a barn.

Thomas could tell the fields had recently been planted, the smell of freshly plowed dirt filled the air. This was definitely a well cared for farm.

Breathing deeply, Thomas started towards the farmhouse, making sure to not step in the furrowed rows. As he drew near, he saw a frail, timeworn woman in a rocking chair on the porch. There was an old, tan hound dog stretched out on the wooden floor at her feet and a tall glass of lemonade on the table by her side. It was a picture-perfect image. Thomas waved at the woman, and she slowly waved back.

"Come over here and have a seat," the woman said as Thomas climbed the small flight of stairs leading up to the porch.

Thomas did as he was told, taking a seat on the railing surrounding the porch. The hound dog raised his eyes, giving Thomas an apathetic glance, as if that small movement was more than the dog had planned on doing today. There was a great similarity between the woman and her dog. They both sat with complete abandon as if they had given up resisting gravity and were waiting to melt into the floor.

The woman, like the dog, barely moved. Thomas could see an almost imperceptible rise and fall of her chest as she breathed. The only attribute that proved she was alive were her eyes. They didn't just sparkle, they burned with life. While everything about her showed signs of age, her eyes looked as young as the day she had been born.

"So, what brings you here, young Thomas?" she asked through lips that barely parted.

Thomas cleared his throat, turning to face the woman more direct as he said, "I'm here for a friend, to find something she needs."

"And you think it's here on my farm, do you?"

"Oh, I'm certain of it. If I've learned one thing that's true these past few years, it's that faith is never wrong. If faith led me here, then what I'm seeking has to be here as well."

The woman made a soft sigh and then turned her eyes towards her fields. Thomas waited, expecting her to say something more, hoping she would tell him where he could find what he sought. When she said nothing more for a long moment, he cleared his throat.

"You wouldn't be able to help me find it, would you?" he asked, sheepishly.

Another sigh.

"You know, you never did change, Brother Thomas. Not in all those years. Always the mission first. That damned quest of yours," she said in exhausted tones, and then quietly corrected herself. "That quest of *ours*."

Thomas leaned back giving her a confused frown. *"Of ours?"* he thought. *Do I know this woman?*

"I'm sorry," he eventually said, "have we met?"

"Oh, my, yes," she sighed, turning her eyes back to his. "Many, many years ago."

Thomas carefully considered the woman before him. She did remind him of someone, he just couldn't place who. As he leaned in closer trying to get a better look, the hound dog growled.

"Oh, hush now, Terence. He won't hurt me."

"Did she say, Terence?" he thought, and then asked the question again, this time out loud. "I'm sorry, but your dog, his name is Terence?"

The old woman laughed.

"It is. Why do you ask?" she said, turning her eyes back to face him.

"I have a friend named Terence. Truth be told, he can be a bit of a hound dog at times, always on the hunt for another date," he said, shaking his head.

"How do you think the dog got his name?" the woman asked, finding the strength to flash a grin.

Thomas gazed deeply into her eyes, wondering once more who she might be. And then, she winked, and suddenly, he knew.

"Gemma?" he asked.

"Who else do you think would be living inside my heart?" she teased him.

Thomas blushed.

"You're right. I should have known. It's just, well, you look so…" he began.

"Old?" she suggested.

"Different," he finished.

"That's just a polite way of saying old."

"Well, I think you look great."

"Oh, Thomas, you always did have a way of making me blush. I always loved that about you."

The two sat in silence, their eyes locked in a friendly embrace. Finally, Thomas broke the silence.

"I remember you telling me on our drive to Houston that this was your dream. You said you couldn't wait to take your inheritance and buy a small plot of land, and that you would use whatever was left to help people in need. Is this it? Is this that farm?"

"The drive to Houston…" Gemma said, wistfully, her eyes taking on a soft glow. "That was when it all began. The Guardians, the battles, our powers."

She looked at Thomas with a smile on her lips and a twinkle in her eyes. Suddenly the smile and twinkle faded, replaced by a gentle frown.

"But you don't remember them yet, because they haven't happened for you. Today's the day it all started for you, the day I became The Paladin."

"Yeah, I guess it is. I'd love to hear your stories, though. Especially those that happened after today. Can you tell me who the other Guardians are? If we were able to fulfill God's plan?"

Gemma shook her head, "I'm sorry, Thomas. You know I can't. If you knew what was ahead, whose lives might be in danger, which of your friends you might lose, my past—and your future—might change. No, you're just going to have to find out for yourself."

"There's nothing you can tell me? Not even a hint? Anything that might give me hope?"

"Hope," Gemma sighed. "That's why you're here today, isn't it? You're here to find my hope. Well, go on inside and get it then. You'll find it in a small box tucked in the back of the bottom drawer of my dresser. When you see it, maybe that will answer your question. Go on, now. Time is growing short."

Thomas stood cautiously, wondering if there was something more he should say. When nothing came, he moved slowly towards the door. Opening the frail screen door, Thomas stepped inside. The interior of the farmhouse was just as he expected. A lot of gingham, lace curtains, and comfortable chairs. The kitchen was on his right. Inside the small room were a round table and two chairs. Pots and pans hung from hooks on the walls, as did a few spoons and ladles. A wooden spice rack hung near the stove, with a large pink mixer just below.

To his left was a hallway leading to two small bedrooms with an even smaller bathroom in between. Thomas entered the bedroom on the right first, finding a small bed set against one wall and, with very little space, not much else. A sewing table, a small chest—most likely filled with fabric, needles, and thread. Two shelves hung on the wall, stacked with candles and books. Crossing back through the hall, he walked into the second bedroom, knowing for certain as he walked in that it was hers. Every wall had a cross hanging on it, some had two, and there was a painting above the bed of a knight in shining armor, a testament to the hero she had become.

Thomas spied the dresser in the back corner of the room and headed that way. On the top he saw a collection of items: a rosary, Bible, small candle, crucifix, and a statue of Our Lady of Guadalupe. As he was about to kneel down and open the drawer, he noticed there were two spots on the faded wood floor that looked more worn than the rest. This, he knew, was where Gemma knelt down to pray. How often and for how long, he didn't know. But the fact that she had worn the finish off the floor in these places told him she must have prayed often.

He felt strange kneeling in the same place she had for so many years, but if he was to retrieve what he had come for, there was no other way. Getting into position, his knees on the well-worn spots, his hands on the knobs of the drawer, Thomas bowed his head for a moment, offering a quick prayer for the friendship he and Gemma had found (and apparently were going to have for many years to come). Sighing deeply, he opened the drawer. Sliding a pair of jeans and a stack of woolen socks out of the way, he found a small square box, just where she had said it would be.

Thomas considered opening the box, revealing what waited inside, but he knew this gift wasn't meant for him. If she wanted him to know, Gemma would tell him at some point in the future. And so instead he simply tucked it into his pocket and closed the drawer. Standing back up, he took a closer look at the medieval painting. The knight, whose face looked just like Gemma's, had a red cloak hanging from metal clasps, one on each shoulder. On the front of each clasp was a symbol that Thomas instantly knew was meant for the Guardians.

The symbol was of a round stone keep, reminding Thomas of the rook piece from the game of chess. A banner hung in the middle of the keep. The banner held the image of a trinity knot emblazoned with a Chi-Rho. Behind the keep were twelve stalks of wheat tied in a sheaf. Six stalks stood on each side, and above each stalk was a star. At the apex, between the rows of stars, was the Star of Bethlehem. Underneath it all was written, *Ex Opere Operato*, meaning, 'By virtue the work performed'.

Thomas made a mental note of the image and then turned and exited the room. He returned to the porch, taking his place once more on the railing. Gemma looked up at him with tired, weary eyes.

"Did you find what you were seeking?" she asked.

Thomas patted his pocket.

"Yes. And one thing more."

Gemma's eyes had that faraway look that gave the impression she was deep in thought, and then, as recognition set in, she smiled.

"Ah…the Guardian's Crest. I always wondered where you had come up with that design. Now, I know," she said, pausing a moment. "Well, you should be going. The younger me will soon need what you have."

"Can I ask you one more question?" Thomas inquired politely.

Gemma nodded, saying, "Yes. But only one."

"Have you always been alone? I mean, besides Terence here. Have you lived out here by yourself all these years?"

Thomas watched as tears formed in Gemma's eyes. With effort, she cleared her throat and then raised a frail, withered hand to wipe at her eyes.

"There is an old saying. *'One can never be alone when you love the one you're with'*. But, to answer your question, yes. Choosing a chaste life and committing oneself to Christ can be a difficult and challenging thing. But that doesn't mean I never felt love," she said, suddenly turning her eyes to Thomas.

Without her saying anything, Thomas understood. He had felt the same way about Gemma, even though he had only known her a short while.

"I understand," he said quietly, and then, quickly changing the subject, he added, "I just can't imagine how you have been able to take care of this large farm by yourself for so long."

Gemma nodded her head gently, looking with admiration over her fields.

"Oh, that's the easy part. This farm is a lot like faith. If you take the time to tend it and care for it early in life, you'll find it takes care of you when you get older. I no longer need to plow, plant, or harvest. The farm does all that on its own. Though, this may be my last season. Terence and I are so very tired. It's time to go home."

Thomas thought about saying something else, but Gemma turned her face away. She didn't want him to see how deeply saddened she had become. Though, at the same time, he knew she was glad. For the life she had lived, for the good she had done, and for the friendships she had made.

Quietly, Thomas stood back up. Before leaving, he knelt down and scratched Terence's ears.

"You take care of her, Terence. Somehow I have a feeling you always have."

The dog looked up at him, raised its head, and then licked his hand and wrist. Thomas smiled, leaning down to kiss the beast on top of his head. Standing back up, he looked once more at Gemma and then leaned forward and kissed her softly on the cheek. His lips felt wet from the tears she shed but his heart told him that her heart was full. Slowly, Thomas turned and walked away.

When he reached the point in the field where he had landed, rather than trying to fly again, he simply willed himself to return. Taking one last look around at the farm, he burned the image in his mind, knowing this woman had greatly changed his life. Then, he closed his eyes and knelt down.

CHAPTER TWENTY
RETURNING HOME

Thomas opened his eyes, seeing that he was once more back with his friends. Gemma still stood on his left, and Theresa was at his right. Their hands were still on his shoulders as his were on theirs. His lips were quietly whispering prayers and every so often a ray of light would shoot forth from the staff in the center of the group. Thomas looked in the direction of where the next ray traveled, seeing it strike one of the many bodies lying motionless on the ground.

As it did, the body moved ever so slightly, and then again, a little bit more. As he watched, the man rolled over, paused a moment, and then sat up. Another of the soldiers wandered over to him, offering him help to stand. The two men hugged each other, celebrating his return to life, and then walked over to help another of their comrades who had also just been revived. As more rays shot forth from the staff, and more men rose from the field, a murmur of conversation began.

Slowly the soldiers began to walk to where the trio of champions stood in their circle. Forming an outer ring around the three, the men drew their swords and knelt down. Placing the point of the sword on the ground and their hands on the hilt, the men bowed their heads, adding their prayers to those Thomas murmured.

The combined prayer lifted Thomas' spirits, giving him courage to pray with even more conviction. As he did, the pure white rays from the staff began firing faster, at times sending two rays at once. The ring of men surrounding them grew thicker as more men continued to rise. For how long this continued Thomas was unaware. He simply continued to pray, watching as the circle of men honoring the Lady of the castle became dense. Then, as quickly as they had started, the vibrations and warmth he had felt from the staff were gone. There were no more dead or wounded left on the field. As the final soldier recovered, following his comrades and finding a place in the outer ring, Thomas ended his prayers, letting the last word echo as a powerful silence fell over the field. After a few moments, Thomas squeezed Theresa's shoulders, waking her from her trance, and then did the same for Gemma. They opened their eyes slowly.

"Did it work?" Gemma asked.

"Look around you," was all he replied.

Gemma turned her head to the left, and then quickly turned it all the way to the right. Letting out a gasp, she took her hand from Theresa's shoulder, wrapping both arms around Thomas' neck. A moment later, Theresa squeezed in between them. The three embraced each other tightly, their tired eyes filled with light. Tears streaked down their faces in celebration of the lives they had saved.

Reaching out his hand, Thomas grasped the staff and pulled it from the ground. Around him, another murmur began to form. Turning to look at the soldiers, he saw they had raised their heads, their eyes fixed on Gemma. Their left hands were still holding their weapons, their right hands were softly thumping their chests.

Gemma let go from the joined embrace, turning to face her men. As she turned from one side to the other, smiling gleefully at her soldiers, they thumped even louder, the murmur growing into a din. One of the soldiers began chanting 'Paladin' on each thump, and the others quickly joined in. Gemma blushed as their chants grew louder, embarrassed to be honored in this way. Thomas leaned over, squeezing her shoulder firmly as once more her eyes released great tears of joy.

"This is your moment, Gemma," he told her.

Gemma turned to him, smiling through her tears. She raised her sword high above her head, causing her army to chant even louder.

"Paladin! Paladin! Paladin!"

The sound echoed through the valley as the townspeople began flowing out from their homes. Gerald was the first one to approach. He had been waiting on the outside of the circle for the soldiers to end their display. With a final united shout, the men raised their weapons above their heads and then grew still.

"Milady, is it done?" the townsman asked her.

"Yes, Gerald," she replied. "The battle is over. Tell the people they are safe. For now."

"That is good news!" Gerald said joyfully. "We must celebrate! Tonight, there will be a feast!"

Before she could tell him 'no', Gerald walked away, barking out commands to those around him. The soldiers also began to disperse, once more forming ranks, preparing to march their Paladin back to the castle with honor. A horse was brought over, and Gemma was helped into the saddle. She turned to Thomas.

"What should I do? We need to get back and help the others! We don't have time for a feast!"

"Though my desire is the same, there is value in celebrating our victory. Every spiritual battle we win needs to be celebrated. Otherwise, we run the risk of leaving a void—an emptiness that the darkness can more easily fill. If we celebrate each victory, regardless of how small, we fill that space with new growth, preventing the Devil's return for a greater amount of time.

"Plus, your presence at the feast will do so much for your townspeople. Remember, this is your spiritual life that we are inside right now. Strengthening the relationships you have here will create a much stronger foundation of faith when we return home. The more you tend to this flock, the easier it will be to remain faithful in the physical world."

Gemma considered what he had just told her, nodding her head in understanding. Then, she turned away from him as she contemplated her reply. When she turned back, a look of excitement was in her eyes.

"Okay. We'll stay for the feast. I've always wanted to be a part of something like this. It really will be a dream come true."

※

The celebration was everything Gemma could imagine. The townspeople had erected an enormous tent outside the castle, decorating it with candles and glass lamps in every hue. Banners and streamers hung from the ceiling and along all of the sides. They arranged rows of tables made from their own front doors resting on sawhorses they had hastily built. A team of ten men built a raised platform for the head table where Gemma, Theresa, and Thomas were to sit alongside the Captain of the Guard, the Mayor, and a few other dignitaries. The platform would give Gemma the ability to see all of her guests, even to the tables at the far end of the tent. And what a crowd it was.

The townspeople attended, the men dressed in their finest attire, the ladies in long, billowing dresses with flowers in their hair. Her entire army came, too. Their metal suits once more clean and polished, though their weapons were left back at their bunks. There would be no need for them. Not for a long, long time.

When everyone was settled, the waiters passed around large silver platters laden with the finest foods. The celebration lasted long into the night. Eventually, the exhaustion of the day won out over the revelry of the night as the people of her town offered their thanks one last time and slowly made their way back home. When only a handful still remained, Gemma said her final goodbyes and then headed to bed. Thomas and Theresa followed closely behind.

In the morning the three met for breakfast in the castle. After their meal, which included several pots of coffee, Thomas pulled the small box he had collected from the back of the dresser drawer. Turning to face Gemma, he held it up.

"While we were gathered together yesterday, healing your troops, I took the liberty of finding this," he said, offering the box to Gemma.

"What is it?" Gemma asked.

"In short, it's your hope. It's all of your dreams, the wishes for your life, everything that you have ever wanted your life to be."

"What am I supposed to do with it?" she asked.

"That, is very much up to you."

Gemma shook the box slightly, holding it close to her ear. The box made a soft, twinkling sound. The sound made her face light up with delight

"Any idea what's inside?" she asked.

"I didn't look. Though, to be honest, I was far more curious than I should have been," Thomas replied.

Gemma held the box before her, her eyes burning with curiosity and anticipation. Slowly, she cracked the box open, taking a quick peek inside. A smile began to grow, and a calm, peaceful glow radiated on her face.

"What is it?" Theresa asked impatiently.

Gemma looked over at her younger friend, then back to Thomas.

"It's absolutely perfect, that's what," she said.

"Aren't you going to share?" Theresa begged.

"No, I don't think so. Not yet, anyway," Gemma said after a moment of consideration.

Closing the box, she reached forward and rang a small bell that called her staff.

"Milady?" the majordomo asked, peeking only his head into the room. "Is there something you need?"

"Take this to the steward. Tell him he must keep it safe. Do not, I repeat, do not open the box, nor tell anyone other than the steward that it exists. I'm sure the Devil would love to get it. And if he does," she said, pausing for a moment, "it could mean my end. Understand?"

"Yes, milady," the man replied, hurrying over and taking the box from her hands. When he left the room, Theresa frowned.

"Well, now what do we do?" she asked.

"Now," Gemma said, "we go rescue our friends."

The story continues in
Book Three – The Guardians Crest

Michael Chrobak has been involved in working with Youth and Youth Ministry programs since he was a teen himself; a long, long time ago. He has held the position of Director of Religious Education and Youth Minister for St. Bonaventure's Parish in Concord, CA, and also as Youth Minister for St. Michael's Parish in Livermore, CA. He has survived raising four children of his own and now lives in Oakley, CA where he continues to stay involved in Youth Ministry through his blogs and books.

How to Connect:

Facebook: https://www.facebook.com/michaelchrobakauthor
Twitter: https://twitter.com/MChrobakAuthor
Instagram: https://www.instagram.com/mchrobakauthor
Website: https://michaelchrobakauthor.com